英诗鉴赏

诸莉　诸光　编著

WUHAN UNIVERSITY PRESS
武汉大学出版社

图书在版编目(CIP)数据

英诗鉴赏/诸莉,诸光编著.—武汉:武汉大学出版社,2024.7(2025.5 重印)
ISBN 978-7-307-24275-3

Ⅰ.英⋯ Ⅱ.①诸⋯ ②诸⋯ Ⅲ.英语—诗歌 —文学欣赏—世界
Ⅳ.①H31 ②I106.2

中国国家版本馆 CIP 数据核字(2024)第 035081 号

责任编辑:李晶晶 责任校对:汪欣怡 版式设计:马 佳

出版发行:**武汉大学出版社** (430072 武昌 珞珈山)
(电子邮箱:cbs22@whu.edu.cn 网址:www.wdp.com.cn)
印刷:武汉邮科印务有限公司
开本:787×1092 1/16 印张:14.25 字数:239 千字 插页:1
版次:2024 年 7 月第 1 版 2025 年 5 月第 2 次印刷
ISBN 978-7-307-24275-3 定价:65.00 元

前　言

　　本教材旨在给学习者提供一个接触英诗的捷径。相较过去，当今的生活变得更为繁忙和高速，加之诗歌课程普设为选修课，只能兼顾极少数学生的兴趣爱好。因此，本教材的编写初衷是：方便更多人学习英语诗歌。本书选择了最具代表性的英美诗人及其作品来作为教学素材，并辅以若干板块的知识支撑，旨在从语言、格律、修辞和人生背景等方面去把握诗歌作品，达到举一反三、窥一斑而知全豹的目的，以帮助大家在认知、审美和情操上实现自我提升。作为英语诗歌鉴赏性教材，本书大部分内容按照文学史脉络，但也兼顾趣味性、代表性和接受性等因素来编排。在此前提下，诗人及其作品的选取难免会挂一漏万，以偏概全。本书无意重述文学史，突出强调的是其教材属性和审美属性。但本书诗歌作品的代表性也是毋庸置疑的，它选取的是英国文艺复兴以降到 20 世纪中叶这一英文抒情诗黄金时代著名诗人的主要作品，其中有格律诗，也有半格律诗和半自由诗。

　　自古以来，诗歌就是人类自我表达的主要方式，无论是抒发情志还是记叙历史，所谓"不学诗，无以言"（《论语·季氏》）。早期的人类还在诗歌的启蒙下得以开化和进步，所以诗歌传统在人类文明化过程中发挥着不可替代的作用。诗歌与语言密不可分，集中了简洁、形象、优美、深情的语言表达。诗歌是历朝历代的诗人们坎坷人生的真实写照。所以古往今来，诗歌一直都是各民族语文学习中不可或缺的文类体裁。它们是我们了解历史、文化和社会，特别是了解诗人的情感以及思想的最佳来源。所谓"诗，可以兴，可以观，可以群，可以怨"（《论语·阳货篇》）就是诗歌社会功能的绝好体现。诗歌对于个体而言，则一直都有抒发情志、怡情悦性、修身养性、提升境界、舒缓压力的作用。时至今日诗歌的实用功能已然不复，但它的精神功能却得到了加强：诗歌已然成为人类精神家园的一种隐喻。"诗和远方"成为一种理想生活的代名词，一种超越现实的精神寄托。

在经济全球化的今天，我们要屹立于世界民族之林，要与其他民族相交相知，就要学习彼此的语言；而语言包含于文化之中，因此学习西方的文化就成为必然。学习英美诗歌不仅可以帮助我们了解英美文化，而且还可以提高我们的英语语言水平。诗歌是中西文明之间相互借鉴、相互交流的一个重要途径。要想讲好中国故事，不了解西方的语言和文化，是很难与世界各民族沟通交流，从而赢得对方的理解和尊重的。而诗歌是语言文化的重要表现形式之一，学习英美诗歌有利于中外各民族之间的相互交流和理解。

本教材共分二十个单元，分别介绍了二十位英美诗人及其作品。每一单元都有诗人简介、推荐作品、中文译文、语言注释、修辞解析、思考题、节奏和韵律图示、作品鉴赏八个部分，外加若干首诗人的其他作品及其译文作为补充和延伸拓展阅读。其中诗人简介、推荐作品、节奏和韵律图示以及诗歌鉴赏为诸光编著，共计11.3万字；语言注释、思考题、修辞解析、其他作品及其译文为诸莉编著，共计12.6万字。由于英语语言对于中国学习者而言是外语，诗歌又是文学中最古老、最浓缩的语言精华，接受起来并不容易，所以需要我们循序渐进，融会贯通，求同存异，理解包容。我们为每个诗歌作品准备了中文译文：有现代散文，也有古典文言形式；其中五言较多，偶尔也用七言；译文尽量恪守"信达雅"标准，在忠实于原作的前提下努力增强归化感，也尽量不喧宾夺主，不过度解读。在此欢迎大家批评指正。

由于时间紧迫，加上编著人员水平有限，本书难免存在各种缺点、错误和瑕疵，还望广大专家、读者和使用者海涵，并提出宝贵的批评意见！在此感谢华中科技大学和武汉纺织大学外经贸学院领导和同事们在成书过程中提供的各种帮助和支持！感谢武汉大学出版社在出版过程中的支持与配合！对于本书引用的各位前辈和专家学者的学术成果和观点，在此对他们表示诚挚的感谢！

诸莉，诸光

2023 年 12 月 27 日

目 录
Contents

Unit 1　Robert Frost　罗伯特·弗罗斯特　　　　　　　　　　　　／001

Unit 2　Alfred Tennyson　阿尔弗雷德·丁尼生　　　　　　　　　／021

Unit 3　Dante Gabriel Rossetti　但丁·加布里埃尔·罗塞蒂　　／029

Unit 4　Christina Georgina Rossetti　克里斯蒂娜·乔治娜·罗塞蒂　／035

Unit 5　John Masefield　约翰·梅斯菲尔德　　　　　　　　　／047

Unit 6　Edgar Alan Poe　埃德加·爱伦·坡　　　　　　　　　／059

Unit 7　Henry Wadsworth Longfellow　亨利·沃兹沃斯·朗费罗　／069

Unit 8　John Donne　约翰·邓恩　　　　　　　　　　　　　　／081

Unit 9　William Shakespeare　威廉·莎士比亚　　　　　　　　／091

Unit 10　Andrew Marvell　安德鲁·马韦尔　　　　　　　　　／105

Unit 11　Robert Burns　罗伯特·彭斯　　　　　　　　　　　　／117

Unit 12　William Blake　威廉·布莱克　　　　　　　　　　　　／133

Unit 13　William Wordsworth　威廉·华兹华斯　　　　　　　　／145

Unit 14　Samuel Taylor Coleridge　塞缪尔·泰勒·柯勒律治　　／157

Unit 15　George Gordon Byron　乔治·戈登·拜伦　　　　　　　／163

Unit 16　Robert Louis Stevenson　罗伯特·路易斯·斯蒂文森　　／173

Unit 17　William Butler Yeats　威廉·巴特勒·叶芝　　　　　/ 179

Unit 18　Alfred Edward Housman　阿尔弗雷德·爱德华·豪斯曼　　/ 191

Unit 19　Emily Dickinson　艾米莉·狄金森　　　　　　　　　/ 201

Unit 20　Edwin Arlington Robinson　埃德温·阿灵顿·罗宾逊　　/ 211

参考文献　　　　　　　　　　　　　　　　　　　　　　　/ 221

Unit 1　Robert Frost

罗伯特·弗罗斯特

罗伯特·弗罗斯特(1874—1963)，美国 20 世纪伟大诗人，被誉为"工业时代的田园诗人"[1]；生于旧金山，长于新英格兰；后迁居伦敦，出版诗集《少年的心愿》和《波士顿以北》，遂一举成名，回国后大受欢迎；曾任教于大学，但一直坚守乡村生活和诗歌创作，四次荣获普利策诗歌大奖，其作品深受美国及世界各国人民的喜爱。

上承英诗传统，背靠新英格兰乡村，弗罗斯特诗歌发展出生活化语言风格与象征主义[2]表现手法；他创作的抒情诗韵律优美、节奏严整、意象清新，以抒情短诗为主，坚守传统格律诗形式，在表面平淡的语句和冷静的叙事背后，往往饱含深情和哲理，需要细细品读。

---

[1] 彭予. 马丽娅·弗罗斯特：工业时代的田园诗人[J]. 中国社会科学院研究生院学报，1994(4)：75-78.

[2] 象征主义：19 世纪后半叶产生于法国的诗歌流派。代表人物是：波德莱尔、魏尔伦、兰波和马拉美。波德莱尔的十四行诗《应和》首次提出著名的象征主义"应和论"。后象征主义主要特点是：创造病态的"美"，表现内心的"最高真实"，运用象征暗示，在幻觉中构筑意象，用音乐性增加冥想效应。(资料来源：百度百科，https://baike. baidu. com/item/% E8% B1% A1% E5% BE% 81% E4%B8%BB%E4%B9%89/1780147？ fr=aladdin)

📖 诗作一

Stopping by Woods on a Snowy Evening
风雪林中夜

Whose woods these are I think I know[①].	我知谁家林，
His house is in the village though;	林主村中寝；
He will not see me stopping here	不知我深夜
To watch his woods fill up with snow.	来看林中雪。
My little horse must think it queer[②]	我马定好奇，
To stop without a farmhouse near	不见农舍迹，
Between the woods and frozen lake	就在湖畔歇，
The darkest evening of the year.	年里最黑夜。
He gives his harness bells[③] a shake	小马轻摇铃：
To ask if there is some mistake.	是否错决定？
The only other sound's the sweep[④]	夜寒万籁寂，
Of easy wind and downy[⑤] flake.	风和绒雪稀。
The woods are lovely, dark and deep,	林幽夜更恬，
But I have promises to keep,	我有诺在先；
And miles to go before I sleep,	寝前行路远，
And miles to go before I sleep.	寝前行路远。

（诺光　译）

✏️ 语言注释

① 宾语从句提前，起强调作用，正常语序为：I think I know whose woods these are。

woods，树林。

② queer：*adj.* 奇怪的，反常的。

③ harness bells：马具(挽具)上的铃(铛；具)。

④ sweep：*n.* 扫，打扫，清扫，扫掠，掠。

⑤ downy：*adj.* 绒毛覆盖的；长着绒毛的；毛茸茸的；柔和的。

? 思考题

1. What would the image "woods" remind you?

2. What might the image "farmhouse" refer to symbolically?

3. What kind of role does "my little horse" play in the poem?

4. What do the image "snow", "easy wind", and "downy flake" stand for?

5. What figure of speech is "dark and deep"?

6. What kind of promises do you think has the speaker already made?

7. What implied meaning would "sleep" have beyond its literal one?

8. What symbolic meanings does this poem have?

✎ 节奏、韵律图示

Stopping by Woods on a Snowy Evening

行数 (Line)	四音步抑扬格 (Iambic Tetrameter)	韵式 (Rhyme Scheme)
1.	Whose woods │ these are │ I think │ I know.	a-/əʊ/
2.	His house │ is in │ the vil │ lage though;	a-/əʊ/
3.	He will │ not see │ me stop │ ping here	b-/ir/

4. To watch │ his woods │ fill up │ with snow. a-/əʊ/
   △ ▲　　　△ ▲　　　△ ▲　　　△ ▲

5. My lit │ tle horse │ must think │ it queer b-/ɪr/
   △ ▲　△ ▲　　　△ ▲　　　△ ▲

6. To stop │ without │ a farm │ house near b-/ɪr/
   △ ▲　　△ ▲　　△ ▲　　　△ ▲

7. Between │ the woods │ and fro │ zen lake c-/eɪk/
   △ ▲　　△ ▲　　△ ▲　　△ ▲

8. The dark │ est eve │ ning of │ the year. b-/ɪr/
   △ ▲　　△ ▲　　△ ▲　　△ ▲

9. He gives │ his harn │ ess bells │ a shake c-/eɪk/
   △ ▲　　△ ▲　　△ ▲　　△ ▲

10. To ask │ if there │ is some │ mistake c-/eɪk/
    △ ▲　△ ▲　　△ ▲　　△ ▲

11. The on │ ly o │ ther sound's │ the sweep d-/iːp/
    △ ▲　△ ▲　△ ▲　　△ ▲

12. Of ea │ sy wind │ and dow │ ny flake. c-/eɪk/
    △ ▲　△ ▲　　△ ▲　　△ ▲

13. The woods │ are love │ ly, dark │ and deep d-/iːp/
    △ ▲　　△ ▲　　△ ▲　　△ ▲

14. But I │ have pro │ mises │ to keep d-/iːp/
    △ ▲　△ ▲　　△ ▲　△ ▲

15. And miles │ to go │ before │ I sleep d-/iːp/
    △ ▲　　△ ▲　　△ ▲　　△ ▲

16. And miles │ to go │ before │ I sleep d-/iːp/
    △ ▲　　△ ▲　　△ ▲　　△ ▲

注：本图引入符号△、▲来分别代表轻、重音。本诗为四音步抑扬格(iambic tetrameter：△▲)，仅有两处例外，为扬扬格(spondee：▲▲)，其余均为抑扬格。尾韵韵式为：aaba bbcb ccdc dddd。

修辞解析

本诗涉及五个诗歌常用的修辞手法：意象、拟人、头韵、悖论和重复。

1. 意象（Image）

意象是一种通过形象语言的运用所激发出的感官印象，表达某种情绪和情感的修辞手法。本诗四度出现的 woods 是弗诗中常见的意象，往往象征着死亡和毁灭。①雪也是常见的意象，而且往往和 woods 同时出现在一首诗中，象征着高洁单纯，但又和死亡相关。②在本诗中它们既象征美，又代表着各种诱惑。

2. 拟人（Personification）

拟人是一种将动物、抽象概念或无生命事物比喻为人类的修辞手法。本诗把小马比喻为一个具有人格的伴侣，会好奇（think it queer，第二节第一行）、会摇铃（gives... a shake，第三节第一行）、会提问（to ask...，第三节第二行）。拟人修辞格的应用能使无生命物体变得像人或动物一般生动有趣起来。

3. 头韵（Alliteration）

头韵是指同一个辅音在一行诗中的两个（或以上）相邻或间隔不远的单词首音上的重复，用来加强语气和气势。③本诗最后一节第一句中的 dark and deep 就是一对典型的头韵词，其中/d/音在 dark 和 deep 的首音位上重复。

4. 悖论（Paradox）

悖论是指一个看似矛盾和荒谬，实则反映了某种真理性的陈述，它反映了事物的复杂性和多面性，首先意在吸引读者的注意力。第四节首句 The woods are lovely, dark and deep 就是一个悖论：一方面树林是美丽可爱的，另一方面它又是深不可测、黑暗神秘的。这二者如何统一，显然需要某种智慧。这种修辞往往表达了对事物既矛盾又统一的辩证的看法。

5. 重复（Repetition）

重复，或反复，是指某个音素、单词、词组或句子的再次（或多次）出现，多为感叹、咏叹，起强调和加强语气、情感的作用。本诗最后两行就是句子的重复：

① 张毓度. 英文名篇鉴赏金库(诗歌卷)[M]. 天津：天津人民出版社，2000：265.

② 张毓度. 英文名篇鉴赏金库(诗歌卷)[M]. 天津：天津人民出版社，2000：266.

③ Chris Baldick. 牛津文学术语词典[M]. 上海：上海外语教育出版社，2000：166.

And miles to go before I sleep/And miles to go before I sleep。重复修辞格的巧妙使用往往具有"一唱三叹"和"回旋往复"的音乐美，同时起到强调和加强意蕴的作用。

作品鉴赏

《风雪林中夜》是弗氏最负盛名的作品，历来深受读者喜爱。究其原因，主要还在于其清新的语言、优美的韵律、深邃的意境和丰富的人生哲理。

该诗通过口语化和生活化语言以及象征主义叙事手法，讲述了一件"迷途知返"的生活轶事：主人公旅行途中偶遇美景而中途下马，在风雪林中流连忘返；终因承诺在先而不得不与美景匆匆别过，凭借神性的自觉而继续前行，去履行自己未尽的职责和义务。该诗通过各种象征意味浓厚的意象，流露出对自然和人生中美的无限向往，以及享乐与义务冲突时的痛苦与无奈。该诗所表现的人生哲理——也是作者的人生顿悟，不经意间弘扬了凡人皆有弱点，而职责高于一切的斯多葛哲学①理念。

这是一首典型的现代格律诗，节奏上严格遵循四音步抑扬格，即每行都有四个音步，八个音节，每两个音节构成一个音步，且都是先抑后扬。全诗共四节，每节四行，是十四行诗的变体；这种十六行诗体流行于浪漫主义时期，其尾韵变化相对随意，并无刻板规定。本诗 aaba bbcb ccdc dddd 的尾韵韵式，大有循环往复、环环相扣、宁静致远的态势，暗示了生命发展的轨迹和事物发展的规律。本诗能兼顾形式与内容，彼此配合默契、相互支撑、相得益彰，读来朗朗上口、回味无穷，是一首富有音乐性、象征性和思想性的经典之作。

---

① 斯多葛主义，或斯多葛哲学学派，是芝诺于公元前300年左右在雅典创立的学派，一直繁盛到罗马帝国时代。该学派主张遵从理性，合乎自然，强调顺从天命，要安于自己在社会中所处的地位，要恬淡寡欲，只有这样才能得到幸福。参见马可·奥勒留. 沉思录[M]. 李娟，杨志译. 上海：上海三联书店，2008：24. （资料来源：https：//www. douban. com/group/topic/179798213/? type = like& _ i = 0104384N9kdY9t)

📖 诗作二

The Road Not Taken
未走之路

Two roads diverged^① in a yellow wood,	林褐分两道，
And sorry I could not travel both	憾难均踏足；
And be one traveler, long I stood	行前我久眺，
And looked down one as far as I could	看尽前路消
To where it bent^② in the undergrowth^③;	渐隐林下木。

Two roads diverged① in a yellow wood,　　林褐分两道，
And sorry I could not travel both　　憾难均踏足；
And be one traveler, long I stood　　行前我久眺，
And looked down one as far as I could　　看尽前路消
To where it bent② in the undergrowth③;　　渐隐林下木。

Then took the other, as just as fair,　　后选另一路，
And having perhaps the better claim④　　芳草嫩又鲜；
Because it was grassy and wanted wear⑤;　　缘由似更足；
Though as for that, the passing there　　若无行人顾，
Had worn⑥ them really about the same,　　踏痕同样浅。

And both that morning equally lay　　清晨路两条，
In leaves no step had trodden black⑦.　　落叶顾自堆；
Oh, I kept the first for another day!　　首路留明朝！
Yet knowing how way leads on to way　　虽知道连道，
I doubted if I should ever come back.　　今生难再回。

I shall be telling this with a sigh　　多年后某地
Somewhere ages and ages hence⑧:　　感叹人生路：
Two roads diverged in a wood, and I,　　两道林中异，
I took the one less traveled by,　　我择旅伴稀，
And that has made all the difference⑨.　　从此运命殊。

（诸光　译）

📝 语言注释

① diverged：*adj.* & *vi.* 分岔。

② bent：bend 的过去式。弯曲，折弯；拐弯，转弯。

③ undergrowth：*n.* 下层灌木丛(指林木下的)。

④ claim：*n.* 理由，缘由。

⑤ wanted wear：人迹罕至的。

⑥ worn：wear 的过去分词。踩出，踩踏。

⑦ had trodden black：踩踏过，留下踩踏的痕迹。trodden 是 tread 的过去分词，表示踩，踏；在……上走；踩实，踩出(道路等)；践踏，蹂躏。

⑧ hence：*adv.* 从此，从那以后。

⑨ make all the difference：关系重大；改变一切；使大不相同。

❓ 思考题

1. What do the image "roads", "woods", and "way" stand for?

2. What might the "travel" and "traveler" refer to?

3. Why does the poet use both "road" and "way" in the poem?

4. What figure of speech is applied in "And be one traveler, long I stood"? What implied meaning does it have by the above figure of speech?

5. What figure of speech as well as the implied meaning would the lines "Two roads diverged in a wood, and I, /I took the one less traveled by" have?

6. What difference might there be if we take different road in life?

7. Have you encountered similar scenarios in life? Share them with others.

📝 节奏、韵律图示

The Road Not Taken

行数 (Line)	四音步抑扬格/抑抑扬格 (Iambic Tetrameter/Anapest)	韵式 (Rhyme Scheme)
1.	Two roads | diverged | in a yel | low wood, ▲ ▲ △▲ △ ▲ ▲ △ ▲	a-/ʊ/
2.	And sor | ry I could | not tra | vel both △ ▲ △△ ▲ △ ▲ △ ▲	b-/əʊ/
3.	And be | one trave | ler, long | I stood △ ▲ △ ▲ △ ▲ △ ▲	a-/ʊ/
4.	And looked | down one | as far | as I could △ ▲ △ ▲ △ ▲ △△ ▲	a-/ʊ/
5.	To where | it bent | in the un | dergrowth; △ ▲ △ ▲ △ △▲ △ ▲	b-/əʊ/
6.	Then took | the o | ther, as just | as fair, △ ▲ △ ▲ △ △ ▲ △ ▲	c-/er/
7.	And hav | ing perhaps | the bet | ter claim △ ▲ △ △ ▲ △ ▲ △ ▲	d-/eɪ/
8.	Because | it was gras | sy and wan | ted wear; △ ▲ △ △ ▲ △ △ ▲ △ ▲	c-/er/
9.	Though as | for that, | the pas | sing there △ ▲ △ ▲ △ ▲ △ ▲	c-/er/
10.	Had worn | them real | ly about | the same, △ ▲ △ ▲ △△ ▲ △ ▲	d-/eɪ/
11.	And both | that mor | ning e | qually lay △ ▲ △ ▲ △ ▲ △ △ ▲	e-/eɪ/
12.	In leaves | no step | had trod | den black. △ ▲ △▲ △ ▲ △ ▲	f-/æ/

13.   Oh, I │ kept the first │ **for ano** │ ther day！   e-/eɪ/
       △ ▲   △ △ ▲   △ △▲   △ ▲

14.   Yet know │ ing how way │ leads on │ to way   e-/eɪ/
       △ ▲   △ △ ▲   △ ▲   △ ▲

15.   I doub │ ted if I │ should e │ ver come back.   f-/æ/
       △ ▲   △ △ ▲   △ ▲   △ ▲ △ ▲

16.   I shall │ be tel │ ling this │ with a sigh   g-/aɪ/
       △ ▲   △ ▲   △ ▲   △ △ ▲

17.   Somewhere │ ages │ and a │ ges hence：   h-/ens/
       ▲ △   ▲ △   △ ▲   △ ▲

18.   Two roads │ diverged │ in a wood, │ and I,   g-/aɪ/
       ▲ ▲   △ ▲   △ △ ▲   △ ▲

19.   I took │ the one │ less trave │ led by,   g-/aɪ/
       △ ▲   △ ▲   △ ▲   △ ▲

20.   And that │ has made all │ the dif │ ference.   h-/ens/
       △ ▲   △ △ ▲   △ ▲   △ ▲

注：本诗总体而言是四音步抑扬格，另外还有一些不规则之处：

① 1-1、18-1 的 Two roads 为扬扬格（spondee：▲ ▲）；

② 17-1 和 17-2 均为扬抑格（trochee：▲△）；

③ 黑体字部分为抑抑扬格（anapest：△△▲），包含三个音节（共 18 个）；

④ 最后一行中 difference 本来发音为/ˈdɪfrəns/，但为了和倒数第四行的 hence（/hens/）押韵，故可读作：/ˈdɪfrens/。

修辞解析

本诗涉及四个诗歌中常见的修辞手法或现象：意象、头韵、停顿和顶针（真）。意象和头韵的概念在前一作品解析中已有解释，下面将举例说明意象和头韵，并重点解释后两个修辞手法，即停顿和顶针（真）。

1. 意象（Image）

本诗中的意象主要有"路"（road）（具体）、"林子"（a yellow wood/a wood）（具体）、"旅行"（travel）（具体）、"旅行者"（traveler）（具体）和"道"（way）（具体）。这

些意象的象征意义是比较明显的，即"路"象征着人生之路（road），或人生之路中的一段（way）。"林子"代表死亡和毁灭、神秘和未知，有时候既象征美，又代表着各种诱惑。"旅行"象征着人生之旅，"旅行者"指代任意一个普通人。

2. 头韵（Alliteration）

头韵修辞格在前一首作品中已有解释，在本诗中仅有一处应用，即第二段第三行末尾的 wanted wear（其中首音是 /w/ 音的重复）。

3. 行中停顿（Caesura）

行中停顿是指诗行中间的停顿，节律的停顿，（韵脚的）休止。它是传统英语诗体学（prosody）中的一个经典术语，指一行诗中间的停顿。在英语诗歌中，这样的停顿不是由韵律（metrical）形式来决定的，而是由句法（syntax）、语义或标点符号来决定的，所以它们的出现无规律可循①。本诗中出现了两处此类现象，表现了说话人在面临选择时的停顿、犹疑和思考：

And be one traveler, long I stood　　　（第一节第三行）

Two roads diverged in a wood, and I,　（第四节第三行）

4. 顶针（真）（Anadiplosis）

用上句结尾的词语作下句的开头，前后顶接，蝉联而下，促使语气衔接。又称联珠、蝉联、连环。本诗最后一节的第三、四行即为一个顶针：

Two roads diverged in a wood, and I,

I took the one less traveled by,

运用顶真修辞手法，不但能使句子结构整齐，语气贯通，而且能突出事物之间环环相扣的有机联系。

作品鉴赏

弗罗斯特在诗歌风格上最大的特点是朴实无华、清新隽永，把深刻的人生哲理寓于平淡的日常琐事和简单的叙事之中。本诗就堪称此方面的典范。

这是一首叙事意味浓厚的抒情诗，描述的是一个随处可见的生活场景，以第

---

① 胡壮麟，等. 西方文体学词典［M］. 北京：清华大学出版社，2004：40.

一人称讲述的一个生活小故事；语气沉静自然、不疾不徐，娓娓道来。该诗语言质朴无华，但在构思上却非常巧妙。诗歌中的林中岔路就是人生岔路的象征。它试图说明在人生的旅途中，每个人常常面临两条道路的选择，而不同的选择将决定不同的人生结局。面对选择时，我们往往会变得犹豫不决、踌躇不前，拿不定主意。这首诗描绘的就是人进行选择时的心态，选择本身所带来的思想波动，以及给读者留下的人生体悟和想象空间。这种每个人都有过的复杂心理体验，被弗罗斯特敏感地捕捉到了，并谱写成一首脍炙人口的佳作。

该诗也是一首现代格律诗，节奏上遵循四音步抑扬格及抑抑扬格，即每行都有四个音步，但有的诗行多达九个到十个音节，因此每两三个音节构成一个音步，且都是先抑后扬。全诗共四节，每节五行；其尾韵韵式为 abaab cdccd efeef ghggh，含蓄沉静、收放有度，揭示了日常生活的自然轨迹和人生哲理，读起来朗朗上口、饱含深情、回味无穷，是一首充满象征性、情感性和哲理性的经典之作。

📖 诗作三

Fire and Ice
火与冰

Some say the world will end in fire	有说世将终于火，
Some say in ice.	有说世将灭于冰。
From what I've tasted of desire,	以我遍尝欲之灼，
I hold with those who favor fire.	总觉大火最无情。
But if it had to *perish* twice,	但若世必毁两遭，
I think I know enough of hate	我知仇恨毒之深，
To know that for destruction ice	为达灭世之奇效
Is also great	冰之无情同样狠，
and would suffice.	分量效果均很好。

（诸莉　译）

📖 诗作四

Nothing Gold Can Stay
并无青绿长久时

Nature's first green is gold,

Her hardest hue to hold.

Her early leaf's a flower;

But only so an hour.

Then leaf subsides to leaf.

So Eden sank to grief,

So dawn goes down to day.

Nothing gold can stay.

自然首绿贵如金，

世间难得其色馨。

嫩叶初现美如花，

却仅鲜活一时寡，

旧叶新叶不停换；

伊甸园里魂已断，

黎明终将迎白日，

并无青绿长久时。

（诸莉 译）

📖 诗作五

Mending Walls
修　墙

Something there is that doesn't love a wall,	不知为何不好墙,
That sends the frozen ground-swell under it,	墙基土壤已冻胀,
And spills the upper boulders in the sun;	日照墙头石块落;
And makes gaps even two can pass abreast.	墙体开裂双人过。
The work of hunters is another thing:	猎人狩猎不一样:
I have come after them and made repair	修修补补不停忙,
Where they have left not one stone on a stone,	石块堆砌留空当,
But they would have the rabbit out of hiding,	宁使兔子无处藏,
To please the yelping dogs. The gaps I mean,	讨好猎狗是裂墙,
No one has seen them made or heard them made,	无人见或闻其筑,
But at spring mending-time we find them there.	春补时分已有墙。
I let my neighbor know beyond the hill;	我将隔山邻居访;
And on a day we meet to walk the line	约好沿墙走一趟,
And set the wall between us once again.	重新垒好两家墙。
We keep the wall between us as we go.	墙在中间人两旁,
To each the boulders that have fallen to each.	掉落石块收妥当。
And some are loaves and some so nearly balls	块状球状均有样,
We have to use a spell to make them balance:	我们念咒求稳当:
"Stay where you are until our backs are turned!"	"离开前别落下!"
We wear our fingers rough with handling them.	手搬石块磨无光。
Oh, just another kind of out-door game,	权当户外游戏忙,
One on a side. It comes to little more:	各站一方内心想:

There where it is we do not need the wall:　　　　其实哪里需要墙:

He is all pine and I am apple orchard.　　　　他种松来我苹果。

My apple trees will never get across　　　　果树不会去闯祸

And eat the cones under his pines, I tell him.　　　　到他院里把松尝。

He only says, "Good fences make good neighbors."　　　　"好篱造就好街坊。"

Spring is the mischief in me, and I wonder　　　　春令我心徒伤悲

If I could put a notion in his head:　　　　如何让他同思维:

"Why do they make good neighbors? Isn't it　　　　"好篱造就好街坊?

Where there are cows? But here there are no cows.　　　　这有牛吗? 没有。

Before I built a wall I'd ask to know　　　　造墙之前我当问

What I was walling in or walling out,　　　　何被围入或围出,

And to whom I was like to give offense.　　　　可能冒犯谁人乎。

Something there is that doesn't love a wall,　　　　不知为何不好墙,

That wants it down." I could say "Elves" to him,　　　　想它倒塌。"会是

But it's not elves exactly, and I'd rather　　　　小精灵? 我宁愿

He said it for himself. I see him there　　　　他自己说。看他

Bringing a stone grasped firmly by the top　　　　紧抓石块死不放,

In each hand, like an old-stone savage armed.　　　　石器时代野人样。

He moves in darkness as it seems to me,　　　　黑暗之中他移动,

Not of woods only and the shade of trees.　　　　并非林中和树下。

He will not go behind his father's saying,　　　　不愿违背父辈话,

And he likes having thought of it so well　　　　照葫画瓢不走样:

He says again, "Good fences make good neighbors."　　　　"好篱造就好街坊。"

(诸光　译)

📖 诗作六

The Gift Outright
全心的礼物

The land was ours before we were the land's.	我先属此地，此地方属我。
She was our land more than a hundred years	她成我家地，一百载有余，
Before we were her people. She was ours	后成她家人。她曾属于我
In Massachusetts, in Virgina,	在马萨诸塞，在弗吉尼亚，
But we were England's, still colonials,	我属英格兰，仍为殖民地，
Possessing what we still were unpossessed by	我们拥有者，自己不屑理，
Possessed by what we now no more possessed	自己着魔者，却已不再有。
Something we were withholding made us weak	自己拥有的，亦使己虚弱，
Until we found out that it was ourselves	及至我发现，原因全在己，
We were withholding from our land of living,	繁衍生息地，并未好打理，
And forthwith found salvation in surrender.	迫急要屈服，藉此觅生机。
Such as we were we gave ourselves outright	空空如我们，全力甘奉献，
(The deed of gift was many deeds of war)	（奉献的礼物为多次战争）
To the land vaguely realizing westward,	献礼致此地，拓展渐向西，
But still unstoried, artless, unenhanced,	未迄经人述，朴素未有奇。
Such as she was, such as she would become.	当时即如此，未来亦如斯。

（诸光　译）

📖 诗作七

Neither Out Far nor in Deep
既不远也不深

The people along the sand	人在沙滩上，
All turn and look one way.	齐转看一方。
They turn their back on the land.	后背朝陆地，
They look at the sea all day.	全天看海洋。
As long as it takes to pass	但凡有船过，
A ship keeps raising its hull;	船体受水托；
The wetter ground like glass	地湿像玻璃，
Reflects a standing gull	恰逢海鸥落。
The land may vary more;	陆地多变幻；
But wherever the truth may be—	真相永流淌——
The water comes ashore,	海水奔向岸，
And the people look at the sea.	人均看海洋。
They cannot look out far.	人既望不远。
They cannot look in deep.	人亦看不深。
But when was that ever a bar	何时可改变
To any watch they keep?	看海的本能？

（诸光　译）

📖 诗作八

Once by the Pacific
太平洋岸边有感

The shattered water made a misty din.	浪花飞溅雾蒙蒙。
Great waves looked over others coming in,	海浪滔天巨潮涌,
And thought of doing something to the shore	海对陆地有图谋
That water never did to land before.	海陆之前从未斗。
The clouds were low and hairy in the skies,	云团飞絮毛绒绒,
Like locks blown forward in the gleam of eyes,	有如毛发嵌眼中,
You could not tell, and yet it looked as if	海岸运气实难测
The shore was lucky in being backed by cliff,	幸有礁石前挡遮
The cliff in being backed by continent;	礁石亦有陆地靠;
It looked as if a night of dark intent	仿佛一夜阴谋到,
Was coming, and not only a night, an age.	恐将持续一世纪。
Someone had never been prepared for rage.	大海风暴从不理,
There would be more than ocean-water broken	远超海面巨浪激,
Before God's last Put out the Light was spoken.	神谕灭灯之前启。

（诸光　译）

Unit 2　Alfred Tennyson

阿尔弗雷德·丁尼生

　　阿尔弗雷德·丁尼生（1809—1892），英国维多利亚时代大诗人，曾是剑桥学子，后因贫辍学；早年诗作被讽为"晦涩"和"矫揉造作"，直至1842年，特别是1850年发表长篇挽诗《悼念》之后才获得好评；同年成为桂冠诗人，从此人生境遇彻底改观，诗歌创作和个人生活都一帆风顺；1884年接受贵族爵位，1892年去世。死后争议颇多，并一直延续至今。

　　作为一代语言大师，其诗坛地位毋庸置疑。他的诗格律齐整，用词讲究，意象鲜明，乐感和画面感极强，文字饱含修辞性和象征性，视野广阔高远，令诗歌充满含混性和张力。作为桂冠诗人，他素以爱国者著称，其诗歌又隐隐带有时代印记和帝国自豪感。

📖 诗作一

The Eagle (A Fragment)
鹰(片段)

He clasps① the crag② with crooked③ hands;　　　　他强力的爪子紧抓峭壁;

Close to the sun in lonely lands,　　　　背靠太阳在孤寂的大地,

Ringed④ with the azure⑤ world, he stands.　　　　蔚蓝海天环绕他的四极。

The wrinkled⑥ sea beneath him crawls;　　　　脚下爬行着褶皱的海面;

He watches from his mountain walls,　　　　他眺望在他陡峭的山岩;

And like a thunderbolt⑦ he falls.　　　　俯冲扑猎时快捷如闪电。

（诸光　译）

✍ 语言注释

① clasp：v. 扣住；扣紧；紧紧抱住；握紧。

② crag：n. 峭壁；悬崖；绝壁。

③ crooked：adj. 弯曲的；扭曲的。v. "crook"的过去式和过去分词。

④ ringed：adj. 被包围的。

⑤ azure：adj. 天蓝色的；蔚蓝色的。

⑥ wrinkled：adj. 有皱纹的；有皱褶的。

⑦ thunderbolt：n. 雷电；霹雳。

❓ 思考题

1. What associations would the image "eagle" remind you?

2. What figure of speech(es) is (are) applied in the first, second and last line?

3. What cultural background is implied here by saying "close to the sun"?

4. Why is the land called "lonely" in the second line?

5. Why does the poet pause in the third line?

6. Why is the eagle personalized?

7. What (or whom) might the eagle symbolize?

8. Why does the poet leave the poem in the form of a fragment?

🖉 节奏、韵律图示

The Eagle (A Fragment)

行数 (Line)	四音步抑扬格 (Iambic Tetrameter)	韵式 (Rhyme Scheme)
1.	He clasps | the crag | with croo | ked hands; △ ▲　△ ▲　△ ▲　△ ▲	a-/ændz/
2.	Close to | the sun | in lone | ly lands, ▲ △　△ ▲　△ ▲　△ ▲	a-/ændz/
3.	Ringed with | the a | zure world, | he stands. ▲ △　△▲　△ ▲　△ ▲	a-/ændz/
4.	The wrin | kled sea | beneath | him crawls; △ ▲　△ ▲　△▲　△ ▲	b-/ɔːlz/
5.	He wa | tches from | his moun | tain walls, △ ▲　△ ▲　△ ▲　△ ▲	b-/ɔːlz/
6.	And like | a thun | derbolt | he falls. △ ▲　△ ▲　△ ▲　△ ▲	b-/ɔːlz/

注：本诗为四音步抑扬格(iambic tetrameter：△▲)，仅黑体词部分(1-2-1、1-3-1)为扬抑格(trochee：▲△)。韵式为 aaa bbb，因为当时是未完成的片段，故此。

🔲 修辞解析

本诗应用了以下八种修辞手法：拟人、头韵、谐元音、移情（转类形容词）、停顿、诗的破格、暗喻（隐喻）、明喻。

1. 拟人（Personification）

该修辞格在弗罗斯特第一首作品中已有界定。本诗一、三、五、六行中的四处主语（He）皆拟人。该诗以男性第三人称将鹰人格化，凸显了男性的力量、机敏以及才华，借此隐喻阿塞·哈勒姆（同学、好友、妹夫）或彼时的大英帝国①。

2. 头韵（Alliteration）

该修辞格在弗罗斯特第一首作品中已有界定。本诗第一行中/kː clasps，crag，crooked 有头韵，第二行中/l/：lonely，lands 有头韵。头韵的使用能起到强调和加强语气、气势的作用。

3. 谐元音（类音、类韵或腹韵）（Assonance）

在两个或更多相邻单词中的重读音节中，元音相同或相似的现象叫类音、类韵、谐元音或腹韵。本诗第一行中的 clasps 和 crag 元音相谐（/æ/），第四行中的 sea 和 beneath 元音相谐（/iː/），第五行中的 watches 和 from 元音相谐（/ɒ/）。元音相谐毫无疑问也增强了诗歌的韵律感。

4. 移情（转类形容词）（Transferred Epithet）

一个修饰语（一个形容词或描述性词组）从一个本来正当描述、修饰或限定的名词前转移到另一个不恰当的名词前面。一般来说，它会从对人的修饰或限定转移到对一个物体或观念的修饰或限定②。本诗中 lonely 一词一般用来形容人或动物，但在诗中创造性地应用于 land，把无感情的自然人格化了，因此属于移情（转类形容词）修辞格。

5. 停顿（Caesura）

该修辞格在弗罗斯特第二首作品中已有界定，应用于此意在强调和突出鹰在大自然中至高无上的尊享地位。

---

① 诸莉. 从形式到内容——鹰（片段）的文学性解读[J]. 外语教育，2009：212-216.
② 冯翠华. 英语修辞大全[M]. 北京：外语教学与研究出版社，2005：234.

6. 诗的破格(Poetic License)

赋予诗人在想象上的和语言上的自由，允许其偏离正常的、在实际准确性、句法、语法或发音方面的散文写作标准，以便达成更令人满意的想象效果或格律效果①。本诗第四行的 wrinkled 一词本来是个单音节词，读作/ˈrɪŋkld/；但为了满足该行八个音节的需要(原本只有七个音节)，以便形成标准的四音步抑扬格(其他各行都已满足)，诗人刻意改变本词的读法，将本词读作/ˈrɪŋkled/，由此 wrinkled 变成双音节词，为该诗行凑满了八个音节。

7. 暗喻/隐喻(Metaphor)

暗喻即省略 like 或 as 的两个事物之间不直接的比较②。本诗中有三处该修辞格：(1) wrinkled sea(第四行)；(2) crawls(第四行)；(3) mountains walls(第五行)。第一个表示"充满褶皱的大海"；第二个表示"像动物或人一样匍匐爬行"；第三个表示"像墙壁一样笔直陡峭的悬崖"。暗喻的特点是它比较间接和含蓄，本体和喻体之间关联性不是很明显，需要读者细细品味。

8. 明喻(Simile)

明喻即两个事物之间的直接比较，常用 like 或 as 引导③。本诗唯一一个明喻是第六行中的 And like a thunderbolt he falls(俯冲捕猎时快捷如闪电)，形容鹰向下俯冲猎食时的迅猛快捷！明喻就是通过通俗和直白的比喻把一个较为复杂抽象的问题或事物说得浅显易懂。

作品鉴赏

《鹰》(片断)是阿尔弗雷德·丁尼生的一首咏物性诗歌小品。长期以来，该诗一直以其优美和谐的韵律、铿锵有力的节奏以及深邃唯美的意境而令人折服，同时也以自身不确定的象征意义及主题思想而令人倍感困惑。尽管它只是一个未完成的片断，"却已可被视为自成起讫的完整诗篇"④。这种未完成的状态不仅没有掩

---

① Baldick Chris. 牛津文学术语词典[M]. 上海：上海外语教育出版社，1999：172.
② Gillespie Sheena, Fonseca Terezinba, Sanger Carol. Literature Across Cultures[M]. Boston：Allyn and Bacon，1998：929.
③ Ibid. 1998：929.
④ 江枫. 英文名篇鉴赏金库·诗歌卷[M]. 辜正坤主编. 天津：天津人民出版社，2001：179.

盖其诗歌的艺术成色；相反，作为诗歌史上罕见的高度浓缩的艺术典范，正是它的未完成才造就了它的艺术成就。正如断臂的维纳斯以残缺之身引起人们无限遐思，并给人以无穷的艺术享受，这个未完成的片段同样使人浮想联翩，欲罢还休……

其实我们不应感到遗憾……因为正是它的未完成造就了诗歌史上罕见的完美和惊人的成就：“这一片段，很像后来的意象派诗人笔下的小品，却有大多数意象派小品难以比拟的恢弘气势。”①就创作时间而言，与其说它像意象派诗人的小品，还不如说意象派诗人的小品像它，或曾以它为典范（它比意象派作品早诞生了半个世纪）。作为格律诗的后期典范，它在诗歌艺术上达到了为后来者难以企及的高度。所以即使后来产生了意象派，主张诗歌以意象为核心来表达思想情感，也未能创作出像《鹰》（片段）这样以音乐性、意象性取胜，形式和内容和谐统一的诗歌精品②。

① 江枫. 英文名篇鉴赏金库·诗歌卷［M］. 辜正坤主编. 天津：天津人民出版社，2001：180.
② 诸莉. 从形式到内容——鹰（片段）的文学性解读［J］. 外语教育，2009：212-216.

📖 诗作二

Break，Break，Break
冲，冲，冲

Break，Break，Break，

On thy cold gray stones，O Sea！

And I would that my tongue could utter

The thoughts that arise in me.

O，well for the fisherman's boy，

That he shouts with his sister at play！

O，well for the sailor lad，

That he sings in his boat on the bay！

And the stately ships go on

To their haven under the hill；

But O for the touch of a vanish'd hand，

And the sound of a voice that is still！

Break，Break，Break，

At the foot of thy crags，O Sea！

But the tender grace of a day that is dead

Will never come back to me.

冲，冲，冲，

　　冲击你黑冷的礁石，喔大海！

但愿我的口舌还能说出

　　我心中涌起的思绪。

看那渔家男儿多骄傲，

　　和其妹玩耍时尽情喊叫！

看那少年水手多自豪！

　　在海湾划船唱歌多美妙！

那一艘艘气派的帆船驶向

　　它们在山下的港湾；

喔多想再抚摸那消逝的手，

　　再聆听那已消停的歌喉！

冲，冲，冲，

　　冲击你悬崖的山脚，喔大海！

但那消逝的优雅温柔

　　却永远回不到这里。

（诸光　译）

诗作三

Crossing the Bar
过沙洲

Sunset and evening star,
And one clear call for me!
And may there be no moaning of the bar,
When I put out to sea,

But such a tide. As moving seems asleep,
Too full for sound and foam,
When that which drew from out the boundless deep
Turn again home.

Twilight and evening bell,
And after that the dark!
And may there be no sadness of farewell,
When I embark;

For though from out our bourne of Time and Place
The flood may bear me far,
I hope to see my pilot face to face
When I have crossed the bar.

夕阳西沉明星启，
一声呼唤多清晰！
每当扬帆要出海，
愿过沙洲无悲哀。

海潮暗涌静似睡，
潮水太满无声推；
满潮来水深悠悠，
水来水往自回流。

夜幕降临晚钟鸣，
钟声响后满天星！
当我登船再出海，
愿人别离不再哀。

时空范围虽有限，
海潮载我去远天；
下次出海过沙洲，
我盼亲遇领航手。

（诸莉　译）

Unit 3 Dante Gabriel Rossetti

但丁·加布里埃尔·罗塞蒂

　　但丁·加布里埃尔·罗塞蒂(1828—1882)，英国维多利亚时代诗人、画家，意大利裔。父亲因参加革命组织而流亡伦敦；自幼喜好诗歌和绘画，尤喜莎士比亚、爱伦·坡等人的作品；在绘画方面，他擅长表现色彩和女性人体，曾大胆表现女性感性美而引发争议；模特娇妻的过早离世使他悲痛欲绝，曾将诗稿殉葬墓中。

　　"前拉斐尔兄弟会"发起人之一；反对学院派刻板呆滞的风格，主张师法拉斐尔等前辈艺术精神，尊重自然和天性，恢复艺术的真诚和纯洁；意大利血统使他拥有南方人的热情、感性和艺术化人格，在诗、画两方面都形成了独特的唯美风格，做到了诗中有画、画中有诗，践行了其一贯的审美主张。

📖 诗作一

Sudden Light
顿　悟

I have been here before,	此地我曾来,
But when or how I cannot tell;	时因已不记;
I know the grass beyond the door,	芳草生门外,
The sweet, keen① smell,	甜香沁心脾,
The sighing② sound, the lights around the shore.	潮泣岸火开。
You have been mine before, —	君曾属于我,
How long ago I may not know:	多久亦不记:
But just when at that swallow's soar③	惊鸿掠飞过,
Your neck turned so,	颈转纱落地,
Some veil④ did fall, —I knew it all of yore⑤.	此景何其多。
Has this been thus before?	此事确曾历?
And shall not thus time's eddying flight⑥	时光若飞旋,
Still with our lives our love restore⑦	可否以命抵,
In death's despite⑧,	舍生续爱缘,
And day and night yield⑨ one delight once more?	日夜结欢喜?

（诸光　译）

📝 语言注释

① keen：*adj.* 热情的，热心的，敏锐的，渴望的。此处意为"强烈的""浓郁的"。

② sighing：sighing 是 sigh 的现在分词。sigh：/saɪ/ *v.* 叹息；悲叹；（风等）呜咽呼啸。此处意为"叹息""低语"。

③ swallow's soar：swallow，*v.* 吞下；咽下；吞没。*n.* 吞；咽；燕。此处为"燕子"。soar：*v.* 翱翔；高飞；猛增；高耸。此处意为"鸿雁掠过"。

④ veil：*n.* （尤指女用的）面纱、面罩；（修女的）头巾。

⑤ yore：*n.* 往昔。all of yore：往昔的一切。此句意为："从前的事情我都想起来了。"

⑥ eddying flight：eddying 为 eddy 的现在分词。eddy：*v.* （使）起旋涡；（使）旋转。flight：*n.* 飞行；班机。此处意为："时光的飞旋（或飞逝）"或"飞旋（或飞逝）的时光"。

⑦ restore：*v.* 恢复（某种情况或感受）；还原。此处意为"重现""再现"。

⑧ In death's despite：despite death，即使死；越过死亡；将生死置之度外。

⑨ yield：*v.* 屈服；让步；放弃；提供，产出。此处意为"生成、化作"。

❓ 思考题

1. Why can't the speaker remember when or how he has been there?

2. Why does the speaker still know many things there so well?

3. What do "the grass", "the smell" and "the sound" signify?

4. Who does the speaker address in the poem?

5. Why can't the speaker remember how long ago she had been his love?

6. Why does the speaker remember some anecdotes so well?

7. What wish does the speaker want to express in the last stanza?

8. What character does the poem reflect about the speaker?

9. What impress you most in the poem?

📝 节奏、韵律图示

Sudden Light/顿悟

音步数 (Foot)	二至五音步抑扬格 (Iambic Dimeter to Pentameter)	韵式 (Rhyme Scheme)
3	I have │ been here │ before, △ ▲　　△ ▲　　△ ▲	a-/ɔː/
4	But when │ or how │ I can │ not tell; △ ▲　　△ ▲　△ ▲　　△ ▲	b-/eɪ/
4	I know │ the grass │ beyond │ the door, △ ▲　　△ ▲　　△ ▲　　△ ▲	a-/ɔː/
2	The sweet, │ **keen smell**, △ ▲　　▲ ▲	b-/eɪ/
5	The sigh │ ing sound, │ the lights │ around │ the shore. △ ▲　△ ▲　　△ ▲　　△ ▲　△ ▲	a-/ɔː/
3	You have │ been mine │ before, — △ ▲　　△ ▲　　△ ▲	a-/ɔː/
4	How long │ ago │ I may │ not know: △ ▲　△ ▲　△ ▲　　△ ▲	c-/oʊ/
4	But just │ when at │ that swal │ low's soar △ ▲　　△ ▲　　△ ▲　　△ ▲	a-/ɔː/
2	Your neck │ **turned so**, △ ▲　　▲ △	c-/oʊ/
5	Some veil │ did fall, │ —I knew │ it all │ of yore. △ ▲　　△ ▲　　△ ▲　▲ ▲　△ ▲	a-/ɔː/
3	Has this │ been thus │ before? △ ▲　　△ ▲　　△ ▲	a-/ɔː/
4	And shall │ not thus │ time's ed │ dying flight △ ▲　　△ ▲　　△ ▲　　△ ▲	d-/aɪt/

4 **Still with** │ our lives │ our love │ restore   a-/ɔː/
   ▲ △   △ ▲   △ ▲   △ ▲

2 In death's │ despite,   d-/aɪt/
   △ ▲   △ ▲

5 And day │ and night │ yield one │ delight │ once more? a-/ɔː/
   △ ▲   △ ▲   △ ▲   △△   ▲

注：本诗每节音步数都遵循 3-4-4-2-5，每音步内的抑扬格格律却比较规律，仅有一处扬扬格（spondee：1-4-2）和两处扬抑格（trochee：2-4-2；3-3-1）。放弃固定音步数的做法实为格律诗向自由诗转变过程中的一个过渡，也是一种新的尝试：用长短句来表现海边波涛起伏、汹涌澎湃的动态图景，也暗示作者内心思绪的起伏不定和情感波澜。

📧 修辞解析

本诗主要应用了以下四种修辞手法：头韵、谐元音（腹韵）、谐辅音和停顿。

1. 头韵（Alliteration）

该修辞格在弗罗斯特第一首作品中已有界定。本诗第一节的第一行中有 have 和 here（/h/），been 和 before 两组交错式头韵（/b/），第二行中 when 和 how（/w/），第四行中 sweet 和 smell（/s/），第五行中 sighing 和 sound（/s/）都是头韵；第二节第三行的 swallow's soar（/s/）也是头韵；第三节第一行的 been 和 before（/b/），第四行的 death's 和 despite（/d/）也是头韵。头韵的使用能起到强调和加强语气、增强气势的作用。

2. 谐元音（类音、类韵或腹韵）（Assonance）

该修辞格在丁尼生作品修辞解析中已有界定。本诗第一节第四行的 sweet 和 keen 元音相谐（/iː/），第五行中的 sighing 和 lights 元音相谐（/aɪ/），第五行中的 sound 和 around 元音相谐（/au/）；第三节第三行中的 time's 和 flight（/aɪ/]）及第五行中的 night 和 delight（/aɪ/）都是元音相谐。元音相谐实质上是一种重复，只不过是元音的重复，但其功能依然是加强语气、增强气势，达到强调的目的。

3. 谐辅音（Consonance）

在两个相邻的词中，辅音完全相同或相近而元音不同的现象我们就称之为谐辅音。第三节第三行中的 lives 和 love 就是一组辅音相谐的案例。辅音相谐实质上是一种重复，只不过是辅音的重复，但其功能依然是加强语气、增强气势，达到强调的目的。

4. 停顿(Caesura)

该修辞格在弗罗斯特第二首作品中已有界定。本诗第二节最后一句有一个停顿，意在强调和突出此情此景给诗人的强烈感受。

作品鉴赏

《顿悟》是罗塞蒂的一首怀念亡妻的悼亡诗，充满了感怀和梦幻的韵调。因为经济困难，罗塞蒂和他的模特女友伊丽莎白·西德尔相爱十年后才结婚，而婚后一年多西德尔因病亡故。罗塞蒂悲痛欲绝，最后以自己的全部诗稿为妻子殉葬，以表达对亡妻的沉痛悼念。

"罗塞蒂是女性的歌者，作为意大利血统的后裔，他的情诗和绘画大多围绕着爱与美来发挥。"[1]罗塞蒂对色彩和女性人体的描绘非常擅长，他对女性的钟爱以及对女性肉体的大胆表现，在"为维多利亚的时空留下了多情的柔美画卷"[2]的同时，也为他带来了非议和指责，使他倍感苦闷和压抑。

该诗在结构上精巧别致，在文字上雕琢讲究，在音韵上优美动听，在意象上梦幻唯美，在情感上浓烈真挚，具有很强的感染力。在修辞上头韵和谐元音的大量使用，使得该诗吟诵起来朗朗上口，韵味无穷。尾韵采用了非常独特的 ababa，acaca，adada 的韵式，在节奏和音律上实现了从格律诗向自由诗的过渡，做出了大胆的创新——没有沿用一齐到底的音步数，而是以每节 3-4-4-2-5 的音步数模式贯穿于全诗。每行音步数的不同使得情感的表达收放有度，挥洒自如：那长短不一的诗句有如高低不平的海浪，波涛汹涌，起伏不定；又恰似诗人内心的强烈思绪，触景生情，睹物思人，久久、久久不能平息……

---

① 王金玲. 从拉斐尔前派画家罗塞蒂的女模特看其女性观[J]. 美与时代(下)，2011(1)：83.
② 王金玲. 从拉斐尔前派画家罗塞蒂的女模特看其女性观[J]. 美与时代(下)，2011(1)：83.

Unit 4　Christina Georgina Rossetti

克里斯蒂娜·乔治娜·罗塞蒂

　　克里斯蒂娜·乔治娜·罗塞蒂(1830—1894)，英国维多利亚时代著名女诗人，前拉斐尔诗派成员，但丁·罗塞蒂的妹妹；诗歌创作受其兄影响颇多，但诗风却不像其兄那样感性、浓情和唯美，比较恬淡、自然和清新，但又不失女性的热情和想象、细腻和敏感。

　　克里斯蒂娜的两次恋爱都因宗教信仰因素而以失败告终，从而终身未嫁，转而专心于诗歌创作和慈善工作，并在家侍奉父母。但爱情主题从未离开她的诗歌，无论是对爱人到来的热烈期待，还是对错失良缘的扼腕叹息，无论是对死后悲境的凄美想象，还是对人生真谛的领悟参透，无不源自其对浪漫爱情和幸福生活的自然向往，以及恋爱挫败给其带来的刻骨铭心的苦痛。

📖 诗作一

The First Day
第一天

I wish I could remember that first day,	一日当铭记,
First hour, first moment of your meeting me,	首次遇见你,
It bright or dim① the season, it might be	季节或明暗,
Summer or winter for aught② I can say;	冬夏均可期;
So unrecorded③ did it slip away,	此日踪难觅,
So blind was I to see and to foresee,	眼盲无先见;
So dull④ to mark⑤ the budding⑥ of my tree.	不觉新芽添,
That would not blossom yet for many a May.	多年花发兮;
If only I could recollect⑦ it; such	但愿拥此日,
A day of days! I let it come and go	我竟得而失;
As traceless as a thaw⑧ of bygone⑨ snow;	融雪般无痕,
It seemed to mean so little, meant so much;	事小却意深;
If only now I could recall that touch,	愿拥触手忆,
First touch of hand in hand did one but know!	首次谁又知!

（诺莉　译）

✍ 语言注释

① bright, dim：原为形容词，此处用作动词，表示"使明亮"和"使暗淡"。

② aught：*n.* 任何事物（等于 anything）。For aught I can say，我只能如此说。

③ unrecorded：*adj.* 未写下的；未记录的；未录音的；未登记的；未注册的。

④ dull：*adj.* 枯燥无味的；迟钝的；乏味的。

⑤ mark：*v.* 纪念；评分；注意；标示。此处为注意，notice 的意思。

⑥ budding：*n.* 发芽；含苞；萌芽。

⑦ recollect：*v.* 记得；回忆起；记起。

⑧ thaw：*n. & v.* 融化，解冻。

⑨ bygone：*adj.* 很久以前的；以往的；过去的；原先的。

？ 思考题

1. How does the speaker feel about the first meeting with her date?

2. What would you imagine about the man she first dated?

3. What possible mistake might the speaker make in her first date?

4. Why couldn't she be aware then that the failure of her first date would mean a lot to her later life?

5. Why does the speaker take the failure of her first date so seriously?

6. Is the speaker to be blamed for the failure of her frist date?

7. Would the speaker definitely gain happiness if her first date was successful?

8. What special expressions and grammatical means does the speaker use to express her deep regret about her first date? How do you like them?

✍ 节奏、韵律图示

The First Day

行数 (Line)	抑扬格五音步 (Iambic Pentameter)	韵式 (Rhyme Scheme)
1.	I wish | I could | remem | ber that | first day, △ ▲ △ ▲ △ ▲ △ ▲ ▲ ▲	a-/eɪ/
2.	First hour, | first mo | ment of | your mee | ting me, ▲ ▲ ▲ ▲ △ ▲ △ ▲ △ ▲	b-/iː/
3.	It bright | or dim | the sea | son, it | might be △ ▲ △ ▲ △ ▲ △ ▲ △ ▲	b-/iː/

4. Summer | or Win | ter for | aught I | can say;　　　a-/eɪ/
　　▲　△　　△　▲　　△　▲　　△　▲　　△　▲

5. So un | recor | ded did | it slip | away,　　　a-/eɪ/
　　△　▲　　△　▲　　△　▲　　△　▲　　△　▲

6. So blind | was I | to see | and to | foresee,　　　b-/iː/
　　△　▲　　△　▲　　△　▲　　△　▲　　△　▲

7. So dull | to mark | the bud | ding of | my tree.　　　b-/iː/
　　△　▲　　△　▲　　△　▲　　△　▲　　△　▲

8. That would | not blos | som yet | for ma | ny a May.　　　a-/eɪ/
　　▲　▲　　△　▲　　△　▲　　△　▲　　△　△　▲

9. If on | ly I | could re | collect | it; such　　　c-/ʌtʃ/
　　△　▲　　△　▲　　△　▲　　△　▲　　△　▲

10. A day | of days! | I let | it come | and go　　　d-/əʊ/
　　△　▲　　△　▲　　△　▲　　△　▲　　△　▲

11. As trace | less as | a thaw | of by | gone snow;　　　d-/əʊ/
　　△　▲　　△　▲　　△　▲　　△　▲　　△　▲

12. It seemed | to mean | so lit | tle, meant | so much;　　　c-/ʌtʃ/
　　△　▲　　△　▲　　△　▲　　△　▲　　△　▲

13. If on | ly now | I could | recall | that touch,　　　c-/ʌtʃ/
　　△　▲　　△　▲　　△　▲　　△　▲　　△　▲

14. First touch | of hand | in hand | did one | but know!　　　d-/əʊ/
　　▲　▲　　△　▲　　△　▲　　△　▲　　△　▲

注：①1-5、2-1、2-2、8-1 和 14-1 大多因为是单音节词，均需重读，所以都是扬扬格（spondee，▲▲）。

②4-1 的 summer 和 6-5 的 foresee 同为双音节词，本身构成一个音步，因其自然重音在第一个音节上，所以只能读作扬抑格（trochee，▲△），但这并不影响全诗抑扬格格律的统一属性。

③8-5 是一个三音节音步，读作抑抑扬格（anapest，△△▲）。

总体而言，该诗为抑扬格五音步的意大利比特拉克式十四行诗（Petrarchan sonnet）。

修辞解析

本诗主要应用了以下四种修辞手法：头韵、谐元音（腹韵）、重复和悖论。

1. 头韵(Alliteration)

本诗第二行中 moment、meeting、me，第七行中 mark、my，第八行中 many、May，第十二行中 mean、meant 都是头韵修辞格的运用(/m/)。头韵的使用能起到强调和加强语气、增强气势和韵律感的作用。

2. 谐元音(类音、类韵或腹韵)(assonance)

该修辞格在丁尼生作品修辞解析中已有界定。第二行中 meeting、me 和第三行中 season、be(/iː/)，第四行中 for、aught(/ɔː/)都是谐元音的运用，起到了增强韵律美感的作用。

3. 重复(Repetition)

某个单字及词组结构或某句诗行以略为改变的形式出现两次以上，称为重复。在该诗第一、二、十四行中 first 共出现了四次，在第五、六、七行开始的位置 so 出现了三次，引导了三个排比句型，第六行中 see 和 foresee 也是重复，第十行中 day 和 days 也是重复，第十二行中 so 出现了两次，第九行和第十三行中 if only 虚拟语气结构出现了两次，最后一行中 hand 出现了两次。大量字词及语法结构的重复无疑增强了韵律感，加强了表达的语气和气势，所谓回旋往复，步步升华，正如某影评人所说，"回旋往复，像每天的日子"①。重复也许就是生活本真的表现。

4. 明喻(Simile)

该修辞格在丁尼生作品修辞解析中已有界定。本诗第十一行的 As traceless as (a thaw of bygone snow)当然不属于那种陈腐的、平庸的、老一套的 as... as 结构的明喻，如：as cold as ice, as good as gold, as strong as an ox, as cunning as fox.② As traceless as 符合一个优质明喻所应具备的条件：freshness 和 originality，即清新度和独创性(参见冯翠华，2005：177)。明喻就是通过通俗和直白的比喻把一个较为复杂的问题说得浅显易懂。

5. 暗喻/隐喻(Metaphor)

暗喻即省略 like 或 as 的不直接比较。③ 本诗中有一处暗喻修辞格，即第七行

① 淡淡的音乐回旋往复，好像日子一天又一天[EB/OL]. (2009-11-28)[2023-01-03]. https://movie. douban. com/review/2800611/.

② 冯翠华. 英语修辞大全[M]. 北京：外语教学与研究出版社，2005：177.

③ Gillespie Sheena, Fonseca Terezinba, Sanger Carol. Literature Across Cultures[M]. Boston：Allyn and Bacon, 1998：929.

的 the budding of my tree。此处当然不是讨论诗人家里的树在春天发芽了，而是在隐喻女诗人青春意识的觉醒，所以是喻指少女青春之树的萌芽。暗喻的特点是其比喻比较间接和含蓄，需要读者细细品味。

6. 悖论(Paradox)

该修辞格在弗罗斯特第一首作品修辞解析中已有界定。该诗第十二行"It seemed to mean so little, meant so much"是一个典型的悖论修辞格(也称似是而非、似非而是)。该句意思是，这一切当时似乎没什么影响，但事后证明其意义极其重大。语法上来说，meant so much 是个过去分词引导的伴随状语，表示一种与主句行为相伴或几乎同时发生的行为或状态。句中的 so little 和 so much 是个对照的概念，因此整句表达的是在时间上几乎同步发生，而在意义上却完全相反的两种判断和认知，反映出女诗人在爱情萌芽上的后知后觉，充满了对痛失良缘的遗憾和叹息。

三 作品鉴赏

《第一天》是一首意大利式彼特拉克十四行诗(Petrarchan sonnet)，英国诗人除莎士比亚创作英式十四行诗以外，基本都写意大利式十四行诗。

同为意大利血统，克里斯蒂娜与其兄但丁的诗风大不相同：如果说哥哥的诗风更唯美和浓情，妹妹则既更清新和自然，体现出哥哥的性格热烈奔放、执着率性，妹妹则多愁善感、细腻温柔。但丁的诗画关注的都是女性，表现的是女性的感性美、人体美以及男女之间刻骨铭心的爱，而克里斯蒂娜关注的是自己的爱情及其内心感受，表现的是爱的遗憾。虽然表现的对象均为女性，但表现视角不同。哥哥是男性视角，妹妹是女性视角；哥哥是第三人称全能视角，妹妹是第一人称有限视角，哥哥是热恋中的爱人视角，妹妹是失恋中的被爱视角。视角不同，落脚点也不同。

本诗文采斐然，文辞优美，情感充沛，充分展现了女诗人过人的语言驾驭能力。例如，该诗的语言表达方式十分丰富：在满足格律前提下，克里斯蒂娜使用了三个虚拟语气(第1、9、13行)，使用了三个排比句式(第5、6、7行：So...)、三个感叹句式(加上 if only 虚拟语气句型共三个：第9、10、13行)、四个对照句式(第3、4、10、12行：bright or dim, Summer or winter, come and go, so little... so much)，还有大量的重复、暗喻(第7行)、明喻(第11行)和悖论(第12行)等修辞格，把内心情感表现得淋漓尽致、分毫毕现。这些表达方式已经达到"妙语生花"的水平，具有很高的清新度和独创性，从此成为隽语或名句，经常为人引用(如to see and to foresee, a day of days, as traceless as a thaw of bygone snow, It seemed to mean so little, meant so much 等)。

该诗是标准的比特拉克十四行诗五音步抑扬格，尾韵为abba abba cdd ccd 的韵式。在修辞上，头韵、谐元音和重复修辞格的大量使用，使得该诗吟诵起来朗朗上口、韵味无穷。

诗作二

Remember
铭 记

Remember me when I am gone away,
记住我，当我离开后，

Gone far away into the silent land;
去那遥远的无声之地；

When you can no more hold me by the hand,
那时你不能再牵我手，

Nor I half turn to go yet turning stay.
我不再犹豫似走非走。

Remember me when no more day by day
记住我，你不用每天

You tell me of our future that you planned:
将美好计划向我倾诉。

Only remember me; you understand
就记住我吧；你知道

It will be late to counsel then or pray.
那时不能忠告或乞求。

Yet if you should forget me for a while
如果你将我一时忘记

And afterwards remember, do not grieve:
后又想起，不必悲伤：

For if the darkness and corruption leave
黑暗和腐败总会残留

A vestige of the thoughts that once I had,
一丝我有的思想痕迹，

Better by far you should forget and smile
宁可你忘掉我并微笑，

Than that you should remember and be sad.
也不愿你记得而悲泣。

（诸莉　译）

📖 诗作三

Song
歌

When I am dead, my dearest,	如果我死了，我最亲爱的，
Sing no sad songs for me;	别为我唱悲哀的歌；
Plant thou no roses at my head,	别在我坟上种玫瑰，
Nor shady cypress tree;	更无需成荫的松柏；
Be the green grass above me	就做我坟上的青草
With showers and dewdrops wet;	既能接雨水，还可沾露珠；
And if thou wilt, remember,	如果你愿意，就记着我，
And if thou wilt, forget.	如果你愿意，就忘了我。
I shall not see the shadows,	我再也见不到树荫，
I shall not feel the rain;	我再也触不到雨水；
I shall not hear the nightingale	我再也听不见夜莺
Sing on as if in pain.	那似在痛中之吟唱；
And dreaming through the twilight	在黄昏或黎明里梦幻，
That doth not rise nor set,	太阳既不升起也不下沉；
Haply I may remember,	或许，我会记得你，
And haply may forget.	或许，我会把你忘记。

（诸莉　译）

📖 诗作四

Up-Hill
上 山

Does the road wind up-hill all the way?	此路蜿蜒可上山？
Yes，to the very end.	山高路长终至头。
Will the day's journey take the whole long day?	今日旅程耗整天？
From morn to night，my friend.	从早到晚慢慢走。
But is there for the night a resting-place?	夜黑尚有休憩处？
A roof for when the slow dark hours begin.	长夜漫漫屋檐护。
May not the darkness hide it from my face?	黑夜会否遮我脸？
You cannot miss that inn.	君慧不至错客店。
Shall I meet other wayfarers at night?	夜晚会否遇他人？
Those who have gone before.	比我先行上路者。
Then must I knock，or call when just in sight?	我须敲门或喊叫？
They will not keep you standing at that door.	不致使君门外漂。
Shall I find comfort，travel-sore and weak?	会有安慰解乏困？
Of labour you shall find the sum.	一日付出终有报。
Will there be beds for me and all who seek?	有床供我及他人？
Yea，beds for all who come.	所有来者皆有份。

（诸莉 译）

诗作五

A Birthday
生　日

My heart is like a singing bird	我心如欢鸟，
Whose nest is in a watered shoot	筑巢嫩芽间；
My heart is like an apple tree	我心像果树，
Whose boughs are bent with thickest fruit；	果实累弯枝；
My heart is like a rainbow shell	我心似彩壳，
That paddles in a halcyon sea；	荡桨静海中；
My heart is gladder than all these	我心欢于此，
Because my love is come to me.	爱人来身边。
Raise me a dais' of silk and down；	垫好绒高座；
Hang it with vair and purple eyes；	挂上皮紫染；
carve it in doves，and pomegranates，	刻上百翎雀，
and peacocks with a hundred eyes；	野鸽石榴饰；
work it in gold and silver grapes，	金银葡萄镶，
in leaves，and silver fleurs-de-lys；	纯银百合叶；
because the birthday of my life	命中福日到，
is come，my love is come to me.	心上人将至。

（诸莉　译）

Unit 5 John Masefield

约翰·梅斯菲尔德

　　约翰·梅斯菲尔德(1878—1967)，英国诗人、小说家和剧作家；1930年被任命为英国第22届"桂冠诗人"；从小丧母，由女管家带大；14岁随商船出海，在海上漂泊3年；1895年去纽约打零工，结识一家书店的主人，得以博览群书；两年后回到伦敦。他的第一部诗集《盐水谣》(1902)描写普通劳动者的生活和工作。《海之恋》是其中最著名的诗，由此，他被誉为"大海的诗人"。该诗至今仍然深受英国及各国人民的喜爱。

　　此外，他还创作了很多戏剧、小说、论文、短篇故事等作品。第一次世界大战后，他的著作大受追捧。第二次世界大战期间，他写了《致水兵》等诗，歌颂英国士兵和水手的勇敢坚毅精神。

诗作一

Sea Fever
海之恋

I must down① to the seas again, to the lonely sea and the sky,　　　　我欲下海去，去看寂海天，

And all I ask is a tall ship and a star to steer her by②,　　　　高船唯我需，孤星为我导；

And the wheel's kick③ and the wind's song and the white sail's shaking,　　　　舵轮踢、海风啸、白帆颤，

And a gray mist on the sea's face and a gray dawn breaking.　　　　海上雾霭灰，黎明待破晓。

I must down to the seas again, for the call of the running tide　　　　我欲下海去，海潮声声唤，

Is a wild call and a clear call that may not be denied;　　　　似狂叫、似清喊，难以拒；

And all I ask is a windy day with the white clouds flying,　　　　唯要大风天，白云翻飞疾，

And the flying spray and the blown spume④, and the seagull's crying.　　　　水雾喷、浪沫飞、海鸥徐。

I must down to the seas again, to the vagrant gipsy⑤ life,　　　　我欲下海去，漂如吉普西，

To the gull's way and the whale's way where the wind's like a whetted⑥ knife;　　　　如鸥徐、如鲸遨、风如刀，

And all I ask is a merry yarn⑦ from a laughing fellow-rover⑧,　　　　唯要开心人，欢乐故事讲，

And a quiet sleep and a sweet dream when the long trick's⑨ over.　　　　长久轮班后，甜美入梦乡。

（诸光　译）

📝 语言注释

① down：有版本用 go down 代替 down 作谓语，但此版亦存；down 既有表示"下降；下去"的意思，又有词性变异的合理性，符合"诗的破格"的概念范畴。

② steer her by = by which to steer her. her 指船（a tall ship）。steer：驾驶。

③ wheel's kick：舵轮反转跳动；舵轮的反冲力。

④ blown spume：喷溅的浪沫。blown：*adj.* 开了花的。spume：（海浪的）泡沫。

⑤ vagrant：*adj.* 流离失所的；gipsy：*n.* 吉普赛人。

⑥ whet：*v.* 磨快。wetted knife：新磨的锋利的刀。

⑦ yarn：*n.*（尤指夸张的或编造的）故事。merry yarn：愉快的海外奇谈。

⑧ fellow-rover：*n.* 船上的伙伴。rover：*n.* 漫游者；流浪者。

⑨ trick's = trick is，系表结构。trick：*n.* 舵手的值班时间，通常为 2 个小时。

❓ 思考题

1. Which do you prefer, traveling on sea, on land or in mountains?

2. Is the speaker very familiar with the sea? Why?

3. Why does the speaker enjoy sailing on the sea even under the severe conditions?

4. Why does the speaker enjoy a very simple and basic life on the ship?

5. Why does the vagrant gipsy life attract the speaker in particular?

6. What kind of life was the speaker probably leading on land while he wrote this poem?

7. Why the hell does the speaker long to go back to the seas again?

📝 节奏、韵律图示

Sea Fever

音步数 (Foot)	抑扬、扬抑、抑抑扬、抑抑扬扬格等 (Iambic, Trochaic, Anapestic, Double Iambic, etc.)	韵式 (Rhyme Scheme)

6　I must down ∣ to the seas ∣ again, ∣ to the lone ∣ ly sea ∣ and the sky,　　a–/aɪ/
　　△△　▲ ∣ △ △　▲ ∣ △ ▲ ∣ △ △　▲ ∣ △ ▲ ∣ △ △　▲

6　And all ∣ I ask ∣ is a tall ship ∣ and a star ∣ to steer ∣ her by,　　a–/aɪ/
　　△　▲ ∣△▲ ∣ △△ ▲　▲ ∣ △ △ △ ∣ △ ▲ ∣ △▲

4　And the wheel's kick ∣ and the wind's song ∣ and the white sail's ∣ shaking,　　b–/eɪkɪŋ/
　　△ △　▲　▲ ∣ △ △ △　▲ ∣ △ △ ▲　▲ ∣ 　▲△

4　And a gray mist ∣ on the sea's face ∣ and a gray dawn ∣ breaking.　　b–/eɪkɪŋ/
　　△ △　▲ ▲ ∣ △△ 　▲ ▲ ∣ △ △ ▲ ▲ ∣ 　▲△

6　I must down ∣ to the seas ∣ again, ∣ for the call ∣ of the run ∣ ning tide　　c–/aɪd/
　　△△　▲ ∣ △ △　▲ ∣ △▲ ∣ △ △　▲ ∣ △ △　▲ ∣ △　▲

5　Is a wild call ∣ and a clear call ∣ that may ∣ not be ∣ denied;　　c–/aɪd/
　　△△▲　▲ ∣ △ △ ▲　▲ ∣ △ ▲ ∣ △ ▲ ∣ △▲

6　And all ∣ I ask ∣ is a win ∣ dy day ∣ with the white clouds ∣ flying,　　d–/aɪɪŋ/
　　△　▲ ∣△▲ ∣ △△ ▲ ∣ △ ▲ ∣ △ △　▲　▲ ∣ ▲△

5　And the fly ∣ ing spray ∣ and the blown spume, ∣ and the seagull's ∣ crying.　　d–/aɪɪŋ/
　　△ △ ▲ ∣ △　▲ ∣ △ △　▲　▲ ∣ △ △ △ ▲ ∣ ▲△

6　I must down ∣ to the seas ∣ again ∣ to the va ∣ grant gi ∣ psy life,　　e–/aɪf/
　　△△　▲ ∣ △ △ ▲ ∣ △▲ ∣ △ △ ▲ ∣ △ ▲ ∣ △ ▲

5　To the gull's way ∣ and the whale's way ∣ where the wind's ∣ like a whet ∣ ted knife;　　e–/aɪf/
　　△ △ ▲　▲ ∣ △ △ ▲　▲ ∣ △ △ ▲ ∣ △ △　▲ ∣ △　▲

7　And all ∣ I ask ∣ is a mer ∣ ry yarn ∣ from a lau ∣ ghing fel ∣ low-rover,
　　△　▲ ∣△▲ ∣ △△ ▲ ∣ △ ▲ ∣ △ △ ▲ ∣ △ △ ▲ ∣ △　▲△

4　And a quiet sleep │ and a sweet dream │ when the long trick's │ over.　　　f-/oʊvər/

　　△　△　▲　▲　│△　△　▲　▲　│　△　△　▲　▲　│　▲△

注：本诗每行的音步数不尽相同（见最左侧栏）；每个音步内的音节数也不尽相同，有 2~4 个不等；每个音步内的韵律模式也不尽相同，从抑扬格到扬抑格（3-4；4-4；7-6；8-5），从抑抑扬格（1-1；1-2；1-4；1-6；2-4；5-1；5-2；5-4；5-5；7-3；8-1；9-1；9-2；9-4；10-3；10-4；11-3；11-5）到抑扬扬格（2-3；3-1；3-2；3-3；4-1；4-2；4-3；6-1；6-2；7-5；8-3；8-4；10-1；10-2；12-1；12-2；12-3），再到抑扬抑扬格（11-7）均有。以上数字第一个代表行数，第二个代表从左向右的音步数。其余均为抑扬格，在此就不标示出来了。

📇 修辞解析

本诗主要应用了以下七种修辞手法：重复、头韵、谐元音（腹韵）、移情（转类形容词）、拟人、暗喻（隐喻）和明喻。

1. 重复（Repetition）

本诗使用了若干个重复的语句和结构。首先，I must down to the seas again 的三次重复，开启了每节第一句的咏叹节奏，但又都不是单纯的重复，因为其后半句各有变化。其次，And all I ask is a... 结构的三次重复，又进一步阐明了下海去的简单而又基本的需求。然后是语词的重复：第一节第一行有 sea(s)，第四行有 gray，第二节第一、二行有 call，第二节第三、四行有 flying，第三节第二行有 way 的重复。这些重复首先在听觉上给人以"一唱三叹"和"回旋往复"的音乐美，其次在意义上也起到了强调的作用。

2. 头韵（Alliteration）

本诗中头韵比较多，如第一节第二行/st/：star，steer；第一节第三行/w/：wheel's，wind's，white；第二节第三行/w/：windy，with，white；第二节第四行/s/：spray，spume，seagull's；第 三 节 第 二 行/w/：way，whale's，way，where，wind's，whetted；第三节第四行/s/：sleep，sweet。这些头韵的大量使用无疑起到了加强语气和气势的作用，使得这首诗读起来朗朗上口、铿锵有力、气势磅礴。

3. 谐元音（腹韵）（Assonance）

谐元音在本诗中有应用，如第一节第四行/eɪ/：gray，face，gray，breaking；第二节第二行/aɪ/：wild，denied；第二节第四行/aɪ/：flying，crying；第三节第一行/iː/：sea，gipsy；第三节第二行/eɪ/：way，whale's；第三节第四行/iː/：sleep，sweet，dream。这些谐元音都有助于增强整个诗歌的韵律节奏感。

4. 移情(转类形容词)(Transferred Epithet)

本诗第一节第一行 lonely sea 中的 lonely，就是一个典型的移情(或叫转类形容词)用法。大自然本身是没有感情的，既不会有喜怒哀乐，也不会有孤独的感觉。而 lonely(孤独的)这一词一般是用来修饰人类或动物的。而现在这一词用来修饰无情感的大海，与其说是修饰大海，还不如说是烘托人类情感，即烘托那些长期在海上漂泊的水手内心的孤独。这就是移情，把修饰人类情感的形容词用来修饰无情感的自然界，使得诗人的情感在大自然上得到体现和映射。

5. 拟人(Personification)

本诗第一节第二行中的 to steer her by 就是一个拟人修辞格。这里 her 代表前面出现过的 tall ship，把船人格化了，而且还是女性，这是一种传统的大男子主义表现。因为船是给人驾驭的，受人驱使的，所以必须逆来顺受，很符合传统女性的特征，以至于人类语言中也有"处女航"(指代船的首航)之类的表达式，所以用女性的第三人称来指代船。

6. 暗喻/隐喻(Metaphor)

本诗第一节第三行和第四行中的 wheel's kick，wind's song，sea's face 就是暗喻修辞格，分别把罗盘的转动、海风劲吹和海面暗比为踢脚、歌唱和人脸。第三节中的 gipsy life 也是一个暗喻，即把自己向往的海上漂泊暗比为吉普赛式的生活。海上的生活孤独而乏味，而且漂泊不定，很像四处流浪和遭人放逐的吉普赛人的生活，貌似自由潇洒，其实并非自己所愿，只是情非得已罢了。

7. 明喻(Simile)

本诗第三节第二行 where the wind's like a whetted knife 中由 like 引导的系表结构，就是一个典型的明喻修辞格。前者用暗喻表达对吉普赛式漂泊生活的向往，而此处用明喻表达风儿像新磨刀枪一般锋利，一个抽象，一个具体，各有千秋，相得益彰。

三 作品鉴赏

《海之恋》是约翰·梅斯菲尔德最著名的诗。被誉为"大海的诗人"的他，在诗中表达了从尘嚣中回归大海，回归大自然的豁达之情。该诗从主题思想意义来说注定不是即景抒情那么简单，它是融合了诗歌语言的外延和内涵的一首张力十分强大的抒情诗。一般的海洋抒情诗都是即景抒情，借海发挥，"以海喻人"①，畅发个人感慨，抒发个人情怀。从时间上来说，该诗的问世正值历史上工业现代性在欧美完全确立的现代文明阶段，所以具有特别的历史意义。同时对于人类个体来说，却是饱受现代性之苦、渴望逃离现实、回归自然母体的进行之时，因为工业现代性的确立虽然使得人类征服自然、战胜自然的能力大为提高，在自然存在中享有越来越大的自由度，但同时它又是一把双刃剑，因为现代性又造成了对人类天性的某种压抑和摧残，造成人类个体在生活中不得不忍受前所未有的孤独、疏离和压抑，因此又具有极大的反讽意义。《海之恋》是一首建立在诗歌意义的外延和内涵之间巨大张力的基础之上，从表层字面意义到深层暗示意蕴完美结合了现实主义和浪漫主义的抒情诗。从诗歌的外延意义来说，叙述者渴望重新回到那朝思夜想的海上，重温年轻时海上工作和生活所带来的那种内心激荡、心情舒畅的美好时光；从诗歌的内涵意义来说，诗歌的叙述者要逃离现代文明下都市生活的喧嚣、污浊和拥挤，还有孤独、疏离和压抑的人性扭曲的环境，渴望回到那曾经滋养过工业文明的前工业化时代，回到那没有污染、没有拥挤、没有孤独的田园牧歌时代。那启蒙时代培育起来的社会理想和科学理性都在工业文明现代性中被碾得粉碎，人们纷纷渴望回归自然状态下简单生活的至真至纯。这不仅仅是对人类社会发展进步的反讽，也是对现代工业文明先进性和合理性的一种颠覆。这既是本诗的主题，也是本诗主题性的张力所在。这种主题性张力体现了人海关系的二元对立与天人合一、现实主义自然观和浪漫主义自然观，过去与现在、现实与理想、物质与精神、现代性与前现代性、工业性与生态性等多重矛盾的对立统一和相辅相成所造成的紧张又和谐的状态，从而允许诗歌在尽情抒发情志的同时，承载较多的思想内容和审美意蕴，并产生广阔的想象空间，使诗人和读者都能收获巨大的精神愉悦和审美享受。

在遣词造句方面，重复句中 down(而非 go down)的用法最为引人入胜。事实上 down 在该诗中的用法既有词典赋予的合法性(如作不及物动词，表示"下降；下

---

① 余光中. 被诱于那一泓魔幻的蓝[J]. 华中科技大学学报(人文社科版)，2002(2)：115-119.

去"的意思），又有诗歌修辞学所赋予的词法（或词性及发音）变异的合理性，即在此符合"诗的破格"这一修辞手法的概念范畴。down 在本诗中这种罕见的用法既符合情感表达的语义需要，也符合诗歌理论所倡导的陌生化和前景化的审美追求，真实体现了诗人千锤百炼的文字表达功力，也恰到好处地传达了诗人所要抒发的反抗现代性的浪漫主义情愫。所以还有什么必要去纠结它是否合乎现代英语语法呢？

除了 down 的妙用之外，诗人在诗中的遣词造句还尽可能使用单音节、具体形象的本民族词汇来构建诗句，尽管还使用了一些双音节词，如 shaking, breaking, running, denied, windy, flying, crying, seagull, merry, laughing, fellow-rover 等，却恰到好处地起到了放缓节奏的作用，但在全诗 158 个词中的比例也只有百分之七，所以总体节奏非常明快而强烈，毫无拖沓逶迤、缠绵阴柔之风，显示了干练、雄健和昂扬奋进的斗志和气节，从遣词造句方面为诗歌的音乐性张力做出了应有的贡献。

该诗的节奏非常富于变化，从抑抑扬格到扬抑格、抑抑扬扬格，甚至再到抑扬抑格，形式十分多样。而音步数量也变化不定，都在 4 到 7 音步之间，每行音节数更是从 13 到 16 个不等。"其节奏犹如大海的波涛一起一伏，不仅读起来朗朗上口，给人以一种音乐美，而且使描写更加生动形象，让读者体验了水手的经历，仿佛亲自去海上遨游了一番。"①该诗节奏的丰富多变，犹如海中波浪一样，长短不一，高低不平，构成了一种犹如一艘小船在大海上漂泊时的那种颠簸摇摆和起伏不定的节奏张力。

---

① 廖永煌.《海恋》赏析［J］. 外国文学研究，1995（1）：52.

📖 诗作二

Trade Winds
贸易风

In the harbor, in the island, in the Spanish Seas,
Are the tiny white houses and the orange-trees,
And day-long, night-long, the cool andpleasant breeze
Of the steady Trade Winds blowing.
There is the read wine, the nutty, Spanish ale,
The shuffle of the dancers, the old salt's tale,
The squeaking fiddle, and the soughing in the sail
Of the steady Trade Winds blowing.

And o'nights there's fire-flies and the yellow moon,
And in the ghostly palm-trees the sleepy tune
Of the quiet voice calling me, the long low croon
Of the steady Trade Winds blowing.

在海港，在岛内，在西班牙海，
有一栋栋小白房和橘树，
无论白天黑夜，总是凉风舒爽——
那就是永不停歇的贸易风。
这里有红酒、果仁味西班牙啤酒，
有曳步舞和老水手的故事
吱吱哑哑的提琴，船帆的嗖嗖——
那就是永不停歇的贸易风。

那儿夜晚会有流萤和黄色月亮，
幽灵般棕榈林里充满倦意的叹息
轻柔地叫唤我，那长长的低吟——
那就是永不停歇的贸易风。

（诺光　译）

📖 诗作三

Beauty
美

I have seen dawn and sunset on moors and windy hills 见过沼泽山丘的晨黎晚夕，

Coming in solemn beauty like slow old tunes of Spain 是庄严慢旧的西班牙旋律；

I have seen the lady April bringing the daffodils, 见过水仙盛开的四月女神，

Bringing the springing graces and the soft warm April rain. 带来温润暖湿的四月细雨。

I have heard the song of the blossoms and the old chant of the sea, 听过花开之歌和古老海谣，

And seen strange lands from under the arched white sails of ships; 也在白帆下见过仙山异地；

But the loveliest things of beauty God ever has showed to me, 而上帝展示的最可爱之美

Are her voice, and her hair, and eyes, and the clear red curve of her lips. 却是她的声、发、眼和唇。

（诸光　译）

📖 诗作四

The Golden City of St. Mary
黄金城市圣玛丽

Out beyond the sunset, could I but find the way,	在夕阳西下处我须找到航路，
Is a sleepy blue laguna which widens to a bay,	去找形如海湾的宁静蓝礁湖，
And there's the Blessed-City—so the sailors say—	那儿有被祝福之城——水手说——
The Golden City of St. Mary.	黄金之城圣玛丽。
It is built of fair marble—white—without a stain,	它由纯净无瑕的大理石筑成；
And in the cool twilight when the sea-winds wane	在海风消退时和舒爽的黄昏，
The bells chime faintly, like a soft, warm rain,	此时如轻柔暖雨的钟声响起，
In the Golden City of St. Mary.	在黄金之城圣玛丽。
Among the green palm-trees where the fireflies shine,	在绿色棕榈树中萤火虫发光，
Are the white tavern tables where the gallants dire,	酒店白餐桌前时髦人士进餐，
Singing slow Spanish songs like old mulled wine,	唱着西班牙慢曲如香甜热酒，
In the Golden City of St. Mary.	在黄金之城圣玛丽。
Oh, I'll be shipping sunset-wards westward-ho	喔我要登船去向落日和西方！
Through the green toppling combers a-shattering into snow,	穿过那飞雪四溅的绿色卷浪，
Till I come to quiet moorings and a watch below,	到达安静之所，再细看下边，
In the Golden City of St. Mary.	在黄金之城圣玛丽。

（诸莉　译）

📖 **诗作五**

The West Wind
西　风

It's a warm wind, the west wind, full of birds' cries;	西风就是暖风啊，风中饱含着鸟鸣；
I never hear the west wind but tears are in my eyes.	我尚未听到西风，却已是热泪满盈。
For it comes from the west lands, the old brown hills.	因为它来自西地，那古老褐色的山。
And April's in the west wind, and daffodils.	四月也在西风里，和四月的黄水仙。
It's a fine land, the west land, for hearts as tired as mine,	那西地可是好地，为疲惫如我打造，
Apple orchards blossom there, and the air's like wine.	那里苹果树花开，空气香甜如美酒。
There is cool green grass there, where men may lie at rest,	那里有芳草萋萋，人们可躺下休息，
And the thrushes are in song there, fluting from the nest.	还有画眉鸟欢唱，如在鸟巢奏长笛。
"Will ye not come home brother? ye have been long away.	"兄弟何不回家？你在外长久漂泊。
It's April, and blossom time, and white is the may;	这是四月花开季，白色的是山楂花；
And bright is the sun brother, and warm is the rain —	那明亮的太阳，温暖的雨，喔兄弟——
Will ye not come home, brother, home to us again?	不回家来吗，兄弟，再和大伙相聚？
"The young corn is green, brother, where the rabbits run.	那玉米还青绿，兄弟，野兔在奔跑。
It's blue sky, and white clouds, and warm rain and sun.	蓝色的天、白色的云、暖暖雨和阳。
It's song to a man's soul, brother, fire to a man's brain,	那是通灵的歌，兄弟，是至脑的火：
To hear the wild bees and see the merry spring again.	去听听那野蜂，看看那快乐的春天。
"Larks are singing in the west, brother, above the green wheat,	云雀西边唱，兄弟，翱翔在青麦上，
So will ye not come home, brother, and rest your tired feet?	你还不回家来，兄弟，把倦足疗养？
I've a balm for bruised hearts, brother, sleep for aching eyes,"	我有疗心药膏，兄弟，让痛眼睡着。"
Says the warm wind, the west wind, full of birds' cries.	那暖风，那西风说着，风中都是鸟鸣。
It's the white road westwards is the road I must tread	那白色路向西，乃我此生必走之路，
To the green grass, the cool grass, and rest for heart and head,	去那绿悠清凉之草，让心与脑休息，
To the violets, and the warm hearts, and the thrushes' song,	和紫罗兰、暖心、话梅鸟歌声一起，
In the fine land, the west land, the land where I belong.	在那美好之地，西地，我的归属地。

（诸莉　译）

Unit 6　Edgar Alan Poe

埃德加·爱伦·坡

埃德加·爱伦·坡(1809—1849)，美国诗人、小说家、批评家。幼年父母双亡，中年丧妻，"凄凉的人生造就了他忧郁敏感的气质，孤僻的个性以及游离主流社会的倾向"①。"一生潦倒，性格又桀骜不驯，为世人所不容"②。爱伦·坡的苦难人生却成就了他不朽的文学创作，所以爱伦·坡又被后世誉为"美国文坛最出色和最具创造力的作家之一"③。在爱伦·坡之前，有人认为"美国无诗"④。爱伦·坡的诗歌体现了其对音乐、美术和忧郁美的不懈追求和执着偏爱。爱伦·坡的短篇小说也成绩斐然，主要有恐怖和推理两大类。此外，爱伦·坡在文学批评方面也颇有建树，著有《创作哲学》和《诗歌原理》，对欧陆文坛影响很大，催生了象征主义文学。

① 刘守兰. 英美名诗解读[M]. 上海：上海外语教育出版社，2003：458.
② 刘守兰. 英美名诗解读[M]. 上海：上海外语教育出版社，2003：459.
③ 刘守兰. 英美名诗解读[M]. 上海：上海外语教育出版社，2003：458.
④ 顾正坤主编. 英文名篇鉴赏金库(诗歌卷)[M]. 天津：天津人民出版社，2000：242.

诗作一

Annabel Lee
安娜贝尔·李

In a kingdom by the sea,
That a maiden[①] there lived whom you may know
By the name of Annabel Lee; —
And this maiden she lived with no other thought
Than to love and be loved by me.

在一个傍海的国度里
你或许认识一位少女
她名叫安娜贝尔·李；
这位少女她活着就没别的念想
唯有爱我和为我所爱。

I was a child and she was a child,
In this kingdom by the sea;
But we loved with a love that was more than love —
I and my Annabel Lee —
With a love that the wingéd seraph[②] in Heaven
Coveted her and me.

我一个孩子，她也一个孩子，
在这傍海的国度里；
我们以一种超乎爱的爱着彼此，
我和我的安娜贝尔·李，
以至于上天的六翼天使
也来把我们妒忌。

And this was the reason that, long ago,
In this kingdom by the sea,
A wind blew out of a cloud, chilling[③]
My beautiful Annabel Lee;
So that her high-born kinsmen[④] came
And bore[⑤] her away from me,
To shut her up in a sepulcher[⑥],
In this kingdom by the sea.

这就是为什么很久以前，
在这傍海的国度里，
云里刮起一阵阴风，冻僵了
我美丽的安娜贝尔·李；
以便她血统高贵的亲戚前来
把她从我身边带离，
将她幽闭在一个墓穴，
在这傍海的国度里。

The angels, not half⑦ so happy in Heaven,   那些上天毫不快乐的天使们

Went envying her and me —   也来把我们的爱妒嫉——

Yes! —that was the reason (as all men know,   是的! 这就是原因(大家都懂的,

In this kingdom by the sea)   在这傍海的国度里)

That the wind came out of the cloud by night,   夜晚一阵阴风刮自云端,

Chilling and killing my Annabel Lee.   冻僵并杀死了我的安娜贝尔·李。

But our love it was stronger by far than the love   但我们的爱它要强烈得多

Of those who were older than we —   相比年长者的爱——

Of many far wiser than we —   相比聪明人的爱——

And neither the angels in Heaven above,   无论是上天的六翼天使,

Nor the demons down under the sea,   还是海底深渊的魔鬼,

Can ever dissever⑧ my soul from the soul   都不能拆分我们的灵魂:

Of the beautiful Annabel Lee: —   美丽的安娜贝尔·李。

For the moon never beams, without bringing me dreams   从此月不再明, 不再于我托梦,

Of the beautiful Annabel Lee;   美丽的安娜贝尔·李;

And the stars never rise, but I feel the bright eyes   星不再升, 我仍感受她的亮眼,

Of the beautiful Annabel Lee: —   美丽的安娜贝尔·李:

And so, all the night-tide⑨, I lie down by the side   因此, 每夜, 我就躺在她的身边,

Of my darling—my darling—my life and my bride,   我亲爱的——我亲爱的——我的生命和我的新娘,

In her sepulcher there by the sea —   在她傍海的墓穴里——

In her tomb by the sounding sea.   在那喧响的海边, 她的坟墓里。

(诸光　译)

📝 语言注释

① maiden：*n.* 少女，处女；未婚女子。

② wingéd seraphs：天堂中群飞的天使们。wingéd：*adj.* 有翼的。seraphs：*n.* 六翼天使。

③ chilling：动词 chill 的现代分词。chill：*vt.* 冷冻，冷藏；使寒心；使感到冷。此处与 killing 形成押韵（腹韵和尾韵都押），意为：冻坏了；使寒（伤）心。

④ high-born kinsmen：血统高贵的男性亲属。high-born：*adj.* 出身名门的；kinsmen：*n.* 亲戚；亲属；男亲属。

⑤ bore sb. away：改变航道；夺走，夺取。

⑥ sepulcher：*n.*〈美〉同 sepulchre，坟墓。

⑦ not half：一点也不；否定词+half 是"一点也不"的意思，而非"一半"的意思。

⑧ dissever：*v.* 使分离；使分裂。

⑨ night-tide：*n.* 夜潮；夜间，夜里。All the night-tide = With all the night-tide，不顾夜晚湿重的潮气。

❓ 思考题

1. Why did the poet set the background of the story in a kingdom by the sea?

2. What kind of family background did Annabel Lee probably have?

3. What atmosphere does the poet create by wind, cloud, night, sepulcher and tomb?

4. Why does the poet say that the angels were "not half so happy in heaven"?

5. What did the angels try to do that chilled and killed Annabel Lee?

6. What attitude did the poet probably hold towards the angels from Heaven?

7. Why don't we feel bored about the repeated vowel sound /iː/ as end rhyme?

8. Which aspect of the poem has touched you, the love story or the rhythm?

📝 节奏、韵律图示

Annabel Lee

音步数 （Foot）	抑扬、扬抑、抑抑扬、抑扬抑、抑扬扬、扬抑扬格等 （Iamb, Trochee, Anapest, Amphibrach, Bacchius, Amphimacer, etc.）	韵式 （Rhyme Scheme）
4	It was ma ｜ ny and ma ｜ ny a year ｜ ago, △ △ ▲　△ △ ▲　△ △ ▲　△ △	b-/əʊ/
3	In a king ｜ dom by ｜ the sea, △ △ ▲　△ ▲　△ △	a-/iː/
4	That a mai ｜ den there lived ｜ whom you ｜ may know △ △ ▲　△ △ ▲　△ ▲　△ ▲	b-/əʊ/
3	By the name ｜ of An ｜ nabel Lee; — △ △ ▲　△ ▲　△ △ ▲	a-/iː/
4	And this mai ｜ den she lived ｜ with no o ｜ ther thought △ △ ▲　△ △ ▲　△ △ ▲　△ ▲	
3	Than to love ｜ and be loved ｜ by me. △ △ ▲　△ △ ▲　△ ▲	a-/iː/
4	I was ｜ a child ｜ and she ｜ was a child, ▲ △　△ ▲　△ ▲　△ △ ▲	
3	In this king ｜ dom by ｜ the sea; △ △ ▲　△ ▲　△ ▲	a-/iː/
4	But we loved ｜ with a love ｜ that was more ｜ than love — △ △ ▲　△ △ ▲　△ △ ▲　△ ▲	c-/ʌv/
3	I and ｜ my An ｜ nabel Lee — ▲ △　△ ▲　△ △ ▲	a-/iː/
4	With a love ｜ that the win ｜ géd seraphs ｜ in Heaven △ △ ▲　△ △ ▲　△ ▲ △　△ ▲ △	d-/v(ə)n/
3	Cove ｜ ted her ｜ and me. ▲ △　△ ▲　△ ▲	a-/iː/

4　And this | was the rea | son that, long | ago,　　b-/əʊ/
　△　▲　　△ △ ▲　　△　△　▲　　△▲

3　In this king | dom by | the sea,　　a-/iː/
　△ △　▲　　△　▲　　△ ▲

4　A wind | blew out | of a cloud, | chilling
　△ ▲　　△　△　△△　▲　　　▲△

3　My beau | tiful An | nabel Lee;　　a-/iː/
　△ ▲　　△△ ▲　　△ △　▲

4　So that | her high- | born kins | men came
　△ ▲　　△　▲　　△　▲　　△　▲

3　And bore | her away | from me,　　a-/iː/
　△　▲　　△ △▲　　△　▲

4　To shut | her up | in a se | pulcher,
　△　▲　　△　▲　　△△▲　　△　△

3　In this king | dom by | the sea.　　a-/iː/
　△ △　▲　　△　▲　　△ ▲

4　The an | gels, not half | so happy | in Heaven,　　d-/v(ə)n/
　△▲　　△　▲　▲　　△　▲△　　△　▲△

3　Went en | vying her | and me —　　a-/iː/
　△　▲　　△△　▲　　△　▲

4　Yes! – that | was the rea | son (as all | men know,　　b-/əʊ/
　△　　▲　　△　△　▲　　△　△　▲　　△　▲

3　In this king | dom by | the sea)　　a-/iː/
　△ △　▲　　△　▲　　△▲

4　That the wind | came out | of the cloud | by night,
　△ △　▲　　△　▲　　△　△　▲　　△　▲

4　Chilling | and kil | ling my An | nabel Lee.　　a-/iː/
　▲△　　△　▲　　△　△　▲△　　△ △　▲

4　But our love | it was stron | ger by far | than the love　　c-/ʌv/
　△ △　▲　　△ △　▲　　△ △　▲　　△　△　▲

3　Of those | who were ol | der than we —　　a-/iː/
　△　▲　　△ △　▲　　△　△　▲

3　Of ma | ny far wi | ser than we —　　a-/iː/
　△　▲　　△ △　▲　　△　△　▲

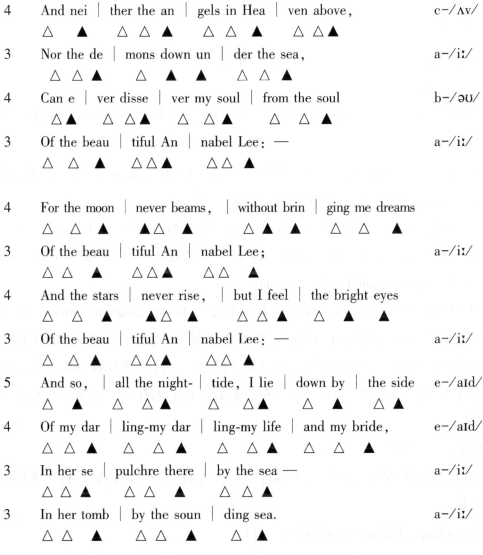

4　And nei | ther the an | gels in Hea | ven above,　　　c-/ʌv/
　△　▲　△　△　▲　△　△　▲　△　△　▲

3　Nor the de | mons down un | der the sea,　　　a-/iː/
　△　△　▲　△　△　▲　△　△　▲

4　Can e | ver disse | ver my soul | from the soul　　　b-/əʊ/
　△　▲　△　△　▲　△　△　▲　△　△　▲

3　Of the beau | tiful An | nabel Lee：—　　　a-/iː/
　△　△　▲　△　△　▲　△　△　▲

4　For the moon | never beams, | without brin | ging me dreams
　△　△　▲　▲　△　▲　△　△　▲　△　△　▲

3　Of the beau | tiful An | nabel Lee;　　　a-/iː/
　△　△　▲　△　△　▲　△　△　▲

4　And the stars | never rise, | but I feel | the bright eyes
　△　△　▲　▲　△　▲　△　△　▲　△　▲　△　▲

3　Of the beau | tiful An | nabel Lee：—　　　a-/iː/
　△　△　▲　△　△　▲　△　△　▲

5　And so, | all the night- | tide, I lie | down by | the side　e-/aɪd/
　△　▲　△　△　▲　△　△　▲　△　▲　△　▲

4　Of my dar | ling-my dar | ling-my life | and my bride,　e-/aɪd/
　△　△　▲　△　△　▲　△　△　▲　△　△　▲

3　In her se | pulchre there | by the sea —　　　a-/iː/
　△　△　▲　△　△　▲　△　△　▲

3　In her tomb | by the soun | ding sea.　　　a-/iː/
　△　△　▲　△　△　▲　△　▲

注：本诗属半格律半自由诗类型，每行的音步数和音律类型（patterns of feet）都不太规律，尾韵更无规律性可言，韵母/iː/的重复特别多，达 21 次，故设为韵式 a，其余也有一些零散的韵式，就归为 b、c、d、e 等，但基本只有 a 是一贯到底的。音步数很有规律性：基本都是 4-3-4-3 模式，只是到了最后几节才有改变，显示出情感的起起伏伏和收放有度。除常见的抑扬格（iamb，△ ▲）和抑抑扬格（anapest，△ △ ▲）之外，在一些音步里还存在一些非典型的音律类型，为方便大家识别，特将这些非典型音律类型及名称列出：

▲ △：扬抑格（trochee）；

△ ▲ △：抑扬抑格（amphibrach）；

△ ▲ ▲：抑扬扬格（bacchius）；

▲ △ ▲：扬抑扬格（amphimacer）。

🗒 修辞解析

本诗主要运用了以下三种修辞手法：重复、谐元音(腹韵)和头韵。

1. 重复(Repetition)

该修辞格在弗罗斯特第一首作品中已有界定。本诗中重复的字、词组、短语等结构相当多。

(1)字词：many(2次)，love(8次，包含不同词性以及动词的不同形态)，chilling(2次)，ever(2次，含 dissever)，soul(2次)。

(2)词组：was a child(2次)，than we(2次)，Annabel Lee(3次)，my darling(2次)，my(2次，my life/my bride)，by the sea(2次，包含 by the sounding sea)，In her(2次，In her sepulcher/In her tomb)。

(3)短语：Of the beautiful Annabel Lee(4次)，In this kingdom by the sea(5次)。

从这些字、词组和短语的重复(最少2次、最多5次，总计多达40次)看来，这些都是诗人为打造哀婉浓情氛围的修辞手段之一。这些重复修辞格首先在听觉上给人以"一唱三叹"和"回旋往复"的音乐美，其次也起到了不断强化和突出主题的作用。

2. 谐元音/腹韵(Assonance)

谐元音的重复使用能极大地丰富行中韵，从而增强诗歌的音乐性。本诗中的谐元音有：

(1)chilling，killing(第四节最后一行)。

(2)beams，dreams(第六节第一行)。

(3)rise，I，bright，eyes(第六节第三行)。

(4)night，tide，I，lie，by，side(第六节第五行)。

(5)life，bride(第六节第六行)。

3. 头韵(Alliteration)

该修辞格在弗罗斯特第一首作品中已有界定。第四节第一行中三个词 half、happy、Heaven 押头韵/h/。此处的头韵毫无疑问起到了加强语气和突出重点的作用。

📑 作品鉴赏

　　《安娜贝尔·李》既是绝世之作也是巅峰之作。爱伦·坡的亡妻被认为是诗中安娜贝尔·李的原型。该诗的创作灵感毫无疑问来源于爱伦·坡的个人经历，如爱妻早亡之殇，对爱的深切怀念，对古典美的偏好，对哥特风的迷恋，对东方神话的熟稔。

　　爱伦·坡有在作品中杜撰悦耳女子姓名的癖好①，本诗亦然。Annabel Lee 连同长元音韵母的单词 sea、me 和 we，共同建构起了贯穿全诗的韵脚/iː/，读来余音袅袅，韵味悠长而深情，表达了诗人对亡妻的忠贞不渝之情。"那低回往复的单一尾音令人耳闻诗人失去爱人后痛不欲生的哀号，也能自然地想起大海波涛幽怨的呜咽声和教堂周围沉重单调的报丧钟声。这样，爱伦·坡所钟情的伤感主题辅以美妙的音韵节奏，构成了一种立体的富于感染力的悲凉韵调，令读者感到欲说还休，难以释怀。"②

　　另外，本诗中仙女和凡夫之间的爱情故事，分明带有一种爱伦·坡版牛郎织女式中国神话的原型：两小无猜、青梅竹马的仙女和凡夫相爱了，可仙女娘家贵为天庭望族，自然不愿此等丑闻发生，遂出面干涉，派其长兄六翼天使出马，将仙女掳走并加以软禁，企图迫使其忘却人间牵挂。不料仙女誓死不从、以死抗争，最终导致悲剧的发生。这个哀婉动人、凄凉无比的爱情故事在多声部复踏的舒缓韵调之下，读来尤为打动人心、感人肺腑。

---

① 刘守兰. 英美名诗解读[M]. 上海：上海外语教育出版社，2003：460.
② 刘守兰. 英美名诗解读[M]. 上海：上海外语教育出版社，2003：460.

Unit 7　*Henry Wadsworth Longfellow*

亨利·沃兹沃斯·朗费罗

　　亨利·沃兹沃斯·朗费罗(1807—1882)，19世纪美国最伟大的浪漫主义诗人之一。1807年出生于缅因州的名门望族，大学曾与霍桑是同班同学；毕业后去欧洲多地，研究语言和文学；1836年开始在哈佛大学讲授语言和文学长达十八年，致力于介绍欧洲文化和浪漫主义作品，在欧美文学之间架构桥梁。他的个人诗风深受欧洲传统影响，注重格律和遣词，追求音韵美。他还创作了艺术性极高的表现印第安人和黑奴主题的诗歌作品，表现了一个作家应有的良知和正义感，在大西洋两岸都享有盛誉。他去世时世界声望很高，在英国能与丁尼生齐名，并被供奉在威斯敏斯特教堂的"诗人角"，其是第一个获此殊荣的美国作家。

📖 诗作一

The Golden Sunset
金色的夕阳

The golden sea its mirror spread①　　　　　　金色大海似平镜，
Beneath the golden skies，　　　　　　　　　映照金色云天，
And but a narrow strip between　　　　　　水天相接岸与影，
Of land and shadow lies②.　　　　　　　　　狭长玉带一线。

The cloud-like rocks，the rock-like clouds　岩如云来云如岩，
Dissolved③ in glory float④，　　　　　　　　壮丽溶于水天；
And midway of the radiant flood⑤，　　　　洪流璀璨海中间，
Hangs silently the boat.　　　　　　　　　静悬小舟一莲。

The sea is but another sky，　　　　　　　海不过另一片天
The sky a sea as well，　　　　　　　　　天亦另一片海；
And which is earth and which is heaven，何为人间何为天，
The eye can scarcely tell.　　　　　　　肉眼何以分开。

So when for us life's evening hour，　　我今桑榆坠西下，
Soft fading⑥ shall descend⑦，　　　　　　晚霞难再满天，
May glory，born of earth and heaven，　天地相交生奇观，
The earth and heaven blend.　　　　　　也把天地熔炼。

Flooded with peace the spirits float，内心平和气如云，
With silent rapture⑧ glow⑨，　　　　　　沉静闪烁如星；
Till where earth ends and heaven begins，何处凡尽天路开，
The soul shall scarcely know.　　　　　我心也难理清。

（诸光　译）

📝 语言注释

① 正常语序为：The golden sea spread its mirror beneath the golden skies。

② 正常语序为：And but a narrow strip of land and shadow lies between (the sea and the sky))。strip：*n.* 带；(陆地、海域等) 狭长地带。

③ dissolve：*v.* 溶解；融化；分解。dissolved in glory：此处为 "化作天边异彩" 的意思。glory：*n.* 光辉灿烂的色彩；奇异的光彩或色彩；意指非常美丽的景象。

④ float：*v.* 浮；浮动；漂浮；漂流。谓语动词，正常语序为 float dissolved in glory。

⑤ radiant：*adj.* 灿烂的；发光的；辐射的；光芒四射。flood：*n.* 洪水；水灾；大批，大量 (的人或事物)。radiant flood 意指灿烂的大海 (强调大海的博大宽广)。

⑥ fading：fade 的动名词。fade：*v.* 使褪色；使凋谢；使衰老。soft fading：逐渐衰老。

⑦ descend：*v.* 下降；下来；降临；来临。

⑧ rapture：*n.* 狂喜；欣喜。silent rapture：沉静的欣喜。

⑨ glow：*v.* 发热；喜形于色。

❓ 思考题

1. Restore the sentence order of the first stanza, and paraphrase it.

2. Paraphrase the second stanza and explain what the poet sees.

3. What is the major difference between the second and the third stanza as far as the content is concerned?

4. What does the fourth stanza try to tell us about the poet himself?

5. What stage of life was the poet in according to the last two stanzas?

6. What attitude does the poet hold towards life and death?

7. Have you found any difference in style of language between the first three stanzas and the last twos? Why is there such a difference?

📝 节奏、韵律图示

The Golden Sunset

行数 (Line)	四/三音步抑扬格交替组合 (Iambic Tetrameter/Iambic Trimeter)	韵式 (Rhyme Scheme)
1.	The gol | den sea | its mir | ror spread △ ▲ △ ▲ △ ▲ △ ▲	a
2.	Beneath | the gol | den skies, △▲ △ ▲ △ ▲	b-/aɪs/
3.	And but | a nar | row strip | between △ ▲ △▲ △ ▲ △ ▲	c
4.	Of land | and sha | dow lies. △ ▲ △ ▲ △ ▲	b-/aɪz/
5.	The cloud | -like rocks, | the rock | -like clouds △ ▲ △ ▲ △ ▲ △ ▲	d
6.	Dissolved | in glo | ry float, △ ▲ △ ▲ △ ▲	f-/əʊt/
7.	And mid | way of | the ra | diant flood, △ ▲ △▲ △ ▲ △ ▲	e
8.	Hangs si | lently | the boat. ▲ ▲ △ ▲ △ ▲	f-/əʊt/
9.	The sea | is but | ano | ther sky, △ ▲ △▲ △▲ △ ▲	g
10.	The sky | a sea | as well, △ ▲ △▲ △ ▲	h-/el/
11.	And which | is earth | and which | is heaven, △ ▲ △▲ △ ▲ △▲△	I
12.	The eye | can scarce | ly tell. △ ▲ △ ▲ △▲	h-/el/

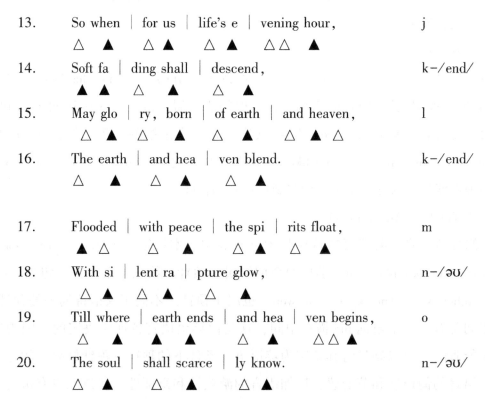

13.　So when │ for us │ life's e │ vening hour,　　　　j

14.　Soft fa │ ding shall │ descend,　　　　k-/end/

15.　May glo │ ry, born │ of earth │ and heaven,　　　　l

16.　The earth │ and hea │ ven blend.　　　　k-/end/

17.　Flooded │ with peace │ the spi │ rits float,　　　　m

18.　With si │ lent ra │ pture glow,　　　　n-/əʊ/

19.　Till where │ earth ends │ and hea │ ven begins,　　　　o

20.　The soul │ shall scarce │ ly know.　　　　n-/əʊ/

注：本诗为四/三音步抑扬格的交替组合；尾韵皆为 abcb 韵式（即所谓一、三不搭，二、四押韵）。但在 4-2-1、5-3-2 是扬扬格（spondee）；5-1-1 为扬抑格（trochee）。在 3-3-4 和 4-3-4 的三音节音步是抑扬抑格（amphibrach）；4-1-4 和 5-3-4 为抑抑扬格（anapaest）；其余音步皆为抑扬格（iamb）。2-4-1 即第二节第四行第一音步；5-1-1 即第五节第一行第一音步，依次类推。

📇 修辞解析

本诗主要运用了以下四种修辞手法：暗喻、明喻、顶针、重复和回环。

1. 暗喻/隐喻（Metaphor）

该修辞格在丁尼生作品中已有界定。本诗第一节第一行 The golden sea its mirror spread（spread its mirror），第三节第一、二行 The sea is but another sky, /The sky a sea as well，第四节第一行 So when for us life's evening hour，都属于暗喻修辞格。第一个暗喻将大海比喻为一面巨大的镜子，展现在我们眼前。第二个暗喻则将大海比喻为又一个天，将天比喻为又一个海（省略 is）。第三个暗喻则将生命说成是傍晚时分。本体和喻体之间省略了"像"，直接将本体说成喻体的修辞效果更简洁，也更有冲击力。

2. 明喻(Simile)

该修辞格在丁尼生作品中已有界定。本诗第二节第一行 The cloud-like rocks, the rock-like clouds 就是明显的明喻。云一般的岩，岩一般的云……这两个用 like 作后缀的复合词(cloud-like, rock-like)其实就是一个浓缩的系表结构：The rocks are like the clouds, the clouds are like the rocks。因此这句话属于明喻的范畴。明喻给人一种强烈的比喻感，属于一种主观性更强的比喻。

3. 顶针(真)(Anadiplosis)

该修辞格在弗罗斯特第二首作品中已有界定。本诗第二节第一句 The cloud-like rocks, the rock-like clouds 前后两个词组属于顶针，第三节第一、二句 The sea is but another sky, /The sky a sea as well，也属于顶针。不同于汉语诗词中的顶针，它们中间都有一个定冠词 the 横在中间，这是由英语语言特征所决定的，因为定冠词不能省略，所以姑且将其认定为英语语言条件下的顶针。顶针修辞格的运用能增强语言的韵律感和节奏感，增加语言的游戏性和辩证性，使诗歌更有审美感染力。

4. 重复(Repetition)

该修辞格在克里斯蒂娜·罗塞蒂的作品中已有界定。本诗的重复有三类：① 词汇的重复；②词组的重复；③语法结构的重复。

(1) 词汇的重复。

The golden sea its mirror spread/Beneath the golden skies(1-1)：golden

The cloud-like rocks, the rock-like clouds(2-1)：cloud, like, rock

The eye can scarcely tell(3-4)/The soul shall scarcely know(5-4)：scarcely

(2) 词组的重复。

May glory, born of earth and heaven, /The earth and heaven blend(4-3)：earth and heaven

Till where earth ends and heaven begins(5-3)：earth + V, heaven + V

(3) 语法结构的重复。

And which is earth and which is heaven(3-3)：which is + n.

The eye can scarcely tell(3-4)．／The soul shall scarcely know(5-4)：scarcely+V。

以上两句除有单词(scarcely)重复之外，最主要是在结构上有相似性，这也是一种重复。

5. 回环(Palindrome)

一行诗、一个单词、一首诗，或一个更长单位的文字，从后往前读和从前往后读是一样的内容。简单地说，回环就是顺读、逆读一个样(如 Bob，dad，deed，peep，level，radar；响水潭中潭水响；黄金谷里谷金黄)。本诗第二节第一行 The cloud-like rocks, the rock-like clouds 就是一个回环修辞手法。后部是前部的逆读，唯一的区别就是中间的组合不同：前部是 cloud-like，后部是 rock-like，还有就是最后那个名词加 s，前面的名词加上 like 后作修饰性的形容词。回环修辞法无疑增加了诗歌语言的趣味性，同时也表达了一种辩证性的逻辑和哲理，值得吟诵和品味。

作品鉴赏

这是朗费罗人生最后一首抒情诗作品，却并无人生末年那种悲天悯人和无病呻吟的消极情绪和面对生命即将消逝发出凄凉的哀嚎。相反，诗人纵情山水，对夕阳西下和金色海洋进行了肆意的泼墨，唯美的描绘和辩证的论说，把一个宁静祥和的落日海景描绘得有形有色，有远有近，有高有低，有大有小，有正有反，可谓情景交融，相得益彰，充满了西哲的辩证和东佛的禅趣，给人以"诗中有画、画中有诗"的审美享受和人生启迪。

本诗前三节对自然美景的描绘可谓气势磅礴、一气呵成，雍容华贵而不失唯美清新。诗句的凝练，语气的酣畅，把诗人博大的胸怀、平和的心境展现得淋漓尽致。优美的韵律和明快的节奏，即一、三不搭，二、四相谐以及四、三音步的交替组合，也将诗人对夕阳海景的咏叹一步步推向高潮。云岩、海天、人间天堂三组形态之间的关系被上升到对立统一的辩证唯物高度，其实是诗人毕生经验和意识的提炼和升华：写夕阳却不带"夕阳"二字，临于岸边却不提岸上的人，真是写得出神入化、丝丝入扣。最后两节诗歌内容比较理性和抽象，意念表述略多，没有能够再造生动具体的意象，以致遣词造句显得干涩勉强、缺乏创意，未能延续前三节那酣畅淋漓的神来之笔，甚为遗憾。

📖 诗作二

The Tide Rises，The Tide Falls
潮汐涨，潮汐还

The tide rises，the tide falls,	潮汐涨，潮汐还。
The twilight darkens，the curlew calls;	黄昏到，杓鹬叫。
Along the sea-sands damp and brown	沿着海滩褐又潮
The traveler hastens toward the town,	旅人急急把路赶，
And the tide rises，the tide falls.	潮汐涨，潮汐还。
Darkness settles on roofs and walls,	暮色降临罩房屋，
But the sea，the sea in the darkness calls;	海风夜黑不停息；
The little waves，with their soft，white hands,	推出浪花小而柔，
Efface the footprints in the sands,	悄悄擦掉沙上迹，
And the tide rises，the tide falls.	潮汐涨，潮汐还。
The morning breaks，the steeds in their stalls	晨将至，马亦起，
Stamp and neigh，as the hostler calls;	马夫吼，嘶又踢；
The day returns，but nevermore	一天又始潮水漫
Returns the traveler to the shore,	旅人一去不再返，
And the tide rises，the tide falls.	潮汐涨，潮汐还。

（诸莉　译）

📖 诗作三

The Arrow and the Song
箭与歌

I shot an arrow into the air,	我向空中射支箭，
It fell to earth, I knew not where;	千寻难知其落点；
For, so swiftly it flew, the sight	因其飞快无所踪
Could not follow it in its flight.	眼力脚步均难从。
I breathed a song into the air,	我向空中唱首歌，
It fell to earth I knew not where;	万觅难晓谁终得；
For who has sight so keen and strong	何人眼力尖又疾
That it can follow the flight of song.	方能乘上歌之翼。
Long, long afterwards, in an oak,	良久之后遇橡树
I found the arrow, still unbroke.	重得我箭新如故。
And the song from beginning to end,	另有我歌首至尾，
I found again in the heart of a friend.	悄然寄寓友心扉。

（诸莉　译）

📖 诗作四

The Slave's Dream
奴隶的梦

Beside the ungathered rice he lay,   躺在未收割的稻谷旁，

His sickle in his hand;   手握镰刀；

His breast was bare, his matted hair   裸露胸膛，脏乱的头发

Was buried in the sand.   埋进沙涛。

Again, in the mist and shadow of sleep,   在睡梦的迷雾幻影里，

He saw his native land.   他看见了故乡。

Wide through the landscape of his dreams   梦中宏大的画面里，

The lordly Niger flowed;   雄伟的尼日尔河奔流不息；

Beneath the palm-trees on the plain   平原的棕榈树下，

Once more a king he strode;   他仍像国王一般大步前进；

And heard the tinkling caravans   听着叮铃声声的驼队

Descend the mountain-road.   沿山路降临。

He saw once more his dark-eyed queen   他又一次见到他的黑眼皇后，

Among her children stand;   站在儿女之中；

They clasped his neck, they kissed his cheeks,   她们抱紧他脖子，吻他脸颊。

They held him by the hand! —   她们紧握他手！——

A tear burst from the sleeper's lids   一滴眼泪从沉睡者眼里涌出，

And fell into the sand.   滴落在沙地。

And then at furious speed he rode   随后，他策马飞奔在

Along the Niger's bank.   尼日尔河河堤。

His bridle-reins were golden chains,   马头缰绳是金色的链条，

And, with a martial clank,
At each leap he could feel his scabbard of steel
Smitting his stallion's flank.

Before him, like a blood-red flag,
Bright flamingoes flew;
From morn till night he followed their flight,
O'er plains where the tamarind grew,
Till he saw the roofs of Caffre huts,
And the ocean rose to view.

At night he heard the lion roar,
And the hyena scream,
And the river-horse, as he crushed the reeds
Beside some hidden stream;
And it passed, like a glorious roll of drums,
Through the triumph of his dream.

The forests, with their myriad tongues,
Shouted of liberty;
And the Blast of the Desert cried aloud,
With a voice so wild and free,
That he started in his sleep and smiled
At their tempestuous glee.

He did not feel the driver's whip,
Nor the burning heat of day;
For death had illumined the Land of Sleep,
And his lifeless body lay
A worn-out fetter, that the soul
Had broken and thrown away!

带着铿锵的马蹄声，
每一次跳跃他都感到
　　剑鞘在马身上的撞击。

在他眼前，像一面血红色大旗，
　　鲜艳的火烈鸟在飞翔，
从早到晚，他跟踪它们的轨迹，
　　在长满罗望子树的平原上。
直到看见卡菲尔人小屋屋顶，
　　远方的海洋映入眼底。

夜晚他听见雄狮的怒吼，
　　鬣狗的嘶叫，
还有那河马，当他踩踏芦苇
　　跨过隐秘的小溪；
路过时发出如同蓬蓬的鼓声，
　　穿过凯旋的梦里。

那森林，以其无数口舌，
　　呼喊着自由；
那沙漠的大风高声啸叫，
　　那嗓音如此狂野和放肆，
以致他从梦中惊起、微笑
　　沉醉于极度的欢喜。

他已感受不到工头的鞭击，
　　也感受不到烈日的炙烤，
因为死亡之光已照亮沉睡大地，
　　那已死的躯体平躺地上，
戴着破旧的镣铐，他的灵魂
　　已然碎裂，并从躯壳中扔弃！

（诸光　译）

Unit 8　John Donne

约翰·邓恩

　　约翰·邓恩(1572—1631)，英国诗人，曾在牛津大学和剑桥大学学习，因不信国教而未获学位；后改信国教，并于1615年担任国教牧师；1621年被任命为伦敦圣保罗大教堂教长。

　　邓恩是最早也是最杰出的"玄学派诗人"的代表。因塞缪尔·约翰逊(Samuel Johnson)不欣赏其作品，文学史上一度受忽视[1]；20世纪获英美新批评派学者高度评价和肯定：艾略特认为玄学派是英国文学的一座高峰，是最能把感觉与思想结合起来的……自玄学派之后，英国诗歌开始变质，出现了"感觉脱节"，并且至今尚未恢复过来[2]。……布鲁克斯说："我们的世纪庆幸重新发现了约翰·邓恩，但我们发现的不只是约翰·邓恩的诗，而是诗本身。"[3]

---

　　[1] 顾正坤主编. 英文名篇鉴赏金库(诗歌卷)[M]. 天津：天津人民出版社，2000：39.

　　[2] 转引自蒋洪新：英诗新方向——庞德、艾略特诗学理论与文化批评研究[M]. 长沙：湖南教育出版社，2001：178-179.

　　[3] 赵毅衡. 新批评———种独特的形式主义文论[M]. 北京：中国社会科学出版社，1988：59-60.

诗作一

Death, Be not Proud
死神别嚣张

Death, be not proud, though some have called thee

Mighty and dreadful, for, thou art not soe[①],

For, those, whom thou think'st, thou dost[②] overthrow,

Die not, poore death, nor yet canst thou kill mee[③].

From rest and sleepe, which but thy pictures bee,

Much pleasure, then from thee[④], much more must flow,

And soonest our best men with thee doe goe[⑤],

Rest of their bones, and soules deliverie[⑥].

Thou art slave to Fate, Chance, kings, and desperate men,

And dost with poison, warre, and sicknesse[⑦] dwell,

And poppie, or charmes can make us sleepe as well,

And better than thy stroake; why swell'st[⑧] thou then?

One short sleepe past, wee wake eternally,

And death shall be no more; death, thou shalt[⑨] die.

死神别嚣张，虽有人说你

很厉害，其实你不过如此；

你以为已把人放倒，未必；

也奈何不了我，可怜的你。

休息和睡眠是你难兄难弟，

但比你可爱，为人也厚道；

英雄豪杰会最先与你比刀，

无非白骨入土，灵魂超替？

受命于厄运杀机暴君狂徒，

与毒药、战争和疾病为伍；

鸦片与巫术亦可催人入眠，

且更灵验，何来嚣张气焰？！

小憩之后，我们永远觉醒，

死将不复；死啊该你消停！

（诸光 译）

📝 语言注释

① thou art：you are。在中世纪英语（Middle English）以及早期现代英语（Early Modern English）里，thou 是 you 的主格形式。soe，同 so。

② thou dost：you do（overthrow）；dost，do 的第二人称单数现在式。

③ canst：can 的第二人称单数现在时。mee：同 me。

④ thee：（thou 的宾格）你（第二人称宾格 you）。then：同 than。

⑤ doe goe：do go。

⑥ deliverie：delivery 的变体，传送；递送；分娩；交付；交货；交割；投递。

⑦ warre，sicknesse：同 war，sickness。

⑧ thy stroake：your stroke，thy 用作第二人称单数所有格形式；stroke，打击，一击。swell'st：第二人称后谓语动词变格形式，同 swell。

⑨ shalt：shall，shall 的第二人称单数陈述语气现在时。

❓ 思考题

1. How many places in the poem can be regarded as personification?

2. When death is personified, what effect can be achieved?

3. What figure of speech is used in the sixth line of the poem?

4. Why are the abstract nouns Fate and Chance listed together with the other two nouns: kings and desperate men?

5. What implied meaning do words "go", "sleep" vs. "wake" have?

6. How do you paraphrase the last two lines of the poem? What figures of speech are used there?

✍ 节奏、韵律图示

Death，Be not Proud

行数 (Line)	五音步抑扬格 (Iambic pentameter)	韵式 (Rhyme Scheme)
1.	Death, be | not proud, | though some | have cal | led thee △　▲　△　▲　　　△　▲　　　△　▲　　　△　▲	a—/iː/
2.	Mighty | and dread | ful, for, | thou art | not soe, ▲　△　△　▲　　△　▲　　　△　▲　　△　▲	b—/oʊ/
3.	For, those, | whom thou | think'st, thou | dost o | verthrow, △　▲　　▲　▲　　▲　▲　　　▲　▲▲　▲　△　▲	b—/oʊ/
4.	Die not, | poore death, | nor yet | canst thou | kill mee. △　▲　　▲　▲　　　▲　▲　　▲　▲　　　▲　▲	a—/iː/
5.	From rest | and sleepe, | which but | thy pic | tures bee, △　▲　△　▲　　　▲　▲　　△　▲　　△　▲	a—/iː/
6.	Much plea | sure, then | from thee, | much more | must flow, △　▲　△　▲　△　▲　　　△　▲　　△　▲	b—/oʊ/
7.	And soo | nest our | best men | with thee | doe goe, △　▲　△　▲　▲　▲　　△　▲　　△　▲	b—/oʊ/
8.	Rest of | their bones, | and soules | deli | verie. ▲　△　△　▲　　　△　▲　　△　▲　　△　▲	a—/iː/
9.	Thou art slave | to Fate, | Chance, kings, | and des | perate men, △　△　▲　△　▲　　▲　▲　　△　▲　　△　△　▲	c—/en/
10.	And dost | with poi | son, warre, | and sick | nesse dwell, △　▲　△　▲　△　▲　　△　▲　　△　▲	d—/el/
11.	And poppie, | or charmes | can make | us sleepe | as well, △　▲　△　△　▲　　△　▲　　△　▲　　△　▲	d—/el/
12.	And bet | ter than | thy stroake; | why swell'st | thou then? △　▲　△　▲　△　▲　　△　▲　　△　▲	c—/en/
13.	One short | sleepe past, | wee wake | eter | nally, △　▲　△　▲　△　▲　　△　▲　△　▲	e—/aɪ/

14. And death │ shall be │ no more; │ death, thou │ shalt die.　　　　e-/aɪ/
　　△　　▲　　　▲　△　　△　▲　　　▲　　　▲　　△　　▲

注：本诗为意大利式比特拉克十四行诗，尾韵押的是 abba abba cdd cee 的韵式。节奏方面大部分是五音步抑扬格（iambic pentameter △▲），也有一些非抑扬格的情况列举如下：

① 扬抑格（trochee ▲△）：2-1；8-1；14-2（行数-音步数，下同）。

② 扬扬格（spondee ▲▲）：3-2；3-3；3-4；4-2；4-3；4-4；4-5；5-3；7-3；9-3；14-4。

③ 抑抑扬格（anapest △△▲）：9-1；9-5。

④ 抑扬抑格（amphibrach △▲△）：11-1。

📑 修辞解析

本诗应用了以下五种修辞手法：拟人、头韵、委婉、双关和悖论。

1. 拟人（Personification）

拟人是一种将动物、抽象概念或无生命事物比喻为人类的修辞格。本诗从第一行开始就将死神人格化，将其比喻为一个势利、膨胀的小人，在普通老百姓面前作威作福，却臣服于厄运、杀机、暴君与狂徒这些恶人……这个人格化死神的意象贯穿于整个作品，不断与"我"或"我们"等众生互动，成为诗歌叙事中的绝对反派主角（特别是第 4、7、9、12 句）。

2. 头韵（Alliteration）

头韵指同一个辅音在一行诗中的两个（或以上）相邻或间隔不远的单词首音上的重复，用来加强语气和气势[1]。本诗第六行就有四个头韵词，其中/m/音在 much、much、more 和 must 的首音上重复。

3. 委婉（Euphemism）、双关（Pun）

用不冒犯人或悦人的表达方式来代替唐突、粗俗或禁忌的言辞[2]就是委婉修辞格。本诗中"goe""sleepe""be no more"就是委婉修辞格，既有睡眠之义又是在暗喻死亡。因此这也是一个语义双关。所谓双关，就是"利用语音和语义条件，使某些词语具有双重意义。所谓双重意义，指表面上说甲，实际上说乙，言在此而意

---

① Chris Baldick. 牛津文学术语词典[M]. 上海：上海外语教育出版社，2000：166.

② 胡壮麟，刘世生. 西方文体学词典[M]. 北京：清华大学出版社，2004：117.

在彼。……运用双关，……使语言幽默、含蓄，富有情趣，耐人品味"①。除了可以是委婉语和双关语之外，这些 sleepe 还有避免重复用词和动名词置换的需要。

4. 悖论(Paradox)

似非而是，一个看似矛盾和荒谬，实则反映了某种真理性的陈述，它反映了事物的多面性和复杂性，目的在于吸引读者的注意力。第十三句就是一个悖论：我们小憩一下之后(意即先死一次)，我们将永远地苏醒(意即再也不会死第二次了)。这二者如何统一，显然需要某种智慧。这种修辞往往表达了对事物既矛盾又统一的辩证的看法。

作品鉴赏

这是 17 世纪"玄学派"代表人物约翰·邓恩的代表作之一，意大利比特拉克十四行诗。说理多过抒情，说理性很强，有论点，有论据，也有结论，宛如一篇论说文。虽然也有强烈的情感因素，但却少了花前月下的浪漫感伤。把死亡比作睡眠，跨越生命从有限到永恒的门槛，是中世纪人类直面死亡的有力盾牌。诗歌通篇都是轻蔑和嘲讽，充满了乐观主义和视死如归的大无畏精神！

对于邓恩来说，写出这种诗歌并不难。他出身于罗马天主教家庭，从小受到正统的宗教熏陶；自己也攻读过神学，并在改信国教后，仕途上一路高歌。他的诗歌多有浓厚的思辩色彩，但并不枯燥。他的诗句力避感伤情调，把情感放在"思想"的容器之中，少了浪漫和感性，多了玄思和理性，是最能把感觉与思想结合起来的②。邓恩的诗歌和马维尔等"玄学派"作品一起，受到英美现代派的推崇。

诗歌说理不容易，因为太抽象，而且有思想性。十四行诗又篇幅有限，还要受格律的羁绊，所谓"戴着镣铐跳舞"。所以本诗的格律并不完美，有很多不规则现象——以抑扬格为主，但还有一些扬抑格、抑抑扬格和抑扬抑格的音步存在；为了满足内容的需要，形式必须作出牺牲。拟人修辞格贯穿全诗，还有委婉、双关和悖论修辞格的运用，使得全诗充满火力、活力和张力。

---

① 吕煦. 实用英语修辞[M]. 北京：清华大学出版社，2004：219.
② 转引自蒋洪新. 英诗新方向——庞德、艾略特诗学理论与文化批评研究[M]. 长沙：湖南教育出版社，2001：178-179.

📖 诗作二

For Whom the Bells Tolls
丧钟为谁鸣

No man is an island,	无人为孤岛,
Entire of itself;	全然靠一己;
Every man is a piece of the continent,	每人是块土,
A part of the main.	大陆地之一。
If a clod be washed away by the sea,	一泥为海掠,
Europe is the less,	欧陆不保昔,
As well as if a promontory were,	正如某海岬,
As well as if a manor of thy friend's or of thine own were:	你我之领地:
Any man's death diminishes me,	人死我亦损,
Because I am involved in mankind,	人人我相系,
And, therefore, never send to know for whom the bell stolls;	莫问丧钟鸣;
It tolls for thee.	为我也为你。

（诸光　译）

诗作三

The Flea
跳 蚤

Mark but this flea, and mark in this,	看呐，注意这跳蚤，
How little that which thou deny'st me is;	你不认可我又有何意义？
It sucked me first, and now sucks thee,	它先吸我的血，后又去吸你，
And in this flea, our two bloods mingled be;	我们的血已在它身上融为一体：
Thou know'st that this cannot be said	你知道，这事儿并非耻辱
A sin, nor shame, nor loss of maidenhead,	或罪过，更不算失去贞操，
Yet this enjoys before it woo,	关键是它未追求就先享受，
And pampered swells with one blood made of two,	将我俩的血融合，撑起它的肚皮，
And this, alas, is more than we would do.	而这，唉，它已大大超越我们自己。
Oh stay, three lives in one flea spare,	喔不，放过一只跳蚤三条命吧，
Where we almost, yea more than married are.	在它身体里，我们岂止是成了亲，
This flea is you and I, and this	它就是你和我，
Our marriage bed, and marriage temple is;	是我们的婚床和婚姻殿堂：
Though parents grudge, and you, we're met,	尽管父母不同意，我们终究相遇，
And cloistered in these living walls of jet.	最终同居在跳蚤身体里。
Though use make you apt to kill me,	按理你杀我之心都有，
Let not to that, self murder added be,	但别把三条命来剥夺，
And sacrilege, three sins in killing three.	不要再添加自杀和亵渎神灵的罪过。

Cruel and sudden, hast thou since

Purpled thy nail, in blood of innocence?

Wherein could this flea guilty be,

Except in that drop which it sucked from thee?

Yet thou triumph'st, and say'st that thou

Find'st not thyself, nor me the weaker now;

'Tis true, then learn how false, fears be;

Just so much honour, when thou yield'st to me,

Will waste, as this flea's death took life from thee.

残忍而突然，你终究还是下了杀手，

用无辜者的血玷污了你的指甲？

这怎能算跳蚤之罪过？

它只吸过你一口，

而你完全可以自豪地说：

你我本来就不比之前虚弱；

另外，说你害怕也太虚假；

就算此时你屈服于我，你的名誉和清白

也都毁于一旦，因为杀死跳蚤也杀死了你。

（诸光　译）

Unit 9　*William Shakespeare*

威廉·莎士比亚

　　威廉·莎士比亚(1564—1616)，英国伟大的剧作家、诗人，欧洲文艺复兴时期最重要的作家，也跟古希腊三大悲剧家合称戏剧史上四大悲剧家。据说出生在英国埃文河畔的斯特拉福镇，幼年在当地上文法学校，后到伦敦从事表演、改编和创作剧本之类。他写了37部无韵体诗剧、两首长诗和154首十四行诗。莎士比亚在意大利比特拉克十四行诗基础上创立了英式或莎士比亚式十四行诗。生前仅发表过少量作品，大部分作品多在去世后由其生前同事和好友们搜集整理而出版，这也是其生平和身份存在很大争议的原因之一。后世学者和诗人蒲柏、约翰逊、斯蒂文斯等也都相继编撰过《莎士比亚全集》。

📖 诗作一

Sonnet 18
十四行诗第 18 首

Shall I compare thee to a summer's day?	佳人可比夏？
Thou art more lovely and more temperate①:	尔比夏更佳；
Rough winds do shake the darling buds of May,	风吹五月蕊，
And the summer's lease② hath all too short a date;	夏驹亦难追；
Sometime too hot the eye of heaven shines③,	天眼时灼热，
And often is his gold complexion dimmed④;	金颜常为遮；
And every fair from fair⑤ sometime declines,	世间美易散，
By chance or nature's changing course untrimmed⑥;	机缘随季翻；
But thy eternal summer shall not fade,	尔夏永不止，
Nor lose possession of that fair thou ow'st⑦;	尔美亦不失；
Nor shall death brag thou wand'rest⑧ in his shade,	死难夸其强，
When in eternal lines to time thou grow'st⑨:	尔与时同昌。
So long as men can breathe, or eyes can see,	凡人一息存，
So long lives this, and this gives life to thee.	诗在赋尔春。

（诸光　译）

✍️ 语言注释

① temperate：*adj.* 气候温和的；温带的；平和的；自我克制的。Thou art：You are。

② lease：*n.* 租约；租用；租契。summer's lease＝the lease of summer，夏天的租约。

③ 正常语序为：Sometime the eye of heaven shines too hot。sometime＝sometimes，下同。

④ 正常语序为：And his gold complexion is often dimmed。dim：*v.* （使）暗淡、朦胧。

⑤ 正常语序为：And every fair sometime declines from fair。前面的 fair 指具体的美人

或美的事物；后面的 fair 指抽象的美。相当于说，美人(美物)的美都会消失。

⑥ 正常语序为：untrimmed by chance or nature's changing course。untrimmed：*adj.* 未修剪的，引申为"被摧残"或"被夺走美貌"的意思，相当于 stripped of beauty。

⑦ thou ow'st：you own。此处用 ow'st 为第二人称单数，省略 e 是为减少一个音节，因为 ownest 是双音节词，如果不减少一个音节就会有十一个音节，就不是完美的五音步抑扬格了。

⑧ thou wand'rest：同上。

⑨ thou grow'st：同上。正常语序为：When in eternal lines thou grow'st to times。

💬 思考题

1. Why does the poet compare his love to a summer's day rather than a spring's day?

2. How does the poet describe summer in his poem?

3. What makes the poet sigh that all beauties in the world decline?

4. Have you ever been in UK in summer? How is summer like in your country?

5. What does it mean by "thou wand'rest in his shade"?

6. What is the logic of the poet in the last two lines of this poem?

📝 节奏、韵律图示

Sonnet 18

行数 (Line)	五音步抑扬格 (Iambic Pentameter)	韵式 (Rhyme Scheme)
1.	Shall I | compare | thee to | a sum | mer's day? △ ▲　△ ▲　　△ ▲　△ ▲　　△ ▲	a-/eɪː/
2.	Thou art | more love | ly and | more tem | perate： △ ▲　△ ▲　　△ ▲　　△ ▲　　△ ▲	b-/eɪt/

3.　Rough winds ｜ do shake ｜ the dar ｜ ing buds ｜ of May,　　　a-/eɪ/
　　▲　▲　　△　▲　　△　▲　　△　▲　　△　▲

4.　And the sum ｜ mer's lease ｜ hath all ｜ too short ｜ a date;　　b-/eɪt/
　　△　△　▲　　△　▲　　△　▲　　△　▲　　△　▲

5.　Sometime ｜ too hot ｜ the eye ｜ of hea ｜ ven shines,　　　c-/aɪnz/
　　▲　△　　▲　▲　　△　▲　　△　▲　　△　▲

6.　And o ｜ ften is ｜ his gold ｜ comple ｜ xion dimmed;　　　d-/ɪmd/
　　△　▲　　△　▲　　△　▲　　△　▲　　△　▲

7.　And e ｜ very fair ｜ from fair ｜ sometime ｜ declines,　　　c-/aɪnz/
　　△　▲　　△　▲　　△　▲　　▲　△　　△　▲

8.　By chance ｜ or na ｜ ture's chang ｜ ing course ｜ untrimmed;　　d-/ɪmd/
　　△　▲　　△　▲　　△　▲　　△　▲　　△　▲

9.　But thy ｜ eter ｜ nal sum ｜ mer shall ｜ not fade,　　　e-/eɪd/
　　△　▲　　△　▲　　△　▲　　△　▲　　△　▲

10.　Nor lose ｜ posses ｜ sion of ｜ that fair ｜ thou ow'st;　　f-/oʊst/
　　△　▲　　△　▲　　△　▲　　△　▲　　△　▲

11.　Nor shall ｜ death brag ｜ thou wand' ｜ rest in ｜ his shade,　　e-/eɪd/
　　△　▲　　△　▲　　△　▲　　△　▲　　△　▲

12.　When in ｜ eter ｜ nal lines ｜ to time ｜ thou grow'st:　　f-/oʊst/
　　△　▲　　△　▲　　△　▲　　△　▲　　△　▲

13.　So long ｜ as men ｜ can breathe, ｜ or eyes ｜ can see,　　　g-/iː/
　　△　▲　　△　▲　　△　▲　　△　▲　　△　▲

14.　So long ｜ lives this, ｜ and this ｜ gives life ｜ to thee.　　g-/iː/
　　△　▲　　△　▲　　△　▲　　△　▲　　△　▲

注：典型的莎士比亚十四行诗，韵式与比特拉克不同：abab cdcd efef gg。除 3-1、5-2(扬扬格 spondee：▲▲)、5-1、7-4(扬抑格 trochee：▲△)、4-1(抑抑扬格 Anapest：△△▲)之外，其他均为五音步抑扬格(Iambic Pentameter△▲)。

修辞解析

本诗运用了六种修辞手法：明喻、暗喻、拟人、提喻、重复和停顿。

1. 明喻(Simile)

明喻即两个事物之间的直接比较，常用 like 或 as 引导①。本诗第一句虽没用 like 或 as，但是用了一个更明显的 compare thee to a summer's day，故可归为明喻修辞格。明喻就是通过通俗和直白的比喻把一个较为复杂抽象的问题或事物说得浅显易懂。

2. 暗喻/隐喻(Metaphor)

暗喻即省略 like 或 as 的两个事物之间不直接的比较②。本诗中第四句、第五句和第九句都属于暗喻修辞格类型。第四句将英国温和的夏季比喻为向上天租借来的一个宝物，所以叫 Summer's lease。第五句将太阳比喻为 the eye of heaven(天堂的眼睛)，一副火眼金睛的样子。第九句 your eternal summer 暗指你永恒的青春。第十一句中宾语从句 thou wand' rest in his shade，字面意义是说"你在死神的阴影中漫步"，实际上是喻指"在死神的掌控中"或"受到死亡的威胁"。这四种暗喻都没有 like 或 as 的引导，而是直接加以陈述，但其实中间跳过了一个比喻的过程，或者说省略了这一过程。这种表述方式既富有文采又具有思想的跳跃性，需要读者慢慢消化。

3. 拟人(Personification)

将动物、抽象概念或无生命事物比喻为人类的修辞格。本诗第六句和第十一句中就包含拟人修辞格。第六句 his gold complexion 就是把太阳形容成是"他的金色容颜"。第十一句 death brag……就是把死神比喻为一个夸夸其谈爱吹牛的人。拟人修辞格能把抽象或无生命的事物人格化，使叙事既有趣味性、生活性又方便理解。

4. 提喻(Synecdoche)

转喻或换喻的一种，用部分的名称来代表整体，反之亦然。第十二句中 eternal lines 是指诗人自己不朽的诗歌，是用部分(不朽的诗行)来代表整体(不朽的诗歌)的修辞格。提喻的意义在于使语言交流更简单具体，通俗易懂。

---

① Gillespie Sheena, Fonseca Terezinba, Sanger Carol. Literature Across Cultures[M]. Boston：Allyn and Bacon, 1998：929.

② Gillespie Sheena, Fonseca Terezinba, Sanger Carol. Literature Across Cultures[M]. Boston：Allyn and Bacon, 1998：929.

5. 重复(Repetition)

重复，或反复，某个音素、单词、词组或句子(结构)的再次(或多次)出现，多为感叹、咏叹，起强调和加强语气和情感的作用。本诗最后两句中的 So long……就是这种句子结构的一种表现。So long (as)是 as long as 的变体，是"只要""只要……就"的意思；但这种用法和 as long as 的现代用法又不尽相同，因此也归为一种重复。本来是一种语法功能，但其实也发挥了重复的情感功能，即强调效果和加强语气的功能。

6. 行中停顿(Caesura)

诗行中间的停顿；节律的停顿，(韵脚的)休止。传统英语诗体学(prosody)中的一个经典术语，指一行诗中间的停顿。在英语诗歌中，这样的停顿不是由韵律形式来决定的，而是由句法、语义或标点符号来决定的，所以它们的出现无规律可循①。本诗中出现了两处诗行中间的停顿，一方面出于句法的需要——前者为并列句，后者为顺承句；另一方面表现了说话人为达强调目的时而加强语气的状态：

So long as men can breathe, or eyes can see,

So long lives this, and this gives life to thee.

▣ 作品鉴赏

本诗为莎翁 154 首十四行诗的第 18 首，也是最为著名的一首。莎士比亚十四行诗大约创作于 1590 年至 1598 年，此时正是欧洲文艺复兴传播到英国的时期；也是意大利十四行诗流传到英国之时。意大利十四行诗也称比特拉克十四行诗，由意大利诗人比特拉克首创，其特点是五音步抑扬格的格律加韵式为 abba abba cde cde(后六个可变异)的尾韵。莎士比亚在此基础上加以改造，创立了莎士比亚十四行诗，其五音步抑扬格的格律不变，但尾韵的韵式变成 abab cdcd ef ef gg。莎士比亚的十四行诗语言丰富而修辞华丽，也反映了该时期的人文主义思想，具有很强的时代气息。莎士比亚的十四行诗在英国诗歌史上具有很高的地位，堪称空前绝后。遗憾的是，莎士比亚十四行诗虽然号称英式十四行诗，但却主要为莎翁本人所钟爱，鲜见其他英国诗人采纳。大多数英国诗人创作的还是意大利十四行诗。

---

① 胡壮麟，等. 西方文体学词典[M]. 北京：清华大学出版社，2004：40.

　　本诗运用了"五音步抑扬格"韵律以及多种修辞手法和句法，使得该诗节奏明快，意蕴丰富，逻辑严谨，立场鲜明。诗的开头将爱慕对象"你"与夏日相比较，因为英国地处高纬度，又是四面环海，属海洋性气候，所以它的夏季气候十分凉爽。加上雨水充沛，所以五月的英国植被繁茂，绿茵醉人，花卉盛开，可谓五彩缤纷，明艳动人。即便如此，"你"却要比这自然的夏日还要"更可爱、更温婉"。又因为是海岛，英国的风一向很强劲，冬春季尤甚，所以五月的风可能大到足以吹落树枝上的娇花嫩蕊，说明自然的夏季也有瑕疵，也时常无情和任性，所以跟"你"没法相比。至于"夏季的租期太短"，当然是一个形象的比喻，仿佛这可爱的夏季是从上天那里租借而来的一个宝物，即英国五六月份的气候和植被都是最美好的时候，是夏季中的"春季"。到了七月份，进入盛夏，太阳光明显变强，所以更为灼热。这时候自然界的植被被强烈的阳光一烤就不再鲜嫩翠绿了，然后随着气温升高，水蒸气上升，云层渐多，所以太阳的"金色容颜"也常常被云所遮挡。因此和五六月份相比，仿佛自然界美好的事物一夜间就蒸发了似的。这一切都让诗人感叹世界上美好的事物太容易消逝了，诗人认为既有机缘巧合的偶然性，又有季节变化的必然性。但"你永恒的夏天"是不会轻易消逝的，你也不会丧失自己的容颜美，即你的青春美貌就如永恒的夏天一样，不会随自然界的季节变化而变化。死神也不能吹牛说"你"被笼罩在它的阴影里，亦即"你"无须担心肉体上的死亡。因为在精神上"你"将在我不朽的诗句里与时共存、共生，与时间一样长生不老。只要世界上还有人类存在，我的诗就一定会存在；而只要我的诗还存在，它就能保佑你与世长存。最后两句既是对爱慕对象的许诺和保证，也是对自己能力的高度自信和肯定：你我物质生命的终结，都不能阻止我的诗歌保佑你继续拥有精神生命和青春。

　　英国文艺复兴继承了欧洲特别是意大利文艺复兴的浪漫风尚，因此爱情诗在莎士比亚所处的时代十分流行。据说，莎士比亚的十四行诗主要为两人而作：前126首献给一位贵族男青年，可能也是莎士比亚戏剧活动的赞助者，后面的则是献给一位黑皮肤女郎。

　　莎士比亚十四行诗除了咏叹人类爱情的至真至纯之外，也高度肯定了人的存在意义，热情赞扬了人的理性作用，尽情抒发了人类的普遍情感，将抽象的情感具象化，通过丰富的词汇和多变的修辞，形象具体地诠释了人文主义的内涵。

📖 诗作二

Sonnet 129
莎士比亚十四行诗第 129 首

Th'expense of spirit in a waste of shame
Is lust① in action, and till action, lust
Is perjured②, murd'rous③, bloody④, full of blame,
Savage⑤, extreme, rude, cruel, not to trust,
Enjoyed no sooner but despised straight,
Past reason hunted, and no sooner had,
Past reason hated as a swallowed⑥ bait⑦,
On purpose laid to make the taker mad;
Mad in pursuit, and in possession so,
Had, having, and in quest to have, extreme,
A bliss⑧ in proof, and proved, a very woe⑨,
Before, a joy proposed, behind, a dream.
All this the world well knows, yet none knows well
To shun⑩ the heav'n that leads men to this hell.

在耻辱之损耗里元气被大伤，
这是情欲在行动；此前就有
伪证、凶杀、血腥等等恶名，
后又粗鲁极端，残暴不可信；
刚品尝甜头，立马又感羞耻；
事前拼命追求，事后又立刻
自我鄙视，仿佛鱼咬饵上钩，
诱饵就是使上钩者忘乎所以：
先拼命追求，后又拼命占有；
已有，正有，还想有，太贪；
先以为甜，后知是悲哀之源；
先以为乐，后才觉虚幻如梦；
这谁人不知；却无人懂怎样
回避那让人堕落地狱的天堂。

（诸光　译）

✍️ 语言注释

① lust: *n.* 性欲；强烈的欲望。

② perjure: *v.* 作伪证；使发伪誓。

③ murderous: *adj.* 杀人的，残忍的；凶残的；蓄意谋杀的。

④ bloody: *adj.* 血腥的；嗜杀的，残忍的。

⑤ savage: *adj.* 野蛮的；残酷的。

⑥ swallow: *v.* 吞下；咽下；燕子。

⑦ bait：*n.* 饵；诱饵；swallowed bait，被咬的诱饵，意为引人上钩的诱饵。

⑧ bliss：*n.* 极乐；天赐的福。

⑨ woe：*n.* 困难，灾难；痛苦，悲伤。

⑩ shun：*v.* 避开，避免；回避。

思考题

1. Why was it a shame of waste for a spirit's expense?

2. Why are following three pairs of things contrasting to each other：enjoyed，despised；bliss，woe；joy，dream?

3. What is that something that the whole world know well，but not well enough…?

4. How do you understand the complex relationship between the heaven and the hell?

5. Do you think that this poem is over critical，because to err is human?

6. What is human nature according to Shakespeare? Do you agree with him?

7. What do you think is the best way to manage and control human nature?

节奏、韵律图示

Sonnet 129

行数 (Line)	五音步抑扬格 (Iambic Pentameter)	韵式 (Rhyme Scheme)
1.	Th'expense ｜ of spi ｜ rit in ｜ a waste ｜ of shame △ ▲　△ ▲　△ ▲　△ ▲　△ ▲	a-/eɪm/
2.	Is lust ｜ in ac ｜ tion, and ｜ till ac ｜ tion, lust △ ▲　△ ▲　△ ▲　△ ▲　△ ▲	b-/ʌst/
3.	Is per ｜ jured, mur ｜ d'rous, bloo ｜ dy, full ｜ of blame, △ ▲　△ ▲　△ ▲　△ ▲　△ ▲	a-/eɪm/

4. Savage, │ extreme, │ rude, cru │ el, not │ to trust,   b-/ʌst/
    ▲ △　　△ ▲　　　△　　▲　　△　▲　　△　▲

5. Enjoyed │ no soo │ ner but │ despi │ sed straight,   c-/eɪt/
    △ ▲　　△　▲　　△　▲　　△▲　　△　　　▲

6. Past rea │ son hun │ ted, and │ no soo │ ner had,   d-/æd/
    △ ▲　　△　▲　　△　▲　　△　▲　　△　▲

7. Past rea │ son ha │ ted as │ a swal │ lowed bait,   c-/eɪt/
    △ ▲　　△　▲　　△　▲　　△　▲　　△　▲

8. On pur │ pose laid │ to make │ the ta │ ker mad;   d-/æd/
    △ ▲　　△　▲　　△　▲　　△▲　　△　▲

9. Mad in │ pursuit, │ and in │ posses │ sion so,   e-/oʊ/
    ▲ △　　△　▲　　△　▲　　△　▲　　△　▲

10. Had, ha │ ving, and │ in quest │ to have, │ extreme,   f-/iːm/
    ▲　▲　　▲　△　　△　▲　　△　▲　　△　▲

11. A bliss │ in proof, │ and proved, │ a ve │ ry woe,   e-/oʊ/
    △ ▲　　△　▲　　△　▲　　△▲　　△　▲

12. Before, │ a joy │ proposed, │ behind, │ a dream.   f-/iːm/
    △ ▲　　△　▲　　△▲　　△　▲　　△　▲

13. All this │ the world │ well knows, │ yet none │ knows well   g-/el/
    ▲ △　　△　▲　　△　▲　　△　▲　　△　▲

14. To shun │ the heav'n │ that leads │ men to │ this hell.   g-/el/
    △ ▲　　△　▲　　△　▲　　△　▲　　△　▲

注：除 4-1、9-1、13-1(扬抑格 trochee：▲△)，10-1、(扬扬格 spondee：▲▲)外其他均为五音步抑扬格(Iambic Pentameter：△▲)，另有 4-4-1、5-5-1 为诗的破格(poetic license)，即此处 e 本不发音，但为满足统一韵式要求而赋予其发音/e/。

修辞解析

本诗运用了 25 个修辞格，共 10 个类型(拟人、排比、对照、重复、头韵、明喻、暗喻、谐元音、顶针、悖论)。

1. 拟人(Personification)

本诗把情欲比喻为一个具有人格的活物，会变得虚伪、凶残、血腥和充满责备，还会变得野蛮、极端、粗暴和不讲信用(第三、四行)，因此具有人格化的特征。

2. 排比(Parallelism)

排比指为达强调或平衡之目的而将两种或两种以上相似或相关的事物或理念置于相似的结构形式之中。本诗在把情欲人格化过程中运用此修辞格来体现其人格化特征：(情欲)会变得虚伪、凶残、血腥和充满责备；还会变得野蛮、极端、粗暴和不讲信用(第三、四行)。这些都是排比。

3. 对照(Antithesis)

对照是一种把意义相对的字词或理念有意安排于一种平衡结构中来达成对比和强调之目的。这种表达方式无论是在判断的深刻性、幽默性或讽刺性等方面都具有极强的对比效果。本诗共有三处对照修辞格应用：第五行、第十一行和第十二行。

4. 重复(Repetition)

本诗第六句和第七句的开头几个词就是典型的重复，或曰部分重复(repetend)：Past reason hunted... /Past reason hated...。重复修辞格的巧妙使用无疑具有"一唱三叹"和"回旋往复"的音乐美，同时起到强调和加强意蕴的作用。

5. 头韵(Alliteration)

本诗第六、九、十、十一、十二、十三、十四行中均有头韵修辞格的运用：hunted，had(第六行)；pursuit，possession(第九行)；Had，having，have(第十行)；proof，proved(第十一行)；Before,... behind,... (第十二行)；the world，well(第十三行)；... heav'n ... hell(第十四行)。丰富的首音重复，能带来同声相谐，回声相衬，铿锵有力，掷地有声的音响美感。

6. 明喻(Simile)

本诗唯一的明喻是第七行的 as a swallowed bait(如被咬的诱饵)。

7. 暗喻/隐喻(Metaphor)

本诗第一行中的 the expense of spirit 指"生气的消耗"，是把 expense 的"开销、消费"引申为"消耗、耗费"，是 spirit(精神、情绪、活力等)的逻辑谓语，暗喻其为一种消耗品。

8. 谐元音(Assonance)

本诗的谐元音是第八行 On purpose laid to make the taker mad 中的/eɪ/：laid，make，taker；还有第十一行中的/u/：proof，proved。

9. 顶针(Anadiplosis)

本诗第八行最后一个词和第九行第一个词即为一个顶针：

On purpose laid to make the taker mad;

Mad in pursuit, and in possession so

运用顶针修辞手法，能使句子语气贯通，可突出事物之间环环相扣的有机联系，亦可起到加强语气的作用。

10. 悖论(Paradox)

概念界定见弗罗斯特诗歌。本诗最后两行中分别各有一个悖论：

All this the world well knows, yet none knows well

To shun the heav'n that leads men to this hell.

一方面说"全世界的人都知道这一点"，另一方面又说"却没有一个人知道……(具体怎么做)"。这是一个典型的悖论表述，表面上看充满了矛盾，但在意义上又具有思辨性和统一性：全世界的人都知道的事情，原来其实只是一种理论知识，或者叫作道理，即虽然明白一个道理或知晓一个理论，却并非一定能实践这个道理或理论。所以这个陈述表面上矛盾但实际上是一种真理性的表述，是一种矛盾统一的说法。因此说它是一个悖论。

第十四行就更好理解了：逃避引人下地狱的天堂，即这个所谓的天堂并不是真的天堂，而是一种看似美好实则丑陋的地狱，是一种假冒的、伪装的天堂。它会勾引意志薄弱者上钩，然后吃亏上当，以为要进天堂而实则是进了地狱。所以这也是一个充满了矛盾的陈述，天堂和地狱这对二元对立的矛盾双方最后就被统一了起来。

📰 作品鉴赏

本诗表现了一些古老的主题，如极端之事都不会长久，任何事物都会物极必反，等等。在爱情方面也就有了类似的说法：太热烈的爱情不一定会长久；爱情要渐入佳境才好。另外，爱情不能墨守成规，它应该是自由奔放、无拘无束的，否则就不能产生必要的火花。最后，爱情多半会先甜后苦，先喜后悲，就如英语谚语所说：Short pleasure, long lament(痛快一时，悲哀一世)①。这些看法都反映了人类早期的一种哲学观、人生观和爱情观。

本诗在主题上一反莎士比亚一贯的歌颂爱情、感叹人生的常态，对人类情欲进行了非常深刻、理性的批判。它首先指出了情欲是不太可靠的一种人性，有其原始野蛮、粗鲁暴力的一面。其次，情欲是人性中非理性的一面，为达目的可以无所不用其极，所以信用极差。最后，情欲还体现了一种贪婪疯狂、永不满足的人性特点。

本诗展现了莎士比亚修辞华丽、语言丰富的创作特点，如应用修辞手法22处，修辞格9种：拟人、排比、对照、重复、头韵、明喻、谐元音、顶针、悖论。其中头韵和谐元音属于语音修辞格，排比、对照、重复和顶针属于句法修辞格，拟人和明喻属于语义修辞格，悖论属于逻辑修辞格。这些修辞格的密集使用使得该诗论证有力、思想深刻，在以情诗著称的十四行诗中可谓独树一帜。

---

① Morris Palmer Tilley. A Dictionary of the Proverbs in England in the Sixteenth and Seventeenth Centuries[M]. Ann Arbor, 1950: 419.

📖 诗作三

Sonnet 29
莎士比亚十四行诗第 29 首

When in disgrace with fortune and men's eyes

I all alone beweep my outcast state,

And trouble deaf heav'n with my bootless cries,

And look upon myself and curse my fate,

Wishing me like to one more rich in hope,

Featured like him, like him with friends possessed,

Desiring this man's art, and that man's scope,

With what I most enjoy contented least;

Yet in these thoughts myself almost despising,

Haply I think on thee, and then my state,

Like to the lark at break of day arising

From sullen earth, sings hymns at heaven's gate;

For thy sweet love rememb'red such wealth brings,

That then I scorn to change my state with kings.

当我时运不济遭人看不起,

就只好哭着哀叹遭人唾弃,

白费哭喊去烦扰聋哑老天,

还顾影自怜痛恨天不我惜,

也想像别人那样充满希望,

要么仪表堂堂或广交云集,

希望拥人才艺或活动能力,

对自己擅长者竟最不满意;

而拥有这自我鄙视之情绪,

一想起你我心情瞬间变好,

如黎明之云雀从阴沉大地

直上云霄,在天堂门口高唱

赞美诗,有你蜜爱之财富

我何曾想与帝王互换境遇。

(诸莉　译)

Unit 10　Andrew Marvell

安德鲁·马韦尔

　　安德鲁·马韦尔(1621—1678)，英国诗人；出生于约克郡的牧师家庭，1638年毕业于剑桥大学；1642年开始从教，曾受雇于托马斯·费尔法克斯和奥利弗·克伦威尔，也曾任共和国拉丁文秘书弥尔顿的助手；王朝复辟后被选为议员，后终身从政；创作了大量政治讽刺诗和小品文，抨击时政和宗教的黑暗；大部分作品都是去世后发表，其中包括脍炙人口的《至他羞涩的情人》《花园》等，以音韵优美、语言自然、比喻奇特和意象新颖著称。

　　马韦尔是17世纪著名的玄学派诗人，在18、19世纪一直被遗忘和忽略，直到20世纪被艾略特发现才得以被重视，并得到越来越高的评价。

诗作一

To His Coy Mistress
致他羞涩的情人

Had we but world enough，and time，	假如我们时空充足，
This coyness①，lady，were no crime.	女士你这矜持就不算添堵。
We would sit down，and think which way	我们可坐下来研究去哪里
To walk，and pass our long love's Day.	漫步，度过我们爱的长日。
Thou by the Indian Ganges'② side	你可去印度恒河边寻找
Should'st rubies③ find；I by the tide	红宝石；我则在老家亨伯河畔
Of Humber would complain. I would	消愁解闷。我会在大洪水
Love you ten years before the Flood，	前十年开始爱你，
And you should，if you please，refuse	而你如愿意可一直拒绝我
Till the Conversion④ of the Jews.	直到犹太人改变信仰。
My vegetable love should grow	我植物般的爱情会发展得
Vaster then empires，and more slow⑤.	比帝国更宽广、更缓慢。
An hundred years should go to praise	我需要百年时间来赞美
Thine eyes，and on thy forehead gaze；	你的眼睛和额头；
Two hundred to adore each breast，	两百年崇拜你每个乳房，
But thirty thousand to the rest；	三万年赞赏完其他地方；
An age at least to every part，	每个部位至少一个时代，
And the last age should show your heart.	最后时代才看到你的心。
For，Lady，you deserve this state，	因为你配得上这种待遇，
Nor would I love at lower rate.	我也不愿降低爱你的规格。
But at my back I always hear	可在背后我总能听见

Time's winged chariot⑥ hurrying near;	时间的带翼风车不断迫近;
And yonder⑦ all before us lie	而展现在我们面前的
Deserts of vast eternity.	却是永恒无边的沙漠。
Thy beauty shall no more be found,	你的美将无迹可寻,
Nor, in thy marble vault⑧, shall sound	我的歌也不回响在你的
My echoing song; then worms shall try	大理石墓穴; 那时蛆虫
That long-preserv'd virginity⑨,	将吞噬你久藏的贞操,
And your quaint⑩ honour turn to dust,	你的矜持将化为灰尘,
And into ashes all my lust.	我的情欲也将燃烧殆尽;
The grave's a fine and private place,	坟墓是个幽静私密的场所,
But none I think do there embrace⑪.	我想无人会在此拥抱。
Now therefore, while the youthful hue⑫	所以趁现在你还年轻美貌
Sits on thy skin like morning dew,	肌肤润泽如晨露,
And while thy willing soul⑬ transpires⑭	趁你周身毛孔所焕发的
At every pore⑮ with instant fires,	即时青春之火,
Now let us sport⑯ us while we may;	让我们都及时行乐;
And now, like am'rous⑰ birds of prey⑱,	现在我们像发情猛兽,
Rather at once our time devour⑲,	宁可马上把自己的时光吞噬
Than languish⑳ in his slow-chapt㉑ pow'r.	也不在细嚼慢咽里消耗。
Let us roll all our strength, and all	让我们凝聚起我们的全部力量,
Our sweetness, up into one ball,	全部爱意, 滚成一个雪球,
And tear our pleasures with rough strife㉒,	粗暴地攫取我们的快乐,
Thorough㉓ the iron gates of life.	通过一道道生活的铁门。
Thus, though we cannot make our sun	这样, 我们即使不能使太阳停下,
Stand still, yet we will make him run.	却可使太阳向前奔跑。

（诸光　译）

107

✍ 语言注释

① coyness：*n.* 羞怯；怕羞。

② Ganges：*n.* 恒河(发源于喜马拉雅山，流经印度和孟加拉国)。

③ ruby：*n.* 红宝石；红宝石色。

④ conversion：*n.* 转换；变换；兑换；改变信仰。

⑤ Vaster, more slow：vaster 同 faster；then 同 than；more slow 的现代形式应该是 slower，为凑音节数而用。

⑥ winged chariot：有(带)翼的战车。chariot：二轮战车。

⑦ yonder：*adv.* (过时语言或方言)那里，在那边；那边的，(在)远处的。

⑧ marble vault：marble，大理石。vault，拱顶；撑杆跳；地下室。

⑨ virginity：*n.* 童贞；处女；纯洁。

⑩ quaint：*adj.* 古雅的；奇怪的；离奇有趣的。quaint honor，此处指矜持。

⑪ embrace：*v.* 拥抱。

⑫ hue：*n.* 色彩；色度；色调。

⑬ willing soul：春心，情思。

⑭ transpire：*n.* 蒸发；泄露；使蒸发；使排出。

⑮ pore：*n.* (皮肤上的)毛孔；(植物的)气孔，孔隙。

⑯ sport：*n.* 运动；游戏；娱乐；玩笑；此处为纵情欢乐的意思。

⑰ am'rous：即 amorous，为减少音节而省略字母"o"；多情的；恋爱的。

⑱ prey：*n.* 猎物；受害者，牺牲品。

⑲ devour：*v.* 吞食；毁灭。

⑳ languish：*v.* 憔悴；凋萎；失去活力。

㉑ slow-chapt：*n.* 慢慢咀嚼吞食的力量。

㉒ strife：*n.* 冲突；斗争；争吵；不和。

㉓ thorough：*prep.* 同 through，穿过；穿行；越过。

❓ 思考题

1. How would you describe the speaker's tone in the first 10 lines?

2. How would you understand the speaker's statements in the 11-20 lines?

3. How would you analyze the structure of the poem?

4. How does the speaker develop his logic of persuasion?

5. What strategy does the speaker employ to persude his mistress to give up her virginity?

6. What part of the poem do you enjoy most? And which part less? Why?

节奏、韵律图示

To His Coy Mistress

行数 （Line）	四音步抑扬格 （Iambic Tetrameter △▲）	韵式 （Rhyme Scheme）
1.	Had we | but world | enough, | and time, 　△　▲　　△　▲　　△ ▲　　　△　▲	a-/aɪm/
2.	This coy | ness, la | dy, were | no crime. 　△　▲　　△　▲　　△　▲　　△　▲	a-/aɪm/
3.	We would | sit down, | and think | which way 　△　▲　　△　▲　　△　▲　　△　▲	b-/eɪ/
4.	To walk, | and pass | our long | love's Day. 　△　▲　　△　▲　　△　▲　　△　▲	b-/eɪ/
5.	Thou by | the In | dian Gan | ges' side 　△　▲　　△　▲　　△　▲　　△　▲	c-/aɪd/
6.	Should'st ru | bies find; | I by | the tide 　△　▲　　△　▲　　▲▲　　△　▲	c-/aɪd/
7.	Of Hum | ber would | complain. | I would 　△　▲　　△　▲　　△　▲　　△　▲	d-/ʊd/
8.	Love you | ten years | before | the Flood, 　▲　△　　▲　▲　　△　▲　　△　▲	d-/ʊd/
9.	And you | should, if | you please, | refuse 　△　▲　　▲　△　　△　▲　　△▲	e-/juːz/

109

10. Till the │ Conver │ sion of │ the Jews.　　　e-/juːz/
　　▲ ▲　　△ △　　　△ ▲　　△ ▲

11. My ve │ geta │ ble love │ should grow　　　f-/oʊ/
　　△ ▲　　△ ▲　　△ ▲　　　△　　▲

12. Vaster │ then em │ pires, and │ more slow.　　f-/oʊ/
　　▲ △　　△ ▲　　△ ▲　　　△　▲

13. An hun │ dred years │ should go │ to praise　　g-/eɪz/
　　△ ▲　　△ ▲　　　△ ▲　　△ ▲

14. Thine eyes, │ and on │ thy fore │ head gaze;　　g-/eɪz/
　　△ ▲　　△ ▲　　△ ▲　　△ ▲

15. Two hun │ dred to │ adore │ each breast,　　h-/est/
　　▲ ▲　　△ △　　△ ▲　　△ ▲

16. But thir │ ty thou │ sand to │ the rest;　　h-/est/
　　△ ▲　　△ ▲　　△ ▲　　△ ▲

17. An age │ at least │ to e │ very part,　　i-/aɪt/
　　△ ▲　　△ ▲　　△ ▲　　△ ▲

18. And the │ last age │ should show │ your heart.　　i-/aɪt/
　　△ △　　▲ ▲　　△ ▲　　△ ▲

19. For, La │ dy, you │ deserve │ this state,　　j-/eɪt/
　　△ ▲　　△ ▲　　△ ▲　　△ ▲

20. Nor would │ I love │ at lo │ wer rate.　　j-/eɪt/
　　△ ▲　　△ ▲　　△ ▲　　△ ▲

21. But at │ my back │ I al │ ways hear　　k-/ɪə(r)/
　　△ ▲　　△ ▲　　△ ▲　　△ ▲

22. Time's win │ ged cha │ riot hur │ rying near;　　k-/ɪə(r)/
　　△ ▲　　△ ▲　　△ ▲　　△ ▲

23. And yon │ der all │ before │ us lie　　l-/aɪ/
　　△ ▲　　△ ▲　　△ ▲　　△ ▲

24. Deserts │ of vast │ eter │ nity.　　l-/aɪ/
　　▲ △　　△ ▲　　△ ▲　　△ ▲

25. Thy beau │ ty shall │ no more │ be found,　　m-/aʊnd/
　　△ ▲　　△ ▲　　△ ▲　　△ ▲

26. Nor, in │ thy mar │ ble vault, │ shall sound　　m-/aʊnd/
　　△ ▲　　△ ▲　　△ ▲　　△ ▲

27. My echo | ing song; | then worms | shall try　　　　　n–/aɪ/
　　△ ▲ ▲　△　▲　　　△　▲　　△　▲

28. That long | -preserv'd | virgi | nity,　　　　　　　　n–/aɪ/
　　△　▲　　△　▲　　△ ▲　△ ▲

29. And your | quaint ho | nour turn | to dust,　　　　o–/ʌst/
　　△　▲　　▲　▲　△　▲　△　▲

30. And in | to a | shes all | my lust.　　　　　　o–/ʌst/
　　△　▲　△ ▲　△　▲　△　▲

31. The grave's | a fine | and pri | vate place,　　　p–/eis/
　　△　▲　　△　▲　△　▲　△　▲

32. But none | I think | do there | embrace.　　　　p–/eɪs/
　　△　▲　△　▲　△　▲　△　▲

33. Now there | fore, while | the youth | ful hue　　q–/juː/
　　▲　△　▲　△　△　▲　△　▲

34. Sits on | thy skin | like mor | ning dew,　　　　q–/juː/
　　▲　△　△　▲　△　▲　△　▲

35. And while | thy wil | ling soul | transpires　　r–/aɪə(r)/
　　△　▲　　△　▲　△　▲　△　▲

36. At e | very pore | with ins | tant fires,　　　　r–/aɪə(r)/
　　△▲　△ ▲　△　▲　△　▲

37. Now let | us sport | us while | we may;　　　　s–/eɪ/
　　△　▲　△　▲　△　▲　△　▲

38. And now, | like am' | rous birds | of prey,　　　s–/eɪ/
　　△　▲　△　▲　△　▲　△　▲

39. Rather | at once | our time | devour,　　　　t–/aʊə(r)/
　　▲ △　△　▲　△　▲　△　▲

40. Than lan | guish in | his slow | - chapt pow'r.　t–/aʊə(r)/
　　△　▲　△　▲　△　▲　△　▲

41. Let us | roll all | our strength, | and all　　　u–/ɔːl/
　　▲ △　△　▲　△　▲　△　▲

42. Our sweet | ness, up | into | one ball,　　　　u–/ɔːl/
　　△　▲　△　▲　△ △　△　▲

43. And tear | our plea | sures with | rough strife,　v–/aɪf/
　　△　▲　△　▲　△　▲　▲　▲

44. Thorough the | iron gates | of life.   v-/aɪf/

      ▲   △   ▲   ▲   △ ▲

45. Thus，though | we can | not make | our sun   w-/ʌn/

      ▲   △   △ ▲   △ ▲   △ ▲

46. Stand still, | yet we | will make | him run.   w-/ʌn/

      △   ▲   △ ▲   △ ▲   △ ▲

注：本诗总体而言是四音步抑扬格 △ ▲(iambic tetrameter)，但有如下例外：① 扬抑格(trochee ▲ △)：8-1、10-1、12-1、24-1、33-1、34-1、39-1、41-1、42-3、44-1、45-1；② 扬扬格(spondee ▲ ▲)：6-3、8-2、15-1、29-2、43-4、44-2；③ 抑抑扬格(anapaest △ △ ▲)：36-2；④抑扬抑格(arnphibrach △ ▲ △)：27-1。尾韵为英雄双行体(heroic couplet)，每两行同韵。

🗒 修辞解析

本诗涉及 7 个诗歌常用的修辞手法：典故(allusion)、嘲讽(irony)、夸张(hyperbole)、明喻(simile)、拟人(personification)、暗喻(metaphor)和诗的破格(poetic license)。

1. 典故(Allusion)

典故通常是一个写作者假定其读者很熟悉的著名历史人物或文学人物，或著名历史事件的随意、简短和含蓄的指称①。本诗第 8 行的 the Flood 和第 10 行的 the Conversion of the Jews 就是典故修辞格。The Flood 显然指《圣经》中记叙的大洪水，而 the Conversion of the Jews 是 "犹太人改变宗教皈依" 的意思，但实际上却是 "不可能" 的意思，因为历史上犹太人在基督教盛行之下坚决不改变其犹太教信仰，所以 Conversion 往往就有了犹太人决不改变其宗教信仰的特指，喻指一件不可能的事。

2. 反讽(Irony)

所谓反讽，就是所用字词要表达的意思与其通常意义正好相反，也叫反话。在英语中 irony 这一类修辞格还有两个极端，轻微一点的叫嘲讽(light irony 或

---

① 张秀国. 英语修辞学[M]. 北京：北京交通大学出版社，2005：202.

innuendo)，严重一点的叫讽刺(heavy irony 或 satire，sarcasm)①。本诗中多处有反讽语气，尤其是从第1行到第20行这一部分。本诗其他地方也有反讽修辞格的运用，如第31行：

The grave's a fine and private place，

反讽修辞格的应用目的主要是幽默②。

3. 夸张(Hyperbole)

所谓夸张，即有意使用夸大其词(主要是数量)的手法来达到强调的目的，也称为 overstatement 或 exaggeration③。哈姆雷特曾这样对他的情人奥菲利亚的哥哥拉奥狄斯说：

I loved Ophelia；forty thousand brothers

Could not，with all their quantity of love，

Make up my sum.　　　　　　　　　　　　　　　　　(Shakespeare)

本诗中既有数量方面的夸张又有质量方面的夸张(5~10行)，如：

Thou by the Indian Ganges' side

Should'st rubies find；I by the tide

Of Humber would complain. I would

Love you ten years before the Flood，

And you should，if you please，refuse

Till the Conversion of the Jews.

4. 明喻(Simile)

本诗中有两处明喻修辞格的应用：Sits on thy skin like morning dew(第34行)，And now，like am'rous birds of prey(第38行)；这两处由 like 引起的介词短语结构在句中都作状语，而非作谓语性表语。这两处都通过形象的比喻来说明抽象复杂的事物。

---

①　张秀国. 英语修辞学[M]. 北京：北京交通大学出版社，2005：217-223.

②　张秀国. 英语修辞学[M]. 北京：北京交通大学出版社，2005：217.

③　张秀国. 英语修辞学[M]. 北京：北京交通大学出版社，2005：210.

5. 拟人(Personification)

本诗中有两处拟人修辞格的运用:

Than languish in his slow-chapt pow'r. (第40行)

Stand still, yet we will make him run. (第46行)

这两处拟人分别代替前面出现过的 am'rous birds of prey 和 sun。拟人修辞的运用比较形象生动,也使诗意更容易理解。

6. 暗喻/隐喻(Metaphor)

本诗第44行 Thorough the iron gates of life 为暗喻修辞格。此处"生活的铁门"形象地喻指生活中的种种条条框框,各种限制和规定,各种风俗习惯。

7. 诗的破格(Poetic License)

为达成英雄双行体尾韵韵式,即两两押韵,本诗有 3 处诗的破格修辞格的应用:Flood(第8行)、eternity(第24行)和 virginity(第28行),分别对应于前一行的would,lie 和 try。这 3 个单词的韵母(或最后一个音节的韵母)原本分别是/ʌ/、/i/和/i/,但为了和前一行的 3 个单词(would,lie 和 try)的韵母押韵,就不得不让它们在发音上改变一下,改发/u/、/aɪ/ 和/aɪ/的音,即/flud/、/ɪ'tɜːnətaɪ/和/və'dʒɪnətaɪ/。这是英语文学中诗人才享有的特权,以使诗歌读起来朗朗上口,更有韵律感。

📋 作品鉴赏

本诗的主题是及时行乐,即求爱者劝其情人放弃矜持而接受他的爱。这类主题在文艺复兴时期较为常见,但本诗的独特之处在于把玄学的理性和田园的野性相结合,男性爱情的炽热和女性矜持的冷漠相对照,相互衬映,产生一种既舒缓又豪放、既浪漫又不失理性的抒情张力。

诗歌是通过一组组陌生化意象来表现这种抒情张力的。一边是情人在印度恒河边淘宝,而另一边是求爱者对着家乡的享伯河发呆,这可是横跨欧亚的异国恋!还有在大洪水前十年就发轫的情愫以及要到三万年后才能完成的对情人身体的赞美,这可是纵横几万年的地老天荒之恋!求爱者还躲在埋葬情人的墓穴中安享幽静与美好,而蛆虫则尽享情人死后躯体的贞操。最后求爱者的情欲和情人的矜持同归于尽、化为灰烬，这是多么哥特式的恐怖之恋呀！还有求爱者呼唤发情的猛禽大口吞掉属于他们的时光，无不体现出求爱者对爱情的渴望和珍惜，以及对时光流逝、青春难续的不甘。

马韦尔的诗热情奔放、构思玄妙，与一般玄学派诗歌的纠结较真不太一样。本诗为四音步抑扬格韵律，尾韵押的是英雄双行体韵式。本诗属于篇幅较长的英美抒情诗作品，虽然文艺复兴后还有诗人，如雪莱、拜伦等喜欢写游记和颂歌等长诗，但总体而言英美现代抒情诗的篇幅还是比较短的。

Unit 11   Robert Burns

罗伯特·彭斯

　　罗伯特·彭斯(1759—1796)，苏格兰最伟大的诗人，英国浪漫主义诗歌的先驱；出生于农民家庭，年少就成为家中主要劳力；从小对苏格兰民歌非常熟悉，27 岁出版著名诗集《苏格兰方言诗集》，轰动苏格兰，受到各界赞誉；出入上层社会和贵族圈子一段时间后，还是回到乡村生活和工作；1789 年被封为收入不高的税收官；他对法国大革命公开发声支持，还曾捐献四门大炮给法国大革命作为礼物；1794 年还曾参加抗法志愿军；最后因过度劳累，积劳成疾，年仅 36 岁就离开了人世。生前受邀创作、收集、整理和改写了三百余首苏格兰民歌，为苏格兰诗歌的继承和发展作出了重大贡献。

📖 诗作一

A Red，Red Rose
一朵红红的玫瑰

O My luve's like a red, red rose,①②	吾爱似红玫，
That's newly sprung③ in June;	六月始绽开；
O My luve's like the melodie,④	吾爱似美乐，
That's sweetly play'd in tune.⑤	甜蜜又合拍。
As fair art thou⑥, my bonie lass⑦	姑娘花般美，
So deep in luve am I;	吾爱深如潭；
And I will luve thee still, my dear,	爱君永不弃，
Till a' the seas gang dry.⑧	纵使海枯干。
Till a' the seas gang dry, my dear,	纵使海枯干。
And the rocks melt wi' the sun:⑨	岩石亦消融；
And I will luve thee still, my dear,	爱君永不弃，
While the sands⑩ o' life shall run.	纵使沙漏空。
And fare thee weel, my only luve,	再会吾之爱，
And fare thee weel a while!⑪	向君告别离！
And I will come again, my luve,	吾将还复来；
Tho' it were ten thousand mile.⑫	不负万里期。

（诸光　译）

📝 语言注释

① O：Oh，感叹词。

② luve：love(古时用法，Old English)。

③ sprung：spring 的过去分词，此处作表语形容词，意为"生出，长出"。

④ melody：*n.* 旋律；歌曲；美妙的音乐。

⑤ play'd：played，演奏。in tune：一致；合调。

⑥ art：be 的现在式第二人称单数形式。thou：第二人称主格(you)；你；尔，汝（古时用法，Old English)。

⑦ bonie lass：可爱的姑娘。bonie：*n.* 可人儿。lass：*n.* 小姑娘；古诗用语。

⑧ a'：all。gang：go。Till a' the seas gang dry＝Till all the seas go dry。

⑨ wi'：with。

⑩ sands：古时用来度量时间的沙漏。

⑪ fare thee weel：fare you well，farewell。本意为"告别，辞别；再见，再会"；"别了！再会！(常含有永别或不容易再见面的意思)"。此处诗人创造性地将该词一分为二，并用作动词。thee，第二人称宾格。

⑫ tho'：though。

❓ 思考题

1. What images in the poem have impressed you? And why?

2. Have you encountered these images in the poetry before?

3. What effect does it have when the images of seas, rocks and sands are applied in the poem?

4. Why does the poet separate the word "farewell" into two words "fare" and "well" in the poem? Is it usual for us to do so in everyday English?

5. There are many repetitions in the poem, can you tell the kinds and significance of these repetitions?

📝 节奏、韵律图示

A Red，Red Rose

行数 （Line）	四、三音步抑扬格 （Iambic Tetrameter & Trimeter）	韵式 （Rhyme Scheme）
1.	O My luve's ∣ like a red，∣ red rose， △ ▲　△ △ ▲　▲ ▲	a
2.	That's new ∣ ly sprung ∣ in June； △ ▲　△ ▲　△ ▲	b—/un/
3.	O My luve's ∣ like the me ∣ lodie， △ ▲　△ △ ▲　△ △	c
4.	That's sweet ∣ ly play'd ∣ in tune. △ ▲　△ ▲　△ ▲	b—/un/
5.	As fair ∣ art thou，∣ my bo ∣ nie lass △ ▲ ▲ ▲　△ ▲ △ ▲	d
6.	So deep ∣ in luve ∣ am I； △ ▲　△ ▲　△ ▲	e—/aɪ/
7.	And I ∣ will luve ∣ thee still，∣ my dear， △ ▲ △ ▲　△ ▲　△ ▲	f
8.	Till a' ∣ the seas ∣ gang dry. △ ▲　△ ▲　△ ▲	e—/aɪ/
9.	Till a' ∣ the seas ∣ gang dry，∣ my dear， △ ▲　△ ▲　△ ▲　△ ▲	g
10.	And the rocks ∣ melt wi' ∣ the sun： △ △ ▲　▲ △ △ ▲	h—/ʌn/
11.	And I ∣ will luve ∣ thee still，∣ my dear， △ ▲ △ ▲　△ ▲　△ ▲	g
12.	While the sands ∣ o' life ∣ shall run. △ △ ▲　△ ▲　△ ▲	h—/ʌn/

13.　And fare ｜ thee weel, ｜ my on ｜ ly luve,　　　　　　　i
　　△　▲　　△　▲　　　△▲　　△▲

14.　And fare ｜ thee weel ｜ a while!　　　　　　　　　j-/aɪl/
　　△　▲　　△　▲　　△　▲

15.　And I ｜ will come ｜ again, ｜ my luve,　　　　　　i
　　△　▲　△　▲　　△　▲　　　△　▲

16.　Tho' it were ｜ ten thou ｜ sand mile.　　　　　　j-/aɪl/
　　△　▲　△　　▲　▲　　△　▲

注：本诗是四音步和三音步的交替组合体，以抑扬格为主。少量不规则音步有：

① 扬抑格(trochee：▲△)：10-2。

② 扬扬格(spondee：▲▲)：1-3；5-2；16-2。

③ 抑抑格(pyrrhic：△△)：3-3。

④ 抑抑扬格(anapest：△△▲)：1-2、3-2、10-1、12-1。

⑤ 抑扬抑格(amphibrach：△▲△)：16-1。

本诗头两节尾韵为 abcb 韵式，即一三不搭，二四押韵：abcb defe；后两节变为 abab 韵式，即 ghgh ijij。

📑 修辞解析

本诗涉及 5 个诗歌常用的修辞手法：明喻(simile)、重复(repetition)、夸张 (hyperboly)、暗喻(metaphor)和诗的破格(poetic license)。

1. 明喻(Simile)

本诗第一节有两处明喻修辞格的应用(第 1 行和第 3 行)：O My luve's like a red, red rose, /That's newly sprung in June; /O My luve's like the melodie, /That's sweetly play'd in tune. 这两个明喻修辞格把自己的恋人描绘得非常生动形象。

2. 重复(Repetition)

本诗有多处重复修辞格的应用：(1)red(第 1 行)；(2)O My luve's like a… (第 1 行、第 3 行)；(3)And I will luve thee still, my dear(第 7 行、第 11 行)；(4) Till a' the seas gang dry (第 8 行、第 9 行)；(5)And fare thee weel(第 13 行、第 14 行)；(6)my dear(第 7 行、第 9 行、第 11 行)；(7)my (only)luve(第 13 行、第 15

行）。一首短短16行的抒情诗就有7处重复的地方，可见这种修辞格应用之广泛。重复的大量使用给人一种民谣般反复吟唱、反复沉吟的感觉，起到不断强化情感、不断深化主题的作用。

3. 夸张(Hyperboly)

本诗有两处夸张修辞格的应用：Till a' the seas gang dry, my dear, /And the rocks melt wi' the sun(第9行、第10行)。显然这是质量方面的夸张，因为提到了"所有"的概念，即全天下的海洋都变干涸了，天底下全部的岩石都被太阳融化了，我也还会爱着你。通过夸大"海枯石烂"的结果来达到强调的目的。

4. 暗喻/隐喻(Metaphor)

本诗第12行中 the sands o' life 属于暗喻(或隐喻)修辞格，暗指生命的尽头。sands 本指沙漏中的沙子，沙漏中的沙子漏光时通常表明一个时辰的终结；后喻指生命即将逝去、人生走到了尽头。

5. 诗的破格(Poetic License)

本诗第13行、第14行有两处诗的破格修辞格的应用：And fare thee weel, my only luve, /And fare thee weel a while! 其中单词 farewell 被创造性地拆分成两个部分：fare 和 weel(即 fare 和 well)，既满足了格律的需要(都是单音节词，轻重相间，非常合适)，同时也满足了诗句句法上的要求(fare 还是谓语动词，而 well 则变成了副词)。这里诗的破格主要体现在构词法方面：原本英文中 farewell 并没有拆分开来使用的先例，但此处创造性地将一词分开来使用，打破了语言的常规，体现了语言应用的创造性、灵活性和审美性。到目前为止也仅有诗歌体裁可以包容这种打破常规的破格用法，在其他文体中几乎不可能出现这种反常的语言现象。

作品鉴赏

这是一首爱情诗，一方面向爱人表达深沉炽热的爱，同时向爱人表达忠贞不二的决心。这类亘古就有的爱情主题在彭斯深情浪漫的笔触之下彰显了农民的本色和艺术的创新。他的艺术灵感常常来自民间，因为他大部分作品来自对民谣、民歌等民间作品的改写和再创。另外他在乡村接触大自然的机会远远多于学院派诗人，能够远离大都市的喧嚣和纷争，所以他的诗歌浸透了民间的风韵和自然的清新，加上他饱含深情的咏叹和一反常规的语言表达，就形成了一种清新脱俗且情感挚热的抒情风格。

　　六月里迎风盛开的红玫瑰，琴弦上奏出的甜美乐曲，都是对美丽爱人的绝佳比喻。对爱人的忠贞不二被表白为：哪怕天下海水全枯干、天下岩石全融化、时间沙漏里的沙子全漏光……这些清新优美的意象从此就经典化了，从此不再对后来者开放，因为彭斯已经使用过了！最经典的还是最后一节里的诗句：And fare thee weel, my only luve, /And fare thee weel a while! 此处运用了诗的破格修辞格。彭斯简直把语言用活了，把 farewell 一词拆分成两个，fare 还是谓语动词，而 well 则变成了副词，即变成了 fare thee weel。这就是陌生化(defamiliarization)①效果，因为它打破了语言的常规，获得了一种特效，具有很强的美感，给人留下了深刻的印象。中国现当代诗人戴望舒也特别擅长使用这种拆分手法(即诗的破格)来表达诗情：

在雨的哀曲里，

消了她的颜色，

散了她的芬芳

消散了，甚至她的

太息般的眼光，

丁香般的惆怅。

(《雨巷》第五节)

　　虽然"消散"一词本来就是动词，可在现代汉语白话文里，人们已经习惯于把"消散"两字连用，不再像古代汉语那样使用单字。但诗人戴望舒创造性地将其一拆为二，单独用作谓语不说(第五节第二、三行)，还拆了又聚，紧接着就用了一个未拆分的原词"消散"作为谓语(第四行)，达到了陌生化的效果，在音韵和意象

---

　　① "陌生化"原本是一个著名的文学理论，它由俄国形式主义评论家什克洛夫斯基提出，是西方"陌生化"诗学发展史上的重要里程碑，也是西方"陌生化"诗学的成熟标志，是俄国形式主义的核心概念，也是形式主义者最关心的问题。这个理论强调在内容与形式上违反人们常见的常情、常理、常事，同时在艺术上超越常境。陌生化的基本构成原则是表面互不相关而内里存在联系的诸种因素的对立和冲突，正是这种对立和冲突造成了"陌生化"的表象，给人以感官的刺激或情感的震动。(参见百度百科陌生化词条。网址：https://baike.baidu.com/item/%E9%99%8C%E7%94%9F%E5%8C%96? fromModule = lemma_search-box.)

两方面都创造了一种一唱三叹和循环往复的意境美，可谓匠心独运、妙笔生花。

　　本诗为四音步与三音步抑扬格的交替韵式，头两节的尾韵为 abcb，后两节又变成 abab，共有四个诗节。大量语句或语词的重复以及诗的破格、明喻和暗喻等修辞格的应用，使得该诗的修辞丰富多变，语言优美自然，共同成就了一个清新脱俗的经典作品。

📖 诗作二

The Slave's Lament
奴隶的悲叹

It was in sweet Senegal①,　　　　　　　　那是在甜蜜的塞内加尔，

That my foes did me enthral②(奴役)，　　我的敌人们将我奴役，

For the lands of Virginia③, -ginia，O!　为了弗吉尼亚、吉尼亚的土地呵！

Torn④ from the lovely shore，　　　　　　我被迫离开这可爱的海岸，

And must never see it more，　　　　　　再也见不到它，

And alas⑤! I am weary⑥, weary，O!　　　唉，我是疲惫、疲惫透了哟！

All on that charming coast　　　　　　　在那迷人的海岸

Is no bitter snow and frost，　　　　　　没有冰冷的雪与霜

Like the lands of Virginia, -ginia，O!　就如在弗吉尼亚、吉尼亚的土地上呵！

There streams for ever flow，　　　　　　那里溪水永远流淌，

And there flowers for ever blow⑦，　　　那里花儿永远开放，

And alas! I am weary, weary，O!　　　　唉，我是疲惫、疲惫透了哟！

The burden I must bear，　　　　　　　　我不得不忍辱负重，

While the cruel scourge⑧(鞭苔) I fear，　还担心残暴的鞭打，

In the lands of Virginia, -ginia，O!　　在弗吉尼亚、吉尼亚的土地上呵！

And I think on⑨ friends most dear　　　我怀念昔日好友啊

With the bitter, bitter tear，　　　　　眼里充满心酸泪花，

And alas! I am weary, weary，O!　　　　唉，我是疲惫、疲惫透了哟！

（诸光　译）

📝 语言注释

① Senegal：*n.* 塞内加尔(非洲国家)。

② enthral：*v.* 迷住；奴役。

③ Virginia：*n.* 弗吉尼亚州(美国最初的十三个州、英国在美国最早的殖民地之一)。

④ Torn：*n.* 撕开；撕掉；扯破；裂开；拉伤(肌肉、韧带)。

⑤ alas：唉(表悲伤、遗憾、恐惧、关切等)。

⑥ weary：*adj.* 疲倦的；厌烦的。

⑦ blow：*v.* (古)开花；同 blossom。

⑧ scourge：*n.* 鞭；鞭子。

⑨ think on：考虑；思量；思念；同 think of。

❓ 思考题

1. As the first person narrator，what kind of person is I in the poem?

2. What kind of people are my foes? Why did they enslave me?

3. Why is everything about Senegal so sweet，lovely and charming to me?

4. Why can't the speaker see it more? And go abroad and would never return?

5. What feelings do you have when you read Virginia，-ginia O?

6. How do you like the figure of speech of repetition? Find out all the repetitions in the poem and discuss the effect of them.

7. Have you ever encountered the interjection word O at the end of the poetic line? What special effect does it have here?

📝 节奏、韵律图示

The Slave's Lament

行数 (Line)	四、三音步抑扬格 (Iambic Tetrameter & Trimeter)	韵式 (Rhyme Scheme)
1.	It was ｜ in sweet ｜ Senegal, △ ▲　△ ▲　▲ △ △	a–/ɔːl/
2.	That my foes ｜ did me ｜ enthral (奴役), △ △ ▲　△ ▲　△ ▲	a–/ɔːl/
3.	For the lands ｜ of Virgi ｜ nia, -gi ｜ nia, O! △ △ ▲　△ △ ▲　△ ▲　△ ▲	b–/oʊ/
4.	Torn from ｜ the love ｜ ly shore, ▲ △　△ ▲　△ ▲	c–/ɔːr/
5.	And must ne ｜ ver see ｜ it more, △ △ ▲　△ ▲　△ ▲	c–/ɔːr/
6.	And alas! ｜ I am we ｜ ary, we ｜ ary, O! △ △ ▲　△ △ ▲　△ △ ▲　△ △ ▲	b–/oʊ/
7.	All on that char ｜ ming coast ▲ △ △ ▲　△ ▲	d–/əʊst/
8.	Is no ｜ bitter snow ｜ and frost, △ ▲　▲ △ ▲　△ ▲	d–/ɔːst/→/əʊst/
9.	Like the lands ｜ of Virgi ｜ nia, -gi ｜ nia, O! △ △ ▲　△ △ ▲　△ ▲　△ ▲	b–/oʊ/
10.	There streams ｜ for e ｜ ver flow, △ ▲　△ △ ▲　△ ▲	b–/oʊ/
11.	And there ｜ flowers ｜ for e ｜ ver blow, △ ▲　▲ △　△ ▲　△ ▲	b–/oʊ/
12.	And alas! ｜ I am we ｜ ary, we ｜ ary, O! △ △ ▲　△ △ ▲　△ △ ▲　△ ▲	b–/oʊ/

13.　　The bur ｜ den I ｜ must bear,　　　　　　　　e-/eə/
　　　　　　△　▲　△　▲　　△　▲

14.　　While the cruel scourge(鞭苔) ｜ I fear,　　　e-/iə/→/eə/
　　　　　　△　　△　▲▲　　▲　　　　　△　▲

15.　　In the lands ｜ of Virgi ｜ nia, -gi ｜ nia, O!　　b-/oʊ/
　　　　　　△　△　▲　　△△　▲　　△　▲　　△　▲

16.　　And I think ｜ on friends ｜ most dear　　　　　f-/ɪːə(r)/
　　　　　　△　△　▲　　△　▲　　　△　▲

17.　　With the bit ｜ ter, bit ｜ ter tear,　　　　　　f-/ɪːə(r)/
　　　　　　△　△　▲　　△　▲　　△　▲

18.　　And alas! ｜ I am we ｜ ary, we ｜ ary, O!　　b-/oʊ/
　　　　　　△　△　▲　　△　△　▲　　△　△　▲　　△　△　▲

注：本诗以抑扬格(iamb△▲)为基调，同时包含了比较多的其他格律：

① 抑抑扬格(anapest△△▲)：2-1、3-1、3-2、5-1、6-1、6-2、6-3、6-4、9-1、9-2、12-1、12-2、12-3、12-4、14-1、15-1、15-2、16-1、17-1、18-1、18-2、18-3、18-4；

② 扬抑扬格(cretic or amphimacer▲△▲)：8-2；

③ 扬抑抑格(dactyl▲△△)：1-3；

④ 扬抑格(trochee▲△)：11-2；

⑤ 扬抑抑扬格(choriamb or choriambus▲△△▲)：7-1。

韵步是从四音步(第3、6、9、11、12、15和18行)到三音步(第1、2、4、5、8、10、13、14、16、17行)。

另外，因本诗每节头两行都有押同韵的需要，故第7、8行和第13、14行必须采用诗的破格手法，让第8行和第14行最后一词的韵母稍作改变，以便与第7行和第13行保持同韵，即让 coast, frost 发相同的音/əv/；让 bear, fear 发相同的音/eə/。

修辞解析

本诗涉及两个修辞手法：重复和诗的破格。

1. 重复(Repetition)

本诗的重复比较频繁，类型也比较多，特分类如下：

(1)诗行的重复

本诗有两行诗分别重复了三遍：

For/Like/in the lands of Virginia, -ginia, O!　　（incremental repetition①）

And alas! I am weary, weary, O!（第6、12、18行）　　　（refrain②）

前者是有变化的重复，故称之为 incremental repetition。后者是没有变化、完全相同的重复，故称之为 refrain。

（2）单词的重复

weary(第6、12、18行)和 bitter(第8、17行)（repetend③）分别重复了 3×2 次和 2 次。

（3）词的部分重复

Virginal, -ginal, O!（第3、9、15行)中的-ginal 不是一个单词，而是 Virginal 中的一个部分。这种词的部分重复，在英诗中是非常罕见的，但是其所达成的回响效果却是非常美妙的。

2. 诗的破格(Poetic Licence)

该修辞格的定义在丁尼生诗歌中已有界定。本诗中诗的破格主要应用在两个方面：韵律方面和语词方面。

（1）韵律方面的诗的破格

第二节头两行即第 7、8 行末尾的 coast 和 frost 本来并不押韵(/əʊst/和/ɔːst/)，鉴于第一节头两行是押韵的，所以为了让这个韵律保持下去，此处就允许 coast 和 frost 在发音上相谐，即都发相同的元音/əʊ/。同理，第三节头两行的末尾两词 bear, fear(第 13、14 行)也不押韵，一个是/eə/，另一个是/iə/。因此我们运用诗的破格手法让 fear 与 bear 发相同的音/eə/，达到本诗每节头两行都押韵的目的。

---

① incremental repetition：A modern term for a device of repetition commonly found in ballads. It involves the repetition of lines or stanzas with small but crucial changes made to a few words from one to the next, and has an effect of narrative progression or suspense. Chris Baldick. 牛津文学术语词典[M]. 上海：上海外语教育出版社，2000：109.

② refrain：A line, group of lines, or part of a line repeated at regular or irregular intervals in a poem, usually at the end of each stanza. It may recur in exactly the same form, or may be subject to slight variations(see incremental repetition). Chris Baldick. 牛津文学术语词典[M]. 上海：上海外语教育出版社，2000：186.

③ repetend：A word, phrase, or a line that recurs in a poem. As distinct from a refrain, a repetend is repeated only partially or only at irregular intervals. Chris Baldick. 牛津文学术语词典[M]. 上海：上海外语教育出版社，2000：187.

（2）语词方面的诗的破格

Virginia, -ginia, O！（第 3、9、15 行）中有 -ginia 的重复，注意是词的一部分的重复，而且巧妙地回避了整个单词的重复。在拆分单词创造同声相谐方面，彭斯毫无疑问是极具创造性的！

作品鉴赏

彭斯同情过法国大革命和巴黎公社，此处同情被贩卖为奴的非洲黑人，实属自然。本诗以第一人称单数为口吻，对自己的悲惨遭遇，对家乡、朋友的无尽怀念都表现得真切自然，感人至深。

写作风格上本诗具有很强的艺术独创性。格律比较多样化，有抑扬格，还有扬抑格、抑抑扬格和扬抑抑格。本诗在尾韵上也灵活多变，不拘一格：aabccb ddbbbb eebffb。在遣词造句方面也打破常规，善于创新：

... Virginia, -ginia, O！　　　　　（第 3、9、15 行）

And alas! I am weary, weary, O！（第 6、12、18 行）

第一行运用了一个重复修辞格，但重复的不是一个词，而是词的后面一部分，但它抓住了读者的神经，因为它是情感的加强型模式。词的后半部分的重复形成一种很强的行内韵律感：腹韵和尾韵的叠加。行尾的 O 则进一步加强了感叹的抒情力度和情感的丰富程度。因为 O 一般都用在行首，而不用在行尾，如 A Red, Red Rose 中：

O My luve's like a red, red rose,

That's newly sprung in June;

O My luve's like the melodie,

That's sweetly play'd in tune.

And alas! 也体现了创新性：alas 是中古时期的感叹语，16 世纪的莎翁常用该词，但彭斯在 19 世纪沿用该词，给人一种古风感，同时也增强了诗歌的历史厚重感。这些表达方式前无古人，后无来者，既强化了情感的力度，也实现了陌生化，令人耳目一新！

📖 诗作三

My Heart's in the Highlands
心系高原

My heart's in the Highlands, my heart is not here;　　心系高原，心不在此；

My heart's in the Highlands a-chasing the deer;　　心系高原，追逐群鹿；

Chasing the wild deer, and following the roe,　　追逐野鹿，跟踪幼鹿，

My heart's in the Highlands wherever I go.　　心系高原，无论何处。

Farewell to the Highlands, farewell to the North,　　再见，高原！再见，北方！

The birth-place of valor, the country of worth;　　美德之家，斗士之乡；

Wherever I wander, wherever I rove,　　何为归途，何处流浪，

The hills of the Highlands for ever I love.　　高原群山，永在心堂。

Farewell to the mountains high cover'd with snow;　　再见，白雪覆盖的高山；

Farewell to the straths and green valleys below;　　再见，河谷与绿色峡谷；

Farewell to the forests and wild-hanging woods;　　再见，森林与藤蔓之树，

Farewell to the torrents and loud-pouring floods.　　再见，急流与轰鸣瀑布。

My heart's in the Highlands, my heart is not here;　　心系高原，心不在此；

My heart's in the Highlands a-chasing the deer;　　心系高原，追逐群鹿；

Chasing the wild deer, and following the roe,　　追逐野鹿，跟踪幼鹿，

My heart's in the Highlands, wherever I go.　　心系高原，无论何处。

（诸莉　译）

Unit 12   *William Blake*

威廉·布莱克

　　威廉·布莱克(1757—1827)，英国前浪漫主义诗人，生活于18、19世纪之交；并未受过正规教育，终生以刻字、雕画为职业；1789年出版《天真之歌》，五年后又刻印《经验之歌》，后来把两者合在一起，取名为《显示人类灵魂两个相反侧面的天真和经验之歌》。《天真之歌》中音乐般的诗句表达了诗人对生活的乐观之情，透露着诗人孩童般的率真与欢快。《经验之歌》则以思想的深刻性和批判性反思见长，反映了现实生活中的贫困与痛苦，语气沉重而激越。

　　布莱克生前并不出名，去世后才被重新发现。20世纪20年代西方学术界才开始对这位"神秘主义诗人"进行系统的研究，肯定了布莱克浪漫主义先驱性诗人的地位。

📖 **诗作一**

London
伦 敦

I wander thro' each charter'd① street,	我游走于每条被占街道，
Near where the charter'd Thames② does flow,	靠近那同样被占的泰河，
And mark③ in every face I meet	注意所遇每个路人面貌
Marks of weakness, marks of woe④.	均带有虚弱哀伤的气色。
In every cry of every man,	从每个人的每一声喊叫，
In every infant's⑤ cry of fear,	从每个婴儿害怕的哭闹，
In every voice, in every ban⑥,	从每个人声，每道禁令，
The mind-forg'd manacles⑦ I hear.	都听到思想铸就的镣铐。
How the chimney⑧-sweeper's cry	扫烟囱少年的每声叫喊
Every black'ning church appals⑨,	震撼着每座暗黑的教堂。
And the hapless⑩ soldier's sigh	还有那不幸士兵的哀叹
Runs in blood down palace walls.	像鲜血冲下那王宫高墙。
But most thro' midnight streets I hear	而午夜街头我常常听到
How the youthful harlot's curse⑪	年轻妓女是如何在诅咒，
Blasts⑫ the new-born infant's tear,	吓得新生婴儿不敢哭闹，
And blights⑬ with plagues⑭ the marriage hearse⑮.	瘟疫人间使婚车变灵柩。

（诸莉 译）

📝 语言注释

① charter：*v.* 包租；发给特许执照；charter'd＝chartered。

② Thames：*n.* (伦敦的)泰晤士河。

③ mark：*v.* 注意；作记号。*n.* 标志；符号；痕迹。

④ woe：*n.* 困难，灾难；痛苦，悲伤，悲哀。

⑤ infant：*n.* 婴儿；幼儿。

⑥ ban：*n.* 禁令。

⑦ manacles：*n.* 镣铐；手铐。mind-forg'd manacles：心灵铸就的镣铐。

⑧ chimney：*n.* 烟囱。

⑨ appals：*v.* 使……大为震惊，使……惊骇；使……厌恶。

⑩ hapless：*adj.* 运气不好的，倒霉的；不幸的。

⑪ harlot：*n.* 娼妓。curse：*v.* 诅咒；咒骂。

⑫ blast：*v.* 爆炸；损害；使枯萎。

⑬ blight：*v.* 破坏；使……枯萎。

⑭ plague：*n.* 瘟疫。

⑪ hearse：*n.* 灵车；棺材。

❓ 思考题

1. The word "mark" is repeated three times. What part of speech is each one?

2. What does the word "charter'd" in the first stanza mean?

3. There are several repeated use of "cry", "voice", "hear", and so on, as if there are many loud speeches taking place. What do these words mean?

4. There are many repetitions in this poem. Find out all of them and discuss what effect they have in expressing the feelings of the poet.

5. What attitude does the poet have towards the city of London? Positive or negative? Extreme or moderate?

6. Can you explain why the poet looks at the city of London that way?

📝 节奏、韵律图示

London

行数 （Line）	四、三音步抑扬格 （Iambic Tetrameter & Trimeter）	韵式 （Rhyme Scheme）

1. I wan │ der thro' │ each char │ ter'd street,　　a－/iːt/
　　△ ▲　△ ▲　　△ ▲　　△ ▲

2. Near where │ the char │ ter'd Thames │ does flow,　　b－/oʊ/
　　▲ ▲　△ ▲　　△ ▲　　△ ▲

3. And mark │ in eve │ ry face │ I meet　　a－/iːt/
　　△ ▲　△ ▲　　△ ▲　　△ ▲

4. Marks of weak │ ness, marks │ of woe.　　b－/oʊ/
　　▲ △ ▲　△ ▲　　△ ▲

5. In eve │ ry cry │ of eve │ ry man,　　c－/æn/
　　△ ▲　△ ▲　△ ▲　　△ ▲

6. In eve │ ry in │ fant's cry │ of fear,　　d－/ɪə(r)/
　　△ ▲　△ ▲　△ ▲　　△ ▲

7. In eve │ ry voice, │ in eve │ ry ban,　　c－/æn/
　　△ ▲　△ ▲　　△ ▲　△ ▲

8. The mind │ -forg'd ma │ nacles │ I hear.　　d－/ɪə(r)/
　　△ ▲　△ ▲　　△ ▲　△ ▲

9. How the chim │ ney-swee │ per's cry　　e－/aɪ/
　　△ △ ▲　△ ▲　△ ▲

10. Every black' │ ning church │ appals,　　f－/ɔːl/
　　▲ △ ▲　△ ▲　△ ▲

11. And the hap │ less sol │ dier's sigh　　e－/aɪ/
　　△ △ ▲　△ ▲　△ ▲

12. Runs in blood │ down pa │ lace walls.　　f－/ɔːl/
　　▲ △ ▲　△ ▲　△ ▲

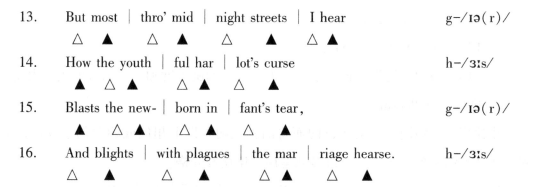

注：本诗格律为四音步抑扬格（iambic tetrameter）（第 1、2、3、5、6、7、8、13、16 行）和三音步抑扬格（iambic trimeter）（第 4、9、10、11、12、14、15 行），且三音步中第一个音步均为三音节，有抑抑扬格（anapest：△△▲）（9-1 和 11-1）和扬抑扬格（amphimacer：▲△▲）（4-1、10-1、12-1、14-1 和 15-1）两类。然后在四音步抑扬格中仅第二行第一音步是扬扬格（spondee：▲▲），其余均为抑扬格（iamb：△▲）。本诗的尾韵为 abab cdcd efef ghgh。

📑 修辞解析

本诗涉及五个修辞手法：重复、排比、隐喻、头韵和矛盾修饰法。

1. 重复（Repetition）

本诗中的重复分两类：语词的重复和结构的重复。

（1）语词的重复

chartered（第 1、2 行）两次重复

mark（第 3、4 行；虽词性不同但词形相同）三次重复

cry（第 5、6、9 行）三次重复

every（第 3、5、6、7 行，且第 5、7 行都有两个）七次重复

thro'（第 1、13 行）两次重复

（2）结构的重复

chartered street/chartered Thames（第 1、2 行）：偏正结构的重复

Marks of weakness, marks of woe.（第 4 行）："of+介词"结构的重复

In every cry of every man,（第 5 行）："in+介词"结构的重复

In every infant's cry of fear,（第 6 行）："in+介词"结构的重复

In every voice, in every ban, (第 7 行)："in+介词"结构的重复

… I hear(第 8 行)：后置主谓

… I hear(第 13 行)：后置主谓

以上两方面的重复都加强了本诗一唱三叹的回旋力度和一气呵成的表达力度。

2. 排比(Parallelism)

排比指为达强调或平衡之目的而将两种或两种以上相似或相关的事物或理念置于相似的结构形式之中。本诗多处运用了排比修辞格。

Marks of weakness, marks of woe(第 4 行)：既是重复又是排比

In every cry of every man(第 5 行)

In every infant's cry of fear(第 6 行)

In every voice, in every ban(第 7 行)

以上第 5、6、7 行既有单词 every 的重复，又有"in+介词"结构的重复，更是三个排比句。三个结构相似的句型读起来极有气势，极有冲击力。

How the chimney-sweeper's cry(第 9 行)

How the youthful *harlot*'s curse(第 14 行)

以上两句虽然相隔较远，但依然是一种排比句式，语气既有哀叹又有强力的揭露。还有两句也是一种排比句式：

Blasts the new-born infant's tear, (第 15 行)

And blights with plagues the marriage hearse. (第 16 行)

Blasts 和 blights 是一对头韵，意思也相近，虽然分处两行。这样的排比句读起来显得非常有气势和力量。

3. 隐喻(Metaphor)

本诗第 12 行 "Runs in blood down palace walls."是一句隐喻，翻译为："(还有那不幸士兵的哀叹)像鲜血冲下那王宫高墙(那么多)。"显然这是一个比喻的说法，指士兵们对自己的工作抱怨颇多，平时在皇宫里执勤站岗的士兵们要遵守刻板的规章制度，过着枯燥乏味的生活，因此常常感叹自己命苦。

4. 头韵(Alliteration)

本诗第 4 行 weakness 和 woe 押头韵(即两词首音/w/的重复)。头韵加上 marks

的重复，加强了作者的感叹语气和表达力度。

5. 矛盾修饰法(Oxymoron)

所谓矛盾修饰法，即把显然矛盾的词语并置以产生强烈的情感效果。

它表现了一种凝练的似非而是(paradox)。①它是悖论(又叫似非而是)修辞格的压缩版，因为悖论修辞格一般而言是一句陈述话语，而矛盾修饰法是一个偏正结构，是一个短语。本诗最后一行 marriage hearse 就属于矛盾修饰法的修辞格，字面意义为"婚姻灵车"。婚姻代表着一种夫妻关系的新生，家庭的新生，也是人类努力繁衍后代的体现。而灵车却是运载亡人的交通工具，代表着生命的逝去和死亡。因此"新生"和"逝去(死亡)"就是一组意义相对的偏正结构，是一对矛盾意义的组合体。

作品鉴赏

这是一首揭露英国社会阴暗面的作品。当时既是资本主义工业化早期，也是瘟疫流行、法国大革命给整个欧洲带来极大震荡的年代。本诗不仅反映社会底层人民的心声和痛苦，更是一枚投枪，一枚匕首，直刺英国的心脏：伦敦。诗歌站在人民的立场，对伦敦城里的英国社会各种不公和丑陋现象进行了无情的揭露和鞭挞。

首先我们看到了一个天怒人怨、黑色恐怖的伦敦。这里既有瘟疫的横行与肆虐，也有血淋淋的资本的无孔不入——它已经深入大街小巷，渗透到泰晤士河。这个城市的男男女女们无不神情虚弱、面有衰容——先是视觉层面，后是声音层面的感受——男人的呼喊、婴儿的啼哭、每一句说话声和每一道禁令的宣读……扫烟囱男孩们的喊叫声震动了墙壁发黑的教堂，倒霉士兵的叹息多如鲜血冲下宫墙。而最让诗人痛彻心扉的却是深夜里年轻妓女们的诅咒声，能把新生婴儿吓得欲哭无泪，其带来的瘟疫能把婚车变成灵柩。这些现在听起来可能非常遥远，但在当时是多么真切和现实。

---

① 胡壮麟，刘世生. 西方文体学词典[Z]. 北京：清华大学出版社，2004：230.

　　这首诗被后世评论家称为"最有力量的小诗"（Oliver Elton）。其实这也是最有战斗力的小诗，是讨伐的檄文，是冲锋的号角，是布莱克希望"坚决摧毁这个地狱式的伦敦……在愉快的绿色英格兰，建立起地上的天国"①的最好写照。

---

　　① 赵洪定. 英文名篇鉴赏金库(诗歌卷)[M]. 天津：天津人民出版社，2000：84.

📖 诗作二

The Chimney-Sweeper
扫烟囱的小男孩

A little black thing among the snow	雪中有一个黑色小东西
Crying "weep!" "weep!" in notes of woe!	悲凉地喊"扫啊，扫啊"！
"Where are thy father and mother, say?"—	"喂，你们父母哪去了？"——
"They are both gone up to the Church to pray.	"他们都去教堂祈祷了。"
"Because I was happy upon the heath,	"我原本在野外很快乐，"
And smil'd among the winter's snow,	我在冬雪里还充满欢笑，
They clothed me in the clothes of death,	他们就用黑衣把我一罩，
And taught me to sing the notes of woe.	还教我唱起悲凉的韵调。
"And because I am happy and dance and sing,	"因为我总是又唱又跳，
They think they have done me no injury,	他们就以为没有伤到我，
And are gone to praise God and His Priest and King,	接着又去赞美上帝国王，
Who make up a Heaven of our misery."	他们用我的苦建了天堂。"

（诸莉　译）

诗作三

The Tyger
老 虎

Tyger! Tyger! Burning bright   老虎，老虎，双眼火亮，
In the forest of the night,   在夜的丛林里
What immortal hand or eye   是什么神奇的手或眼
Could frame thy fearful symmetry?   打造了你这恐怖的匀称？

In what distant deeps or skies   是什么深海或高天
Burnt the fire of thine eyes?   燃烧着你双眼的火焰？
On what wings dare he aspires   靠什么翅膀他敢在空中翱翔？
What the hand dare seize the fire?   什么样的手敢去抓这火焰？

And what shoulder, and what art,   什么肩膀，什么手艺
Could twist the sinews of thy heart? 能把你心脏之肌扭动？
And when thy heart began to beat, 当你心脏开始跳动，
What dread hand? And what dread feet? 什么可怕的手？什么可怕的脚？

What the hammer? what the chain?   什么铁锤？什么铁链？
In what furnace was thy brain?   什么熔炉炼成你的大脑？
What the anvil? What dread grasp?   什么铁砧？什么恐怖的紧握？
Dare its deadly terrors clasp?   胆敢抓住这致命的恐怖？

When the stars threw down their spears, 当群星投下长矛，
And water'd heaven with their tears, 用泪水浇灌长空，
Did he smile his work to see?   他可见到自己的杰作而微笑？
Did he who made the Lamb make thee? 是否造出羔羊的他也造出了你？

Tyger! Tyger! Burning bright   老虎，老虎，双眼火亮，
In the forests of the night,   在夜的丛林里，
What immortal hand or eye   是什么神奇的手或眼
Dare frame thy fearful symmetry?   打造了你这恐怖的匀称？

              （诸莉　译）

📖 诗作四

Holy Thursday
神圣的星期四

Is this a holy thing to see	圣洁事一桩？
In a rich and fruitful land,	富庶多产地，
Babes reduc'd to misery,	婴儿状可悲，
Fed with cold and usurous hand?	高利贷维系？
Is that trembling cry a song?	颤哭成歌唱？
Can it be a song of joy?	欢乐之歌兮？
And so many children poor?	众童陷贫困？
It is a land of poverty!	贫穷国度里！
And their sun does never shine,	太阳从不升，
And their fields are bleak and bare,	田地遭废弃，
And their ways are fill'd with thorns:	道路荆棘布：
It is eternal winter there.	永恒寒冬季。
For where'er the sun does shine,	愿阳光普照，
And where'er the rain does fall,	愿雨水润地；
Babe can never hunger there,	婴儿不忍饥，
Nor poverty the mind appal.	贫穷迹难觅。

（诸莉　译）

诗作五

A Poison Tree
有毒的树

I was angry with my friend:	我怒怨我友:
I told my wrath, my wrath did end.	直言怒即休。
I was angry with foe:	我怒怨我敌:
I told it not, my wrath did grow.	隐忍怒反积。
And I watered it in fears,	心惧以水浇,
Night and morning, with my tears;	朝夕以泪洗;
And I sunned it with smiles,	日照沐以笑,
And with soft deceitful wiles.	温柔欺骗计。
And it grew both day and night,	从此日夜长,
Till it bore an apple bright;	结出苹果光;
And my foe behold it shine,	我敌睹其亮,
And he knew that it was mine.	知是我种养。
And into my garden stole	入我花园窃,
When the night had veiled the pole;	夜深人已歇;
In the morning glad I see	天明我欣狂
My foe outstretched beneath the tree.	见敌树下躺。

（诺莉 译）

Unit 13　*William Wordsworth*

威廉·华兹华斯

　　威廉·华兹华斯(1770—1850)，英国浪漫主义诗歌重要代表，"湖畔派"领袖；生于英格兰西部湖区的一个律师家庭，曾在剑桥大学学习古典文学，毕业后数次游历欧洲大陆；1795年他与其妹及诗人柯勒律治和骚塞逃离城市，隐居湖区，"湖畔派"由此得名；1798年与柯勒律治共同发表《抒情歌谣集》，倡导情感论，一反简洁典雅的诗风，动摇了古典主义诗学基础，开创了抒发个人强烈情感的浪漫主义诗风；此后十余年为华兹华斯诗歌创作的全盛期，其在此期间创作了大量的抒情诗歌作品；1843年被封为"桂冠诗人"；自此其诗歌创作开始走下坡路，诗才逐渐枯竭，创作内容流于说教；其于1850年去世。

诗作一

Composed upon Westminster Bridge
威斯敏斯特桥上有感

Earth has not anything to show more fair[①]:	大地无法展现更多美,
Dull would he be of soul who could pass by	无感而过必心灵麻痹;
A sight so touching[②] in its majesty[③]:	风景如此壮观而动人。
This City now doth, like a garment[④], wear	这城市就如披上外衣:
The beauty of the morning: silent, bare,	清晨之美: 洁净整齐;
Ships, towers, domes[⑤], theatres and temples lie	船、塔、剧院和寺庙
Open unto the fields, and to the sky,	全都面向田野和天际,
All bright and glittering[⑥] in the smokeless air.	在朝气中明亮而闪烁。
Never did sun more beautifully steep[⑦]	太阳从未如此美丽地
In his first splendour[⑧] valley, rock, or hill;	将幽谷山岗罩上晨曦;
Ne'er saw I, never felt, a calm so deep!	我从未感受如此静谧!
The river glideth[⑨] at his own sweet will:	河水流淌, 悠缓慢徐;
Dear God! The very houses seem asleep;	亲爱的神! 万家正困,
And all that mighty heart is lying still!	硕大的心脏仍在休息。

（诸光　译）

语言注释

① fair: *adj.* 公平的; 美丽的, 白皙的。此处作名词, 同 beauty, fairness。

② touching: *adj.* 动人的, 令人同情的。

③ majesty: *n.* 威严; 雄伟; 最高权威, 王权; 权威。

④ garment: *n.* 衣服, 服装; 外表, 外观。

⑤ domes: *n.* 圆屋顶; 穹顶。

⑥ glittering: *adj.* 闪闪发光的; 辉煌的, 显赫的; 盛大的, 华丽的。

⑦ steep：*v.* 泡；浸；使……充满；此处作及物动词，有"普照"的意思。

⑧ splendour：*n.* 显赫；光彩壮丽。

⑨ glideth：*v.* 滑翔；滑行。th＝s，第三人称单数。此处指河水的流动。

❓ 思考题

1. What personality would the word "dull" refer to according to the poem?

2. Why are "towers", "domes", "theatres" and "temples" mentioned?

3. What elements of Nature are mentioned in the poem?

4. What attitude does the poet hold towards London?

5. Why doesn't the poet describe any human activity in the poem?

6. What does the mighty heart in the last line refer to?

✒ 节奏、韵律图示

Composed upon Westminster Bridge

行数 (Line)	五音步抑扬格 (Iambic Pentameter)	韵式 (Rhyme Scheme)
1.	Earth has | not a | nything | to show | more fair： ▲ △ △▲ △ ▲ △ ▲ △ ▲	a-/eə(r)/
2.	Dull would | he be | of soul | who could | pass by ▲ △ △ ▲ △ ▲ △ ▲ △ ▲	b-/aɪ/
3.	A sight | so tou | ching in | its ma | jesty： △▲ △ ▲ △ ▲ △ ▲ △▲	b-/aɪ/
4.	This Ci | ty now | doth, like | a gar | ment, wear △ ▲ △ ▲ △ ▲ △▲ △ ▲	a-/eə(r)/
5.	The beau | ty of | the morn | ing： si | lent, bare, △ ▲ △ ▲ △ ▲ △ ▲ △ ▲	a-/eə(r)/

6. Ships, tow | ers, domes, | theatres | and tem | ples lie   b-/aɪ/

    ▲ ▲ △ ▲   ▲ △ △ ▲   △ ▲

7. Open | unto | the fields, | and to | the sky,   b-/aɪ/

    ▲ △ ▲ △ △ ▲   △ ▲ △ ▲

8. All bright | and glit | tering in | the smoke | less air.   a-/eə(r)/

    △ ▲ △ ▲ △ △ ▲   △ ▲   △ ▲

9. Never | did sun | more beau | tiful | ly steep   c-/iːp/

    ▲ ▲ △ ▲ △ ▲   ▲ △ ▲ △ ▲

10. In his | first splen | dour val | ley, rock, | or hill;   d-/ɪl/

    △ ▲ ▲ ▲ △ ▲ △ ▲   △ ▲

11. Ne'er saw | I, ne | ver felt, | a calm | so deep!   c-/iːp/

    ▲ ▲ △ ▲ △ ▲   △ ▲   △ ▲

12. The ri | ver gli | deth at | his own | sweet will: d-/ɪl/

    △ ▲ △ ▲ △ ▲   △ ▲   ▲ ▲

13. Dear God! | The ve | ry hou | ses seem | asleep;   c-/iːp/

    △ ▲ △ ▲ △ ▲ △ ▲   △ ▲

14. And all | that migh | ty heart | is ly | ing still!   d-/ɪl/

    △ ▲ △ ▲ △ ▲ △ ▲   △ ▲

注：本诗以比特拉克五音步抑扬格（iambic pentameter：△ ▲）为基调，同时包含了一些其他格律形式：

① 抑抑扬格（anapest：△ △ ▲）：8-3

② 扬抑格（trochee：▲ △）：1-1、2-1、6-3、7-1、7-2、9-1

③ 扬扬格（spondee：▲ ▲）：6-1、10-2、11-1、12-5

修辞解析

本诗涉及六个修辞手法：诗的破格、明喻、并列、排比、拟人、隐喻。

1. 诗的破格（Poetic License）

本诗有两处诗的破格。

（1）本诗第 3 行 majesty 词尾发音本来为/ti/，但因为本诗是意大利比特拉克十四行诗，头四行押 abba 韵，也就是 majesty 必须与上一行的 by 押韵，所以 majesty 最后一个音节发音变/taɪ/。这就是诗的破格。

2）另外，因本诗第 12 行仅有 9 个音节，必须采用诗的破格手法，让第三个音步中的 glideth 的后半部分 deth 中的 e 从不发音到发 /e/ 音，从而使得 glideth 具有两个音节，以满足五音步抑扬格的格律要求。

2. 明喻（Simile）

本诗第 4 行 like a garment 就是明喻。明喻给人明确无误的信息，清楚明白，容易理解。

3. 并列（Juxtaposition）

并列由两个或两个以上的词组或分句并列组合而成，叙述相关的事情，或说明相关的情况，它们之间没有主次之分。本诗第 5 行的 silent，bare；第 7 行的 unto the fields，and to the sky；第 8 行的 All bright and glittering；第 11 行的 Ne'er saw I，never felt 都属于并列结构，彼此没有主次之分，也互不相关，都是描绘事物的性状，有加强语气的作用。

4. 排比（Parallelism）

本诗第 6 行中的 ships，towers，domes，theatres and temples 和第 10 行中的 valley，rock，or hill 就是排比修辞格，即利用三个或三个以上意义相关或相近、结构相同或相似的词组或句子的排比组合，以达到一种加强语气的效果。排比可加强文章的节奏感，使文章更具条理性，也更有利于表达强烈的感情。

5. 拟人（Personification）

本诗第 10 行和第 12 行的 in his first splendour 和 at his own sweet will 中的两个 his 就是拟人修辞格。这里分别把太阳和河流拟人化了。该诗以男性第三人称单数将太阳和河流人格化，凸显了男性的威力、博大及壮丽。

6. 暗喻/隐喻（Metaphor）

本诗最后一行中的 mighty heart 暗喻伦敦这座首都及大都市是这个国家的强大的心脏。

📑 作品鉴赏

这首十四行诗对伦敦充满了由衷的赞誉。湖畔派诗人以酷爱自然山水、逃避城市喧嚣而著称，所以这首诗也是华兹华斯为数不多的城市书写之一。据华氏自己说，这首诗是他去法国途中，坐马车经过威斯敏斯特大桥，从桥上远眺泰晤士河两岸的凌晨景象而写就。那时的伦敦有一种恬静、壮丽和庄严的美。昨日的喧嚣都已散去，今日尚未开始。

　　这首诗是纯粹地写景抒情；没有像布莱克那样去批判和揭露社会问题。虽然描绘了城市景象如桥梁、塔楼、教堂、穹顶等，但因为没有涉及人类社会关系，所以与描绘纯粹自然山水并无二致，实际上是对人类社会生活的一种逃避。湖畔派逃避的并不是单纯物理意义上的城市，而是充斥于城市间的那种资本主义的尔虞我诈、虚伪算计的功利主义人际关系。这也解答了为什么一向纵情于山水的华兹华斯也会偶尔咏叹一下大都市的疑惑。他清晨看到的其实是剥离了一切社会关系的物理意义上的伦敦。这也是高尔基将湖畔派界定为消极浪漫主义诗歌的原因——他对英国资本主义社会缺乏批判和揭露，对当时的社会采取一种消极逃避的态度，对普罗大众的疾苦缺乏同情和理解。所以他描写的虽然是伦敦城，但其实他歌咏的只是物理意义上的伦敦，和自然山水书写并无区别，符合湖畔派的一贯主张。

📖 诗作二

My Heart Leaps up
我心必颤动

My heart leaps up when I behold	我心必颤动，
A rainbow in the sky：	每当见彩虹：
So was it when my life began，	人之初如此，
So is it now I am a man，	成年后亦同，
So be it when I shall grow old	惟老后依旧，
Or let me die！	否则毋宁死！
The child is father of the Man；	儿为成人父；
And I could wish my days to be	但愿我余生
Bound each to each by natural piety.	充满天地诚。

（诸莉　译）

📖 诗作三

The Solitary Reaper
孤独高原女

You solitary Highland Lass!	孤独高原女!
Reaping and singing by herself;	劳作在麦地;
Stop here, or gently pass!	经过勿扰伊!
Alone she cuts and binds the grain,	独自忙收割,
And sings a melancholy strain;	哀怨曲调唱;
O listen! For the Vale profound	歌声满山谷,
is overflowing with the sound.	忧愁四处溢。
No nightingale did ever chaunt	夜莺岂能敌,
More welcome notes to weary bands	歌声慰商旅;
Of travelers in some shady haunt,	暂栖树荫下,
Among Arabian sands;	阿拉伯沙地!
A voice so thrilling ne'er was heard	嗓音动人心—
In springtime from the Cuckoo bird,	杜鹃亦不及,
Breaking the silence of the seas	打破海上寂,
Among the farthest Hebrides.	遥远赫布里!
Will no one tell me what she sings? —	天知她唱啥?
Perhaps the plaintive numbers flow	曲调或凄惨,
For old, unhappy, far-off things,	讲述遥远事,
And battles long ago;	征战在往昔?
Or is it some more humble lay,	曲调或一般,

Familiar matter of today?　　　　　　　今日话平凡？

Some natural sorrow, loss, or pain,　　　痛苦或忧伤，

That has been, and may be again?　　　　新旧皆一样？

Whate'er the theme, the Maiden sang　　无论何主题，

As if her song could have no ending;　　歌唱无绝期；

I saw her singing at her work,　　　　　边唱边劳作，

And o'er the sickle bending —　　　　　弯腰挥镰兮；

I listened, motionless and still;　　　　不动静静听；

And, as I mounted up the hill,　　　　　直到来山顶，

The music in my heart I bore,　　　　　歌声久已寂，

Long after it was heard no more.　　　　余音在心底。

（诸莉　译）

📖 诗作四

I Wander'd Lonely as a Cloud
逍遥如浮云

I wandered lonely as a cloud	逍遥如浮云，
That floats on high o'er vales and hills,	游荡山谷间，
When all at once I saw a crowd,	突见水仙花，
A host, of golden daffodils;	金色一大片；
Beside the lake, beneath the trees,	湖边或树下，
Fluttering and dancing in the breeze.	颤舞风中颠。
Continuous as the stars that shine	连绵不断线
And twinkle on the milky way,	银河星眨眼，
They stretch'd in never-ending line	伸展无止境，
Along the margin of a bay:	绕沿湖湾边：
Ten thousand saw I at a glance,	一瞥有千万，
Tossing their heads in sprightly dance.	摇摆舞翩跹。
The waves beside them danced, but they	旁有波浪跳，
Out-did the sparkling waves in glee:	不及亮水仙。
A poet could not but be gay,	诗人开怀乐，
In such a jocund company!	欢乐侣伴兼！
I gazed—and gazed—but little thought	此景久凝视—
What wealth the show to me had brought:	宝物落九天！
For oft, when on my couch I lie	我常卧沙发，
In vacant or in pensive mood,	茫然或沉湎，
They flash upon that inward eye	心有水仙亮
Which is the bliss of solitude;	独处极乐添；
And then my heart with pleasure fills.	我心满欢悦，
And dances with the daffodils.	起舞伴水仙。

（诸莉　译）

📖 诗作五

She Dwelt Among the Untrodden Ways
她居幽僻地

She dwelt among the untrodden ways　　　　她居幽僻地，

Beside the springs of Dove,　　　　　　　多佛小溪边；

A Maid whom there were none to praise　　无人夸其好，

And very few to love.　　　　　　　　　更少放心间。

A violet by a mossy stone　　　　　　　苔石紫罗兰，

Half hidden from the eye!　　　　　　　半掩人难见！

Fair as a star, when only one　　　　　　貌美如孤星，

is shining in the sky.　　　　　　　　　夜空独闪现。

She lived unknown, and few could know　　生时无人知，

When Lucy ceased to be;　　　　　　　　死亦无人晓；

But she is in her grave, and, oh,　　　　今葬坟茔中，

The difference to me!　　　　　　　　　余我空寂寥！

（诸莉　译）

Unit 14　Samuel Taylor Coleridge

塞缪尔·泰勒·柯勒律治

塞缪尔·泰勒·柯勒律治(1772—1834)，英国浪漫主义诗歌主要代表人物之一；"湖畔派"主要成员；生于英格兰乡村牧师家庭，曾学习古典文学，年轻时深受启蒙主义思想影响，同情法国革命；1789年与华兹华斯共同出版《抒情歌谣集》，对英国浪漫主义诗歌产生深远影响；柯勒律治想象力丰富，认为文学没有想象力就没有了灵魂。"在艺术风格上，华兹华斯的诗歌以清新、自然见长，柯勒律治的诗歌则以想象奇特、情节怪诞、超自然色彩浓厚著称。"①他的代表作有《古舟子咏》和《忽必烈汗》等。此外，他还从事文艺批评，《文学传记》是他的主要文艺理论著作，同时代及后代的诗人和批评家们也多受其影响。

---

① 黄宗英. 英文名篇鉴赏金库(诗歌卷)［M］. 天津：天津人民出版社，2001：99.

📖 诗作一

The Rime of the Ancient Mariner（Selections of Part Ⅱ）
古舟子咏（第 2 章选段）

The fair breeze blew, the white foam[①] flew,	微风轻拂，白沫四溅，
The furrow[②] followed free;	船儿飞快地勇往直前；
We were the first that ever burst[③]	我们闯入这寂静之海，
Into that silent sea.	首批不速之客已到来。
Down dropt the breeze, the sails dropt down,	风也停了，帆也收了，
'Twas sad as sad could be;	当时的情形实在悲惨；
And we did speak only to break	我们偶尔开口说说话，
The silence of the sea!	就为消除航行的孤单。
All in a hot and copper sky,	炎热、黄铜色的天空
The bloody Sun, at noon,	有正午血淋淋的太阳，
Right up above the mast did stand,	此时正立在桅杆顶上，
No bigger than the Moon.	大小不会超过一月亮。

（诸莉　译）

✍ 语言注释

① foam：*n.* 泡沫；水沫；灭火泡沫。

② furrow：*n.* 皱纹；犁沟；车辙。

③ burst：*v.* 爆裂；突然爆发(某种感情)；爆发出；冲开。

？ 思考题

1. What is the tone in the line "We were the first that ever burst/into that silent sea"?

2. What figures of speech does the poet apply in the first two lines of the first stanza?

3. Why does the poet feel sad very quickly in the next stanza?

4. How do you feel about the image of "the silent sea"?

5. What roles does "the silent sea" each play in the first two stanzas? Are there any differences between them?

6. Have you felt the mood in each stanza? Can you interpret all the moods?

📝 节奏、韵律图示

The Rime of the Ancient Mariner（Selections of Part Ⅱ）

行数 （Line）	四、三音步交替抑扬格 （Alternated Iambic Tetrameter & Trimester）	韵式 （Rhyme Scheme）
103.	The fair ｜ breeze blew, ｜ the white ｜ foam flew, △ ▲ △ ▲ △ ▲ △ ▲	a-/uː/
104.	The fur ｜ row fol ｜ lowed free; △ ▲ △ ▲ △ ▲	b-/iː/
105.	We were ｜ the first ｜ that e ｜ ver burst △ ▲ △▲ △ ▲ △ ▲	c-/ɜːst/
106.	Into ｜ that si ｜ lent sea. ▲△ △▲ △ ▲	b-/iː/
107.	Down dropt ｜ the breeze, ｜ the sails ｜ dropt down, ▲ ▲ △ ▲ △ ▲ △ ▲	d-/aʊn/
108.	'Twas sad ｜ as sad ｜ could be; △ ▲ △ ▲ △ ▲	b-/iː/

109. And we │ did speak │ only │ to break   e-/eɪk/
    △ ▲ △ ▲ △▲ △ ▲

110. The si │ lence of │ the sea!   b-/iː/
    △▲ △ ▲ △ ▲

111. All in │ a hot │ and cop │ per sky,   f-/aɪ/
    △ ▲ △ ▲ △ ▲ △ ▲

112. The bloo │ dy Sun, │ at noon,   g-/uːn/
    △ ▲ △ ▲ △ ▲

113. Right up │ above │ the mast │ did stand,   h-/ænd/
    △ ▲ △ ▲ △ ▲ △ ▲

114. No big │ ger than │ the Moon.   g-/uːn/
    △▲ △ ▲ △ ▲

🔲 修辞解析

本诗涉及五个诗歌常用的修辞手法：头韵、重复、谐元音、暗喻和拟人。

1. 头韵(Alliteration)

本诗共有五组头韵词：① breeze, blew(第 103 行：/b/)；② foam, flew(第 103 行：/f/)；③ furrow, followed, free(第 104 行：/f/)；④ silent, sea；(第 106 行：/s/)；⑤ silence, sea；(第 110 行：/s/)。这么密集地使用头韵修辞格，烘托了疾风劲吹、浪花飞溅情形下乘风破浪的速度和快感，也强化了探索新天地、首入无人之境的豪迈语气。

2. 重复(Repetition)

本诗有两处词语的重复：the silence of the sea(第 110 行)重复了之前出现过的 that silent sea(第 106 行)。此外还有 'Twas sad as sad could be(第 108 行)中 sad 的重复。由此可见，海上的寂静是多么地令人绝望，由此产生的孤独和寂寞又是多么地深切和浓烈。

3. 谐元音(Assonance)

本诗短短三节却包含了较多的谐元音(也包含双元韵和谐辅音)：

① blew, flew：/uː/(第 103 行)

② furrow，follow：/ʌ/，/əʊ/（第 104 行）

③ breeze，free，be，sea，speak，sea：/iː/（第 103—110 行）

④ first，burst：/əːst/（第 105 行）

⑤ hot，copper：/ɔ/（第 111 行）

⑥ bloody，up，above：/ʌ/（第 112—113 行）

⑦ silent，silence，right，sky：/aɪ/（第 106—113 行）

⑧ mast，stand，than：/æ/（第 113—114 行）

大量的元音相谐无疑极大地增强了诗歌的韵律感。

4. 暗喻/隐喻(Metaphor)

在所选三节诗歌中，第三节集中运用了三个与颜色有关的暗喻修辞格：in a hot and copper sky，the bloody Sun 和 no bigger than the Moon。第一个暗示天空像铜一样(铜镜一般的天空，橙黄清澈透明)；第二个暗示太阳像血一样(毛主席有诗："苍山如海，残阳如血。"——《忆秦娥·娄山关》)；第三个暗示太阳如月亮一样大小(译者之所以翻译为"大小不会超过一月亮"，是因为其本身就是一个比喻，虽然原文并无"like"存在)。暗喻的特点是它比较间接和含蓄，有时候本体和喻体之间关联性不是很明显，需要读者细细品味。

5. 拟人(Personification)

在本诗第 113 行里有 "Right up above the mast did stand"，其中 stand 指的就是太阳像一位威严的将军高高在上，仿佛就站在桅杆的顶上一样，俯瞰着他们的一举一动。而灼热的阳光直射着船上的一切，直烤得水手们头皮发麻，酷热难当，他们还不敢吭声。

作品鉴赏

《古舟子咏》是一首六百多行的叙事长诗，以想象力丰富而著称，特别是它那离奇曲折的故事情节，怪诞恐怖的灾难场面，皆以诗歌的形式刻画得生动细腻。该诗的一大特点是它的夹叙夹抒情，即叙事之中有抒情，抒情之中不忘叙事。其中有些章节或诗句的精彩程度，绝不亚于同类题材的抒情诗，堪称海洋抒情诗的绝唱。

本部分选自原诗第 2 章,共 3 小节。其中通过歌谣体 abcb 的韵式及四、三音步抑扬格的变奏,还有丰富的头韵、腹韵、重复、暗喻、拟人等修辞手法,烘托出海洋诗歌丰富的音乐变奏性和新天地豪迈的开拓者形象。本书选段第一节堪称叙事诗中的精彩抒情华章:

The fair breeze blew, the white foam flew,

The furrow followed free;

We were the first that ever burst

Into that silent sea.

一切是那么地轻松愉快而且还豪气冲天。海上和风劲吹,白浪翻飞,船儿奋力前行:我们是最先进入这个寂静海域的第一批人!后两节则反映了言说者明显的情绪变化,前面刚刚表达了闯入无人之境而滋生的无比骄傲的自豪之情,转瞬间就陷入一种令人绝望的孤独寂寞之中,连说话都是为了打破可怕的沉默……然后还得忍受海上烈日的炙烤:天是炎热而呈古铜色的,太阳是血腥色的,仿佛就悬在桅杆顶上照射着船上生活、工作的人们……一副生不如死的炼狱情景!

丰富的想象力赋予了该诗鲜明的浪漫主义色彩。从人物到背景到情节,都是离奇、怪诞和超自然的。首先,诗中的主人公老水手并没有具体的名字、年龄和身份,只有一个职业,是故事的经历者。这个人物本身就充满了离奇、神秘和超自然的色彩,此乃一。其次,故事背景以他们的船只出海航行为主要线索,但此次航行并不在英国领海或附近海域展开,而是穿越到了遥远的魔域,故带有神秘、陌生和新奇的异域风光和色彩,此乃二。另外,故事情节十分离奇和曲折。他们的航船离港出海后不久就遭遇灭顶之灾,是一只信天翁的到来才使航船化险为夷。可老水手偏偏用弓箭射杀了信天翁,于是航船又陷入绝境:水手们先后死去。最后老水手良心发现,爱怜生命,才换来了他们重归故土。此乃三。最后,无所不在的超自然力量:航船出发不久就天降大难,多亏信天翁飞临相救,可老水手却错杀信天翁使得航船马上又陷入绝境,最后老水手爱怜生命感动了上苍,最终赎回了水手们的生命。这离奇的情节背后似乎有一只无形的手在操纵着人间的一切恩怨情仇,但唯有克服私欲、诚心热爱生命才能感动上苍,保佑平安。此乃四。总而言之,本诗中神秘的人物、新奇的异域、离奇的情节、神奇的超自然力量共同构成了该诗鲜明的浪漫主义色彩。

Unit 15　*George Gordon Byron*

乔治·戈登·拜伦

　　乔治·戈登·拜伦（1788—1824），英国 19 世纪伟大浪漫主义诗人；出生于没落贵族家庭，曾求学于哈罗公学和剑桥大学三一学院，后从政，曾任上议院议员；由于其个人生活放浪形骸，还有离婚和不伦之恋等丑闻不断，因而为英国社会所不容，从此远走他乡，漫游欧陆；拥有强烈的民主意识和正义感，曾为破坏机器的劳工辩护，也曾加入意大利烧炭党抗击奥地利占领者的地下活动，最后为了民族独立赴希腊驰骋疆场而不幸染疾身故；主要成就为长篇游记诗、东方叙事诗以及一些诗剧和抒情诗；其在长诗中塑造的"拜伦式英雄"也是其自身生活的写照，这种英雄形象对后世和其他国家影响都很大。

📖 **诗作一**

So We'll Go No More A-Roving
我将不再游——

So we'll go no more a-roving[①]	我将不再游——
So late into the night,	夜深人该休,
Though the heart be still as loving,	内心依有爱,
And the moon be still as bright.[②]	月明皎如旧。
For the sword outwears[③] its sheath[④],	剑欲磨破鞘,
And the soul wears out the breast,	魂欲胸中脱;
And the heart must pause to breathe,	心累必缓跳,
And love itself have rest.	爱鸟须回窝。
Though the night was made for loving,	夜为爱而造,
And the day returns too soon,	昼却回太急,
Yet we'll go no more a-roving	我将不再游,
By the light of the moon.	月光下依依。

（诸莉　译）

✍ **语言注释**

① rove：*v.* 漫游；流浪；漂泊。roving，现在分词或动名词；前缀 a-，表示动作正在进行之中；a-roving 有凑音节的作用。该行原本仅 7 个音节，现在用了 a-就凑满了 8 个音节 4 个音步。本诗为四、三音步交替成节。

② Though the heart be still as loving, ／And the moon be still as bright：让步状语从句；早期英语中这种让步状语从句为虚拟语气，动词须用原形，此处 be 为系动词原形。

③ outwear/wear out：穿破，穿坏；比……经久耐用；用旧；使筋疲力尽。

④ sheath：*n.* 鞘；护套；叶鞘。

思考题

1. What is the connection between night and the moon?

2. Why will we go no more a-roving according to the poet?

3. Will it be easy for the poet to go no more a-roving? Why?

4. What is the purpose that night was made for according to the poet?

5. What do you think are the uses of the night for mankind today?

6. What are the dualities of night to mankind?

节奏、韵律图示

So We'll Go No More A-Roving

行数 (Line)	三音步抑扬格 (Iambic Trimeter)	韵式 (Rhyme Scheme)
		a
1.	So we'll | go no more | a-roving △ ▲　△ ▲ ▲　△ ▲ △	-/oʊvɪŋ/
2.	So late | into | the night, △ ▲　▲ △　△ ▲	b-/aɪt/
3.	Though the heart | be still | as loving, △ △ ▲　△ ▲　△ ▲ △	a-/ʌvɪŋ/
4.	And the moon | be still | as bright. △ △ ▲　△ ▲　△ ▲	b-/aɪt/
5.	For the sword | outwears | its sheath, △ △ ▲　▲ △　△ ▲	c-/iːð/

165

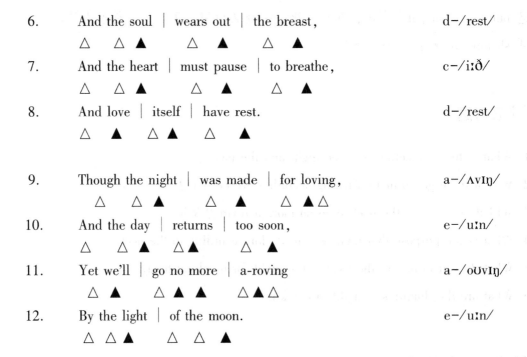

6. And the soul | wears out | the breast,   d-/rest/
7. And the heart | must pause | to breathe,   c-/iːð/
8. And love | itself | have rest.   d-/rest/
9. Though the night | was made | for loving,   a-/ʌvɪŋ/
10. And the day | returns | too soon,   e-/uːn/
11. Yet we'll | go no more | a-roving   a-/oʊvɪŋ/
12. By the light | of the moon.   e-/uːn/

注：本诗基本上是抑扬格三音步(iambic trimeter)，但也有抑抑扬格 9 个、抑扬抑格 4 个、扬抑格 2 个、抑扬扬格 2 个等其他格律模式。音步方面的唯一例外是最后一行(第 12 行)，为两音步(dimeter)。所以本诗节奏并不太规律，但尾韵却相当严谨讲究。

修辞解析

本诗涉及四种诗歌常用修辞手法：重复、谐元音、并列和暗喻；且前两种类型比较多样化。

1. 重复(Repetition)

(1)单词或词组的重复：night(2 次：2-3、9-1)、moon(2 次：4-1、12-2)、love/loving(3 次：3-3、8-1、9-3)、outwears/wears out(2 次：第 5、6 行)。

(2)语法结构的重复：Though the heart be still as loving, /And the moon be still as bright。（第 3、4 行）这两句为让步状语从句。早期英语中这种让步状语从句为虚拟语气，动词须用原形，此处 be 为系动词原形。

(3)句子的重复：So we'll go no more a-roving(第 1 行)/Yet we'll go no more a-roving(第 11 行)，这两行基本完全相同，仅一词之差(so 和 yet)。

重复修辞格的使用往往具有"一唱三叹"和"回旋往复"的音乐美，同时起到强调和加强意蕴的作用。

2. 谐元音（Assonance）

本诗中共有三个谐元音：

① /oʊ/：So, go, no, roving（第 1 行）；go, no, roving（第 11 行）。

② /uː/：too, soon（第 10 行）。

③ /aɪ/：by, light（第 12 行）。

元音相谐毫无疑问极大地增强了诗歌的韵律感。

3. 并列（Juxtaposition）

Though the heart be still as loving, /And the moon be still as bright（第 3、4 行）与 For the sword outwears its sheath, /And the soul wears out the breast（第 5、6 行），以及 And the heart must pause to breathe, /And love itself have rest（第 7、8 行）不仅仅是重复修辞格，也是并列修辞格。并列修辞格具有加强语气、增强论说力度的作用。

4. 暗喻（Metaphor）

For the sword outwears its sheath, /And the soul wears out the breast，此两行不仅是重复和并列，而且还是暗喻。此处的"剑欲磨破鞘，魂欲胸中脱"都是在暗喻爱情过于炽烈会损伤身体，从而为加强论点作论证。

作品鉴赏

本诗属抒情小品，因为拜伦的作品都很长且以叙事为主，所以这种短小精悍的抒情诗就属于小品了。这种小品诗言简意赅、优美隽永，具有满满的正能量，所以流传至今还能获时代的认同。

众所周知，拜伦是位风流多情的人，所以该诗也多半带有个人自传性质，表达了个人的真实感受。诗意的指向既有忠告他人，更在提醒自己：不要纵欲，不要滥情，不要毫无节制。从诗歌抒情手法来看，本诗是相当节制的和理性的，可以说一反浪漫主义作品多愁善感的常态。本诗异常冷静和理性，提出不要过度夜游和过度滥情，而且诗人论证的方式有着严密的逻辑性和丰富的修辞性，想象力丰富，情感细腻且论证有力，是典型的西方论辩传统的体现。

  该诗格律不甚整齐但样式繁多；尾韵规则且很有个性；修辞不甚华丽但简单
实用；遣词造句接近日常口语，可谓老少皆宜；想象力丰富且论证有力；主题人
人皆懂，揭示普遍常理。

📖 诗作二

She Walks in Beauty
她走在美的光彩中

She walks in beauty like the night	她从美中来，
Of cloudless climes and starry skies;	无云满天星；
And all that's best of dark and bright	明暗或正好，
Meet in her aspect and her eyes;	妆魅秋波现；
Thus mellowed to that tender light	柔美如晨曦，
Which heaven to gaudy day denies.	却比晨曦浅。
One shade the more, one ray the less,	增减俱有损，
Had half impaired the nameless grace	难言之美韵，
Which waves in every raven tress,	波动在乌发，
Or softly lightens o'er her face;	柔亮散于脸；
Where thoughts serenely sweet express	恬静现忧思，
How pure, how dear their dwelling-place.	内心纯又甜。
And on that cheek, and o'er that brow,	眉眼及脸颊，
So soft, so calm, yet eloquent,	柔和又多情，
The smiles that win, the tints that glow,	微笑发肤亮，
But tell of days in goodness spent,	养尊处优静：
A mind at peace with all below,	平和待世界，
A heart whose love is innocent!	纯真见爱心！

（诸莉　译）

📖 诗作三

When We Two Parted
当初我们分别

When we two parted	当我俩分别，
In silence and tears,	只有无语和眼泪，
Half broken-hearted	心也几乎破碎，
To sever for years,	要分别多年，
Pale grew thy cheek and cold,	你的脸又白又冷，
Colder thy kiss;	你的吻更冷，
Truly that hour foretold	那时刻也预示着
Sorrow to this.	今日的哀伤。
The dew of the morning	凌晨的露水
Sunk, chill on my brow—	滴到我的眉头——
It felt like the warning	感觉像是警告
Of what I feel now.	今日我一切的感受。
Thy vows are all broken.	你彻底违背了誓言，
And light is thy fame;	你的名誉也变轻浮；
I hear thy name spoken,	每当别人提起你，
And share in its shame.	我都承受了你的耻辱。
They name thee before me,	每当别人当面提起你，
A knell to mine ear;	犹如丧钟鸣响耳边；
A shudder comes o'er me—	我不禁浑身战栗——
Why wert thou so dear?	你为何还要那么亲密？
They know not I knew thee,	他们不知我对你的了解，
Who knew thee too well—	还有谁对你如此熟悉——

Long, long shall I rue thee,	我会长久为你哀伤,
Too deeply to tell.	如此深沉，难以言表。
In secret we met—	我们当年秘密幽会——
In silence I grieve	此刻却静静悲泣
That thy heart could forget,	你的心却已忘记,
Thy spirit deceive,	你的灵魂竟也欺骗！
If I should meet thee	如果多年之后,
After long years,	你我再次相聚,
How should I greet thee?	我该如何向你问好？
With silence and tears.	沉默与眼泪。

（诸莉　译）

Unit 16　Robert Louis Stevenson

罗伯特·路易斯·斯蒂文森

　　罗伯特·路易斯·斯蒂文森（1850—1894），英国19世纪著名小说家、诗人，生于苏格兰爱丁堡；代表作有《金银岛》《化身博士》和诗集《儿童诗苑》《矮树丛》等；父亲和祖父都是灯塔设计师与工程师，所以养成了其热爱冒险、喜爱海洋的性格；因从小身体不好，可能从母亲那里传染了肺结核，所以形成了其到国外温暖的南方去居住和旅行的爱好；由于具有丰富的海外经历，其创作了很多探险传奇小说，并受到少年儿童在内的大众的欢迎；其诗歌创作也获得了很高的成就，虽然不能同其小说相比，但因讲究格律和音韵美，以及对儿童生活描写深刻，所以其创作的儿童诗在英国家喻户晓，深受人们的喜爱。

📖 诗作一

Bed in Summer
夏日难眠

In winter I get up at night	冬日凌晨起,
And dress by yellow candle-light.	秉烛来穿衣。
In summer, quite the other way,	夏日昼未尽,
I have to go to bed by day.	天明须就寝。
I have to go to bed and see	寝中可见鸟,
The birds still hopping① on the tree,	尚在树上跳;
Or hear the grown-up people's feet	街上踏脚声,
Still going past me in the street.	床上依可闻。
And does it not seem hard to you,	于君或不难,
When all the sky is clear and blue.	天空晴又蓝。
And I should like so much to play,	玩兴犹未尽,
To have to go to bed by day?	日寝何甘心?

（诺莉　译）

✏️ 语言注释

① hopping：hop 的现在分词。hop：单脚跳行；齐足(或双足)跳行。

❓ 思考题

1. Why does the speaker have to get up at night in winter?

2. Why does the speaker have to go to bed by day in summer?

3. Why are the birds still hopping on the tree when he goes to bed?

4. Why is all the sky clear and blue in summer when he goes to bed?

5. Is it hard for all children in the world to get up in winter and go to bed in summer ?

6. Is this phenomenon more popular in UK? Why?

✍ 节奏、韵律图示

Bed in Summer

行数 （Line）	四音步抑扬格 （Iambic Tetrameter）	韵式 （Rhyme Scheme）
1.	In win │ ter I │ get up │ at night △ ▲　△ ▲　△△ ▲　△ ▲	a−/aɪt/
2.	And dress │ by yel │ low can │ dle-light. △　▲　△ ▲　△ ▲　△ ▲	a−/aɪt/
3.	In sum │ mer, quite │ the o │ ther way, △　▲　△　▲　△△ ▲　△ ▲	b−/eɪ/
4.	I have │ to go │ to bed │ by day. △ ▲　△△ ▲　△ ▲　△ ▲	b−/eɪ/
5.	I have │ to go │ to bed │ and see △ ▲　△ ▲　△ ▲　△ ▲	c−/iː/
6.	The birds │ still hop │ ping on │ the tree, △ ▲　△ ▲　△ ▲　△ ▲	c−/iː/
7.	Or hear │ the grown │ -up peo │ ple's feet △ ▲　△ ▲　△ ▲　△ ▲	d−/iːt/
8.	Still go │ ing past │ me in │ the street. △ ▲　△ ▲　△△ ▲　△ ▲	d−/iːt/
9.	And does │ it not │ seem hard │ to you, △ ▲　△△ ▲　△ ▲　△ ▲	e−/uː/

10.   When all │ the sky │ is clear │ and blue.   e-/uː/

               △ ▲   △ ▲   △ ▲   △ ▲

11.   And I │ should like │ so much │ to play,   b-/eɪ/

               △ ▲   △ ▲   △ ▲   △ ▲

12.   To have │ to go │ to bed │ by day?   b-/eɪ/

               △ ▲   △ ▲   △ ▲   △ ▲

修辞解析

本诗涉及一个诗歌常用的修辞手法：重复。

本诗第 4 行、第 5 行和第 12 行就是句子的重复：I have to go to bed by day. /I have to go to bed and see... To have to go to bed by day？本诗这三个句子的重复并非完全相同的重复，而是围绕核心成分 I have to go to bed 的反复述说，后面的状语或同位语成分以及语境也在不断变化，所以这个重复丝毫不显呆板和累赘，起到了反复咏唱、不断强化主题的作用。

作品鉴赏

这是一首脍炙人口的儿童诗，写得简短、清新而优美。诗中从一个儿童视角把冬日早起和夏日早睡的两段痛苦经历进行了对照，最后以一个反问句结束，具有普遍性、讽刺性和教育性。所谓普遍性，就在于很多地方冬天的夜间温度比较低，所以冬天早起就比较痛苦。所谓讽刺性，就在于夏天又要早睡，英国的夏天日照时间较长——晚上十点钟天才黑！孩子们因为天太亮或外面太吵而睡不着就成了家常便饭。该诗的教育性在于，把一件生活里很小、很普通的事情写得清新脱俗，辩证理性，寓教于乐，使家长和教育者们意识到：让孩子们过得太刻板了也是不快乐、不科学的，毕竟他们童心未泯，玩兴正大，不可能像成年人一样自律，过刻板的生活。

该诗一共三节，每节四行；四音步抑扬格，尾韵押 aabb ccdd eebb 的双行体韵。该诗用词地道、平易，没有一个生僻词，没有一个复杂的语言结构，使用的是英语中最普通、最地道的词汇。三音节及以上词汇一个没有；双音节词有 9 个，在全诗 86 个词汇中仅占 10.5%；其余全是单音节词，满足了英语格律诗最基本的要求：词汇本土化与最简化。这样既能满足格律要求，又能表现儿童诗特有的单纯、天真的风格。

📖 诗作二

Young Night-Thought
少年夜奇思

All night long and every night,　　　　　　每夜皆如此，

When my mama puts out the light,　　　　妈妈熄灯后，

I see the people marching by,　　　　　　就见人行军，

As plain as day, before my eye.　　　　　清晰如白昼。

Armies and emperors and kings,　　　　　皇帝国王兵，

All carrying different kinds of things,　　　全都携武器，

And marching in so grand a way,　　　　　行军多威武，

You never saw the like by day.　　　　　　白昼全无戏。

So fine a show was never seen　　　　　　阅兵从未见，

At the great circus on the green;　　　　　马戏团不演；

For every kind of great and man　　　　　各类人与兽，

Is marching in that caravan.　　　　　　　列队齐向前。

At first they move a little slow,　　　　　开始行动慢，

But still the faster on they go,　　　　　随后愈渐快，

And still beside them close I keep　　　　伴行挨其旁

Until we reach the town of sleep.　　　　直到入梦乡。

（诸莉　译）

Unit 17   *William Butler Yeats*

威廉·巴特勒·叶芝

威廉·巴特勒·叶芝(1865—1939)，爱尔兰大诗人、剧作家，生于都柏林一个新教画师家庭；早年诗歌创作带有浪漫主义色彩，并深受唯美主义和象征主义影响；年轻时喜好艺术和文学，厌恶商业文明；中后期逐步回归现实，并投入爱尔兰民族自治运动，在此期间结识了爱尔兰剧作家格雷戈利夫人，与其一起创办了亚培剧院，并上演了很多自己创作的反映爱尔兰民族生活的戏剧作品，二者还和其他作家一起发起了爱尔兰文艺复兴运动；早期诗歌倾向于浪漫主义的含蓄和脱俗，中后期诗歌逐渐走向现实主义的明朗和直率，晚期诗歌则带有更多的神秘主义和象征主义色彩；1932 年获得诺贝尔文学奖。

📖 **诗作一**

The Lake Isle of Innisfree
茵涅斯弗里岛

I will arise and go now, and go to Innisfree,①	我欲起身去，茵涅斯弗里，
And a small cabin build there, of clay and wattles② made;	岛上棚屋建，黏土藤条砌；
Nine bean-rows will I have there, a hive for the honeybee③,	豌豆种九行，蜂巢搭枝上，
And live alone in the bee-loud glade④.	林中空地住，蜜蜂转悠忙。
And I shall have some peace there, for peace comes dropping⑤ slow,	安宁或许有，时光缓慢滴，
Dropping from the veils⑥ of the morning to where the cricket sings;	滴自晨帷幔，蟋蟀幽幽泣；
There midnight's all a glimmer⑦, and noon a purple glow,	子夜微光闪，午后强光劲，
And evening full of the linnet's⑧ wings.	黄昏有红雀，斑斓彩翼馨。
I will arise and go now, for always night and day	我欲起身去，昼夜响不停，
I hear lake water lapping⑨ with low sounds by the shore;	耳畔湖水声，低回拍岸轻；
While I stand on the roadway⑩, or on the pavements grey,	不论走大路，还是穿小径，
I hear it in the deep heart's core.	心中常回响，湖岛召唤情。

（诸莉 译）

✏️ **语言注释**

① Innisfree：*n.* 茵涅斯弗里岛，是爱尔兰北部湖中的一个小岛。

② clay：*n.* 黏土，陶土。wattle：*n.* 编条结构(用于编筑篱笆、围墙等)。

③ hive：*n.* 蜂房；蜂箱；蜂群；一箱蜜蜂。honeybee：*n.* 蜜蜂。

④ bee-loud glade：glade，指林中空地，bee-loud，指蜜蜂嗡嗡叫的。两者合在一起
　指蜜蜂嗡嗡叫的林中空地。

⑤ dropping：drop 的现在分词，表示滴、滴下、滴落。dropping slow：非常缓慢地

降临。

⑥ veil：*n.* 面纱；幔；遮布；遮蔽物。cricket：*n.* 蟋蟀。

⑦ glimmer：*n.* 微弱的闪光；闪烁的微光；微弱的迹象；一丝。glow：*n.* 微弱稳定的光。

⑧ linnet：*n.* 赤胸朱顶雀，红雀。

⑨ lap：*v.*（水）轻拍，轻打；*n.* 膝上；膝头。lapping，现代分词，拍打；低舔。

⑩ roadway：*n.* 道路；车行道；车道；巷道；路面。

? 思考题

1. Where did the poet probably stay when he would to arise and go?

2. What do you imagine would the lake Isle of Innisfree be like?

3. What characteristics of the Isle of Innisfree attracted the poet?

4. Did the poet finally fulfill his wish or dream of living a simple life on the Lake Isle of Innisfree? Why or why not?

5. Does the life that the poet described attract you? Why or why not?

6. How do you feel about the long poetic lines of the poem, which are essay-like and loose and not so compact?

节奏、韵律图示

The Lake Isle of Innisfree

行数 （Line）	六音步抑扬格、抑抑扬格 （Iambic Hexameter, Anapaestic Hexameter）	韵式 （Rhyme Scheme）
1.	I will ǀ arise ǀ and go ǀ now, and go ǀ to In ǀ nisfree, △ ▲　△▲　△ ▲　△ △ ▲　△▲　△ ▲	a-/iː/
2.	And a small ǀ cabin ǀ build there, ǀ of clay ǀ and wat ǀ tles made； △ △ ▲　▲△　△ ▲　△ ▲　△ ▲　△ ▲	b-/eɪd/

181

3. Nine bean- | rows will | I have | there, a hive | for the ho | neybee,　　a-/iː/

   ▲　△　　△　　▲　△　▲　　　△　△　▲　　△　△　▲　　△　▲

4. And live | alone | in the bee- | loud glade.　　b-/eɪd/

   △　▲　　△　△　△　△　▲　　△　　▲

5. And I | shall have | some peace | there, for peace | comes drop | ping slow,　　c-/əʊ/

   △　▲　　△　▲　　△　▲　　△　△　▲　　△　▲　　△　▲

6. Dropping | from the veils | of the morn | ing to where | the cri | cket sings;　　d-/ɪŋ/

   ▲　△　　△　△　▲　　△　△　▲　　△　△　▲　　△　▲　　△　▲

7. There mid | night's all | a glim | mer, and noon | a pur | ple glow,　　c-/əʊ/

   △　▲　　△　▲　　△　▲　　△　△　▲　　△　▲　　△　▲

8. And e | vening full | of the lin | net's wings.　　d-/ɪŋ/

   △　▲　　△　△　▲　　△　△　▲△　　△　▲

9. I will | arise | and go | now, for al | ways night | and day　　e-/eɪ/

   △▲　　△△　　△　▲　　△　△　▲　　▲　△　　△　▲

10. I hear | lake wa | ter lap | ping with low | sounds by | the shore;　　f-/ɔː/

   △　▲　　△　▲　　△△　　△　△　▲　　△　▲　　△　▲

11. While I | stand on | the road | way, or | on the pave | ments grey,　　e-/eɪ/

   △　▲　　△　▲　　△　▲　　△　▲　　△　△　▲　　△　▲

12. I hear | it in | the deep | heart's core.　　f-/ɔː/

   △　▲　　△▲　　△　▲　　△　▲

　　注：本诗总体而言是六音步抑扬格，但有 15 个抑抑扬格（1-4；2-1；3-4；3-5；4-3；5-4；6-2；6-3；6-4；7-4；8-2；8-3；9-4；10-4；11-5），有 3 个扬抑格（2-2；3-1；6-1），所以格律不是很规整。尾韵很整齐：abab cdcd efef。

📑 修辞解析

本诗涉及四个诗歌常用的修辞手法：重复、头韵、尾韵和谐元音。

1. 重复（Repetition）

（1）本诗第一节和第三节首句就是一个重复（I will arise and go now）：

I will arise and go now, and go to Innisfree. （第一节）

I will arise and go now, for always night and day. （第三节）

（2）本诗第二节有一个核心词汇的重复：peace（第二节第一句）：

And I shall have some peace there, for peace comes dropping slow.

（3）本诗第二节有一个重复（dropping）：

And I shall have some peace there, for peace comes dropping slow.

Dropping from the veils of the morning to where the cricket sings.

（4）本诗第三节第一、三行中有一组重复（I hear）：

I hear lake water lapping with low sounds by the shore.

I hear it in the deep heart's core

诗中 I will arise and go now 这个句子的重复并非完全相同的重复，而是围绕核心成分 I will arise and go now 这个句段的反复述说，后面的状语或同位语成分以及语境也在不断变化，所以这个重复丝毫不显呆板和累赘，起到了反复咏唱、不断强化主题的作用。

2. 头韵（Alliteration）

本诗共有三组头韵修辞格的应用，但都比较散漫，在同一行诗句中彼此相距较远，因此其音响效果自然就较弱：

（1）/k/：cabin—clay（间隔 3 个词）（第一节第二行）。

（2）/h/：have—hive—honeybee（间隔 2 个词）（第一节第三行）。

（3）/g/：glimmer—glow（间隔 4 个词）（第二节第三行）。

（4）/l/：lake—lapping—low（分别间隔 1 个词）（第三节第二行）。

3. 尾韵（End Rhyme）

一般同一行中押尾韵的不多，但本诗有一个/ɪŋ/，也都比较散漫，在同一行诗句中彼此相距较远，因此其音响效果自然就较弱：

（1）/ɪŋ/：dropping—morning—sings（第二节第二行）。

（2）/ɪŋ/：evening—wings（第二节第四行）。

4. 行中韵、谐元音或腹韵（Internal Rhyme, Assonance）

（1）/aɪ/：I—arise（间隔 1 词）（第一节第一行）。

（2）/æ/：cabin—wattles（间隔 5 词）（第一节第二行）。

（3）/eɪ/：clay—made（间隔 2 词）（第一节第二行）。

（4）/aɪ/：nine—I（间隔 3 词）（第一节第三行）。

（5）/i：/：bean-rows—honeybee（间隔 8 词）（第一节第三行）。

（6）/ɒ/：dropping—from（间隔 0 词）（第二节第二行）。

（7）/aɪ/：I—arise—night（间隔 1 词和 5 词）（第三节第一行）。

（8）/eɪ/：always—day（间隔 2 词）（第三节第一行）。

（9）/aɪ/：while—I（间隔 0 词）（第三节第三行）。

（10）/eɪ/：roadway—pavements—grey（间隔 2 词和 0 词）（第三节第三行）。

以上谐元音或腹韵，皆为行中韵，除了少数几个外（第一行、第六行、第七行和第九行），其他都在同一行诗句中彼此相隔较远，比较散漫，其音响效果自然就较弱。

作品鉴赏

显然，本诗作者渴望过上一种陶渊明式"采菊东篱下，悠然见南山"般的田园生活，其核心是逃离大都市的喧嚣，逃离名利场，逃离尘世的纷扰，重新投入大自然的怀抱，求得心灵的抚慰。

本诗可以比肩约翰·梅斯菲尔德的《海之恋》：I must down to the seas again，to the lonely sea and the sky（我欲下海去，去看寂海天）。两者都是同样的主题，即逃离城市，回到乡村或海洋，回到大自然中去；挣脱束缚，实现人性的回归！这两首诗发表时间也比较接近，刚刚进入 20 世纪，西方的资本主义社会进入高速发展阶段，资本对人性的压抑和扭曲也开始变本加厉，导致人们对社会的不满和反抗也愈加激烈。浪漫主义诗歌就是这种反抗精神在文学中的最佳表现形式。无独有偶，这两位大诗人，一位成为桂冠诗人，一位成为诺贝尔文学奖获得者，同时创作了主题相似的两首诗歌来表达自己的苦闷和不满。

这两首作品的一个共性就在于，它们都产生于喧嚣嘈杂的大都市环境，而非浪漫诗意的乡村，但都表达了逃离大都市、回归自然（海洋或湖岛）、过一种田园式宁静安详生活的强烈愿望。所谓田园式生活，就是一种与世无争，自给自足的生活方式，生产力水平虽然不高，但节奏舒缓，故乐得其所，安于清贫，富于精神。中国传统文人向往的桃花源或理想地其实也就是人少地多，自然资源丰富，有山有水、有树有林且远离喧嚣的地方。所以这两个作品中的湖岛和海洋，基本都属于这种类型，即与世隔绝，与世无争，舒缓放松。这也是中国道家理想中的桃花源地和理想国——东西方文化异曲同工，都有这种消极遁世的理想存在。生活于大都市的白领人群，工作和生活压力比较大时，往往就容易产生这种理想和追求。

　　本诗的格律音响，在某种意义上属于半格律、半自由状态。从尾韵来看，格律是很整齐规律的；但从行中韵来看，虽然有多达十组的谐元音及多组头韵和重复等修辞手法，但都不是特别强烈和规律，总的来说比较散漫和随意，因此格律就属于半自由状态。除此之外，该诗另外一个特点也使得其半自由状态越发明显，即它的散文化趋势。所谓散文化就是指诗歌创作不再受格律、节奏约束的影响，在结构和语言上，它更多受散文创作的影响……也就是说诗歌写得无韵无律，或半韵半律，句式结构比较松散随意，即本来跳的是有节奏有规律的舞步，最后却成了随心所欲的漫步，从行中到行尾的韵律没有那么严谨或讲究了，最后格律诗就写成了散文诗。归纳起来就是，艺术形式上不合格律规范的诗歌创作都可以称为"散文化"。从前文分析可以看出，本诗的主流韵律是六音步抑扬格，这本身就比更主流的四音步和五音步多出来一两个音步，使每一个诗行的长度更长。然后还不止于此，根据节奏、韵律图示部分的注释，还有共 15 个三音节音步夹杂于全诗，可见诗句句型的构造方面比较松散和自由。最直观的一个表现就是它的诗行都比较长，或长短不一，颇有起伏不定的意味——因为每一诗行的音节数并不完全相同——最多的一行(第 6 行)有 3 个三音节音步，比其他行多出了 3 个音节。当然，决定一个诗行长度的因素还有其单词长度。以第 5 行为例，它是本诗最长的一行，但其音节数比第 6 行还少 2 个。所以音节数不是影响诗行长度的决定性因素。除诗行音节数因素外，该诗散文化趋向还表现在每节前 3 行全部是复合句型，除包含两个简单句(第 5、7 行)外，要么带有省略主语的平行简单句(第 1、3 行)，要么带有一个限制性定语从句(第 6 行)，要么带有一个时间状语(第 9 行)，要么带有一个 with 引导的方式状语(第 10 行)，要么带有一个地点状语(第 11 行)。这样就使得每句诗行都变得比较长，在节奏上就显得比较拖沓，不那么紧凑。这也是其散文化趋势的表现之一。

　　至于这种散文化趋向是否是作者有意而为之，这就是一个很有意思的问题了。因为从作者的工作和生活环境以及他一贯的人生追求来看，他非常渴望过上那种

"采菊东篱下，悠然见南山"般的田园生活，他渴望逃离城市的喧嚣、名利的羁绊和尘世的纷扰，回到自然的怀抱。因此我们也就不难理解这种比较松散拖沓的句式结构和散漫随意的韵律节奏，其实可能是作者的匠心独运，刻意用来体现其心心念念的田园生活的自由自在、轻松随意……

从音乐性审美来说，这些半自由、半格律的散文化趋向还是比完全不讲究格律的自由诗强多了，因为它还是可以给人一种或隐或现的同声相谐的节奏感、韵律感，对诗歌意义也会有一些支持和烘托，使之更加和谐、美妙和有意义。所以该诗依然属于英国文学史上难得的佳作之一，值得大家细细品味。

📖 诗作二

When You Are Old
当你老了

When you are old and gray and full of sleep,	人老发白睡意浓,
And nodding by the fire, take down this book,	炉边读书常浑慵,
And slowly read, and dream of the soft look	慢读慢忆君昔眉,
Your eyes had once, and of their shadows deep;	忧郁深深柔眼中;
How many loved your moments of glad grace,	多少爱君怡人雅,
And loved your beauty with love false or true,	多少爱君美人貌,
But one man loved the pilgrim soul in you,	唯我爱你圣洁气,
And loved the sorrows of your changing face;	爱你愁容日渐老;
And bending down beside the glowing bars,	火光炉旁腰躯弯,
Murmur, a little sadly, how Love fled	凄凄低诉爱已散,
And paced upon the mountains overhead	越过头顶登上山,
And hid his face amid a crowd of stars.	掩面藏于星灿烂。

（诸莉　译）

📖 诗作三

The Wild Swans at Coole
库尔的野天鹅

The trees are in their autumn beauty,	树着秋装美,
The woodland paths are dry,	林中小径干,
Under the October twilight the water	十月黄昏下,
Mirrors a still sky;	倒映寂静天。
Upon the brimming water among the stones	鹅卵映水秋,
Are nine-and-fifty swans.	天鹅顾自游。

The nineteenth autumn has come upon me	十九秋已过,
Since I first made my count;	自我来数鹅。
I saw, before I had well finished,	未等我数毕,
All suddenly mount	天鹅群飞起,
And scatter wheeling in great broken rings	散开又绕圈,
Upon their clamorous wings.	扑翅闹腾喧。

I have looked upon those brilliant creatures,	目睹天鹅景,
And now my heart is sore.	此刻多伤心。
All's changed since I, hearing at twilight,	一切均已变,
The first time on this shore,	首次湖畔听,
The bell-beat of their wings above my head,	头顶翅震颤,
Trod with a lighter tread.	我步多轻盈。

Unwearied still, lover by lover,	比翼从不倦,
They paddle in the cold	荡桨寒中情,
Companionable streams or climb the air;	凌空双飞远,
Their hearts have not grown old;	心气贯长天;
Passion or conquest, wander where they will,	不论去何地,
Attend upon them still.	激情永不息。

But now they drift on the still water,	幽静水面游,
Mysterious, beautiful;	神秘又美好;
Among what rushes will they build,	湖边芦苇荡,
By what lake's edge or pool	如何来筑巢,
Delight men's eyes when I awake some day	某天我醒来,
To find they have flown away?	鹅已无踪杳?

（诸莉　译）

📖 **诗作四**

The Old Men Admiring Themselves in the Water
老人们自赏水中倒影

I heard the old, old men say,　　　　　　　常听老人言：

"Everything alters,　　　　　　　　　　　"一切均会变，

And one by one we drop away."　　　　　　个个都消失。"

They had hands like claws, and their knees　手若动物爪，

Were twisted like the old thorn trees　　　膝盖若枯藤

By the waters.　　　　　　　　　　　　　曲折难扭直。

I heard the old, old men say,　　　　　　　常听老人言：

"All that's beautiful drifts away　　　　　"凡美均将逝，

Like the waters."　　　　　　　　　　　　河水般流弃。"

（诸光　译）

Unit 18　*Alfred Edward Housman*

阿尔弗雷德·爱德华·豪斯曼

　　阿尔弗雷德·爱德华·豪斯曼(1859—1936)，英国现代学者，杰出诗人，19世纪末开始发表作品，到20世纪初"一战"后才大放异彩，广受欢迎；曾在牛津大学学习，后成为著名古罗马文学校勘学家，并在剑桥大学终生任教；工作之余共创作近200首诗歌作品，1896年自费出版第一部诗集《什罗普郡少年》，从此一发不可收拾；1922年出版《最后的诗》，成为绝唱；去世后其胞弟整理《集外诗作》，于1936年出版，并作为其传记；豪斯曼诗风独特，喜好模仿传统民谣，追求朴实平易，使用地道英语词汇，既满足格律要求，又实现音韵美；诗歌主题大多哀叹青春易逝，鸳梦难续和人心不古，充满了悲观主义色彩。

📖 诗作一

Loveliest of Trees
最可爱的树

Loveliest of trees, the cherry① now	樱树最可爱,
Is hung with bloom② along the bough③,	枝头花正开;
And stands about the woodland④ ride⑤	傲立林中道,
Wearing white for Eastertide⑥.	复活穿白袄。
Now, of my threescore⑦ years and ten,	人活七十岁,
Twenty will not come again,	二十已难追;
And take from seventy springs a score⑧,	七旬二十去,
It only leaves me fifty more.	仅余五十许。
And since to look at things in bloom	欲穷花间美,
Fifty springs are little room,	五十岁何为?
About the woodlands I will go	我先林中走,
To see the cherry hung with snow.	樱雪看个够。

（诸光　译）

✍ 语言注释

① cherry：n. 樱桃；樱桃树；樱桃木；樱桃色，鲜红色。

② bloom：n. 花，花朵；花期；v. 开花，绽放。in bloom：盛开；开着花。

③ bough：n. 树枝。

④ woodland：n. 林地，森林。

⑤ ride：n. (尤指林中的) 骑马道。

⑥ Eastertide：*n.* 复活节季。

⑦ threescore：*n.* 六十；六十岁。

⑧ score：*n.* <正式>二十，约二十个。

⑦ 思考题

1. Why does the speaker say that the cherry now is the loveliest of trees?

2. Why is it special that it snowed for Eastertide?

3. What do we know about the life expectancy then from the poem?

4. Is there any change in life expectancy today? What is the tendency of the change?

5. Why does the speaker feel that fifty years are not enough?

6. How do you feel about the general mood of the speaker in the poem?

✍ 节奏、韵律图示

Loveliest of Trees

行数 (Line)	四音步抑扬格 (Iambic Tetrameter)	韵式 (Rhyme Scheme)
1.	Loveliest ｜ of trees, ｜ the cher ｜ ry now ▲ △　△ ▲　　△ ▲　△ ▲	a-/aʊ/
2.	Is hung ｜ with bloom ｜ along ｜ the bough, △ ▲　△ ▲　△▲　△ ▲	a-/aʊ/
3.	And stands ｜ about ｜ the wood ｜ land ride △ ▲　△▲　△ ▲　△ ▲	b-/aɪd/
4.	Wearing white ｜ for Eas ｜ tertide. △ △　▲　△ ▲　△▲	b-/aɪd/
5.	Now, of ｜ my three ｜ score years ｜ and ten, △ ▲　△ ▲　▲ ▲　△ ▲	c-/en/

193

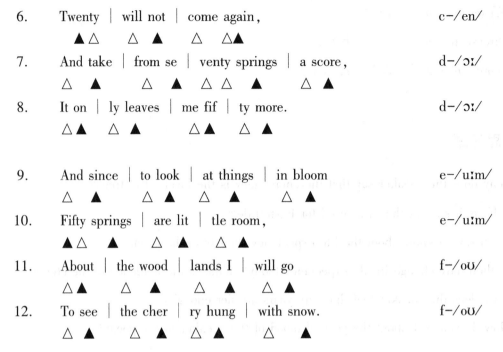

6.　Twenty ｜ will not ｜ come again,　　　　　c-/en/
　　　▲△　　△　▲　　△　▲▲

7.　And take ｜ from se ｜ venty springs ｜ a score,　d-/ɔː/
　　　△　▲　　△　▲　△　▲　　△　▲

8.　It on ｜ ly leaves ｜ me fif ｜ ty more.　　　d-/ɔː/
　　　△▲　△　▲　　△▲　▲　△　▲

9.　And since ｜ to look ｜ at things ｜ in bloom　e-/uːm/
　　　△　▲　　△　▲　△　▲　　△　▲

10.　Fifty springs ｜ are lit ｜ tle room,　　　e-/uːm/
　　　▲▲　▲　　△　▲　△　▲

11.　About ｜ the wood ｜ lands I ｜ will go　　f-/oʊ/
　　　△▲　△　▲　　△　▲　△　▲

12.　To see ｜ the cher ｜ ry hung ｜ with snow.　f-/oʊ/
　　　△　▲　△　▲　△　▲　　△　▲

注：本诗总体而言是四音步抑扬格，但有三个抑抑扬格（4-1；6-3；7-3），有两个扬抑格（1-1；6-1）；一个扬扬格（5-3）；一个扬抑抑格（10-1），所以格律还是相当规整的。韵式也很规律：aabb ccdd eeff（英雄双行体，heroic couplet）。

修辞解析

本诗仅涉及一个诗歌常用的修辞手法：头韵修辞格。这个头韵是第四行的 wearing white（4-1）。有关头韵的概念及作用在弗罗斯特诗歌里已有讨论，在此不再赘述。

作品鉴赏

本诗在豪斯曼诗歌中占有重要地位。在《什罗普郡少年》诗集里位列前位，是诗人的最爱之一。

一首赏樱小品，带出美景易逝、只争朝夕的主题。本是意气风发、人生起航的追风少年，竟也感叹岁月易逝，人生无常。诗人认为必须珍惜当下才能遍赏林中樱花，才能阅尽人间美景。人生在世，若想有所成就，又何尝不是如此？本诗与其他豪诗不同之处在于，如果说他的作品大多悲天悯人，絮叨冷峻，常常感叹世风日下、人心不古，这首诗歌却洗练劲爽、清新洒脱、朗朗上口、立意高远，堪称诗人最有青春朝气的作品之一。尤其是那种时不我待、只争朝夕的追风少年的气势，充分体现了诗人热爱生活、珍爱生命的积极向上的人生态度，与其他表现生命易逝、爱情不忠等主题的诗风形成鲜明对比。

豪斯曼诗歌是简短的、冷峻的。它的抒情意味隐藏在叙事情节之下，埋得很深。在它冷峻、悲情的叙事之下往往隐藏着一颗炽热的心。

本诗是一首现代格律诗，格律严谨，音调优美，文风淳朴，不加雕饰，基本不用传统修辞格。抒情与叙事风格也极尽含蓄、低调，刻意模仿民谣歌调，仅使用最淳朴地道的本民族英语词汇(基本不用英语中的外来语如法语、拉丁语词汇)，诗歌带有一种格言般的简洁和庄重。

📖 诗作二

With Rue My Heart is Laden
我心满悲叹

With rue my heart is laden	我心满悲叹，
For golden friends I had,	昔日好伙伴，
For many a rose-lipt maiden	多少红唇女，
And many a lightfoot lad.	多少敏捷男。
By brooks too broad for leaping	宽宽小河旁，
The lightfoot boys are laid;	敏捷男儿躺；
The rose-lipt girls are sleeping	红唇女长眠
In fields where roses fade.	玫瑰谢田上。

（诸莉　译）

📖 诗作三

Along the Fields as We Came by
田地正路过

Along the fields as we came by	田地正路过，
A year ago, my love and I,	恋人她和我。
The aspen over stile and stone	墙边白杨树，
Was talking to itself alone.	自言自语说：
"Oh who are these that kiss and pass?	"是谁过而吻？
A country lover and his lass;	小伙及情人；
Two lovers looking to be wed;	看似要成婚；
And time shall put them both to bed,	到时即共枕，
But she shall lie with earth above,	女卧黑土下，
And he beside another love."	男又牵手她。"
And sure enough beneath the tree	此事真不假，
There walks another love with me,	她我又树下，
And overhead the aspen heaves	头上白杨叶，
Its rainy-sounding silver leaves;	轻叹如雨下；
And I spell nothing in their stir,	而我全不懂，
But now perhaps they speak to her,	或许向她诉，
And plain for her to understand	也仅她明通，
They talk about a time at hand	预言不久后，
When I shall sleep with clover clad,	我眠墓草下，
And she beside another lad.	女又牵手他。

（诸莉　译）

197

📖 诗作四

To an Athlete Dying Young
致英年早逝的运动员

The time you won your town the race	故乡赢比赛
We chaired you through the market-place;	过市把卿抬;
Man and boy stood cheering by	须眉均叫好
And home we brought you shoulder-high.	举卿齐肩高。
Today, the road all runners come,	今日跑手到,
Shoulder-high we bring you home,	举卿齐肩高,
And set you at your threshold down,	置卿宅门前,
Townsman of a stiller town.	故乡邻里奠。
Smart lad, to slip betimes away	机灵及时溜,
From fields where glory does not stay	赛场誉难久;
And early though the laurel grows	桂冠早长熟,
It withers quicker than the rose.	凋零快于露。
Eyes the shady night has shut	眼为长夜闭,
Cannot see the record cut,	不见记录易;
And silence sounds no worse than cheers	寂静胜欢呼,
After earth has stopped the ears:	双耳塞满土:
Now you will not swell the rout	从此不烦躁
Of lads that wore their honour out,	不惧旧荣消,

Runners whom renown outran	声望跑更快
And the name died before the man.	名姓早忘怀。
So set，before its echoes fade，	回音尚未散，
The fleet foot on the sill of shade，	捷足登门槛；
And hold to the low lintel up	举高低门楣，
The still-defended challenge-cup.	奖杯仍捍卫。
And round that early-laurelled head	桂冠加冕早
Will flock to gaze the strengthless dead，	众聚睹亡夭；
And find unwithered on its curls	卷叶尚未枯，
The garland briefer than a girl's.	花环却已腐。

（诸光　译）

📖 诗作五

Home is the Sailor, Home from Sea
水手海上归

Home is the sailor, home from sea:	水手海上归：
Her far-borne canvas furled	远航帆已垂，
The ship pours shining on the quay	货自四方卸，
The plunder of the world.	亮闪码头堆。
Home is the hunter from the hill	天罗地网布，
Fast is the boundless snare	猎人山里回，
All flesh lies taken at his will	鸟兽难逃脱
And every fowl of air.	猎杀之追随。
'Tis evening on the moorland free,	荒原夜无际，
The starlet wave is still:	星辰浪波息：
Home is the sailor from the sea,	水手海上归，
The hunter from the hill.	猎手山里回。

（诸莉 译）

Unit 19 *Emily Dickinson*

艾米莉·狄金森

　　艾米莉·狄金森(1830—1886)，美国 19 世纪女诗人，英美现代派诗歌先驱；从小家境优越，因此受过良好教育；因情场失意，遂退隐闺中，追求个人兴趣，终身未嫁；创作诗歌 1700 多首，大多发表于去世之后，生前仅发表 8 首；年轻时受清教主义影响，后来受艾默生的超验主义哲学和玄学派诗歌影响，并富有时代正义感；因社会活动范围有限，诗歌题材多局限于个人的玄思冥想，主题包括爱情、死亡、永恒、美等；其诗歌创作带有很多反传统手法：以破折号代替标点符号，所有名词都大写，以半韵和近韵代替传统格律，诗歌韵律以半格律、半自由形式为主，富于个性且勇于创新。

诗作一

I Died for Beauty
我为美而死

I died for Beauty, — but was scarce[①]	我为美而死,
Adjusted in the Tomb,	才歇坟墓里,
When one who died for Truth was lain[②]	他为真理亡
In an adjoining[③] Room —	来躺我隔壁——
He questioned softly why I failed?	问我何至此?
"For Beauty." I replied —	我说为了美。
"And I — for Truth, —Themself are one —	"而我为真理——
We brethren[④] are," he said —	我俩是兄弟。"
And so, as kinsmen[⑤], met a Night[⑥]—	亲戚夜相逢——
We talked between the Rooms—	隔墙也聊天——
Until the Moss[⑦] had reached our lips,	青苔爬上唇,
And covered up — our names —	终将名字掩——

（诸光　译）

语言注释

① scarce：*adv.* 相当于 scarcely，副词。

② lain：*v.* 躺，位于(lie 的过去分词)。

③ adjoining：*adj.* 邻接的；毗连的。

④ brethren：（旧式或老式用法）兄弟们，同胞；同党，会友。相当于 brothers。

⑤ kinsmen：*n.* 亲戚(kinsman 的复数)。

⑥ a night：at night。

⑦ moss：*n.* 苔藓，青苔；藓类植物。

✍ 节奏、韵律图示

I Died for Beauty

行数 （Line）	四、三音步抑扬格 （Iambic Tetrameter & Trimeter）	韵式 （Rhyme Scheme）
1.	I died ｜ for Beau ｜ ty— but ｜ was scarce △ ▲　△ ▲　△ ▲　△ ▲	a－/ers/
2.	Adjus ｜ ted in ｜ the Tomb △ ▲　△▲　△ ▲	b－/uːm/
3.	When One ｜ who died ｜ for Truth， ｜ was lain △ ▲　△ ▲　△ ▲　△ ▲	c－/eɪ/
4.	In an ｜ adjoi ｜ ning Room— △ ▲　△▲　△ ▲	b－/uːm/
5.	He ques ｜ tioned soft ｜ ly "Why ｜ I failed"？ △ ▲　△ ▲　△ ▲　△▲	/eɪld/
6.	"For Beau ｜ ty," I ｜ replied— △ ▲　△ ▲　△ ▲	/aɪd/
7.	"And I ｜ — for Truth— ｜ Themselves ｜ are One— △ ▲　△ ▲　△ ▲　△ ▲	/ʌn/
8.	We Bre ｜ thren are," ｜ He said— △ ▲　△ ▲　△ ▲	/ed/
9.	And so， ｜ as Kins ｜ men，met ｜ a Night— △ ▲　△ ▲　△ ▲　△▲	/aɪt/
10.	We talked ｜ between ｜ the Rooms— △ ▲　△ ▲　△ ▲	b－/uːmz/

11.　Until ｜ the Moss ｜ had reached ｜ our lips— 　　　　　/Ips/
　　△ ▲　　△ ▲　　　△ ▲　　　△ ▲

12.　And co ｜ vered up ｜ — our names— 　　　　　/neImz/
　　△ ▲　　△ ▲　　　△ ▲

注：本诗为四三音步交替抑扬格(alternated iambic tetrameter and trimeter)。每节一、三行为四音步抑扬格，二、四行为三音步抑扬格。尾韵第一节为 abcb，其他均无规律。

本诗虽然韵式不整，但韵律均为抑扬格，格外整齐规律。

修辞解析

本诗仅使用明喻和拟人两个修辞格。

1. 明喻(Simile)

本诗唯一的一个明喻修辞格是第三节第一行中的 And so，as Kinsmen，met a Night —，意思就是"亲戚夜相逢"。明喻就是通过一个比喻把一个较为复杂抽象的问题说得浅显易懂。

2. 拟人(Personification)

本诗的一个拟人修辞格就是第三节第三行的 Until the Moss had reached our lips—中的 Moss(苔藓、青苔)。此处虽然苔藓也会蔓延，缓慢扩大面积，但 reach 一词把 Moss 的行为人格化了，使其动态化：仿佛它是人或动物，主动有意够着了我的嘴唇，而非慢慢生长、蔓延到那里去的。拟人修辞格的应用能使无生命物体变得像人或动物一般生动有趣起来。从广义来说，整首诗其实都弥漫着拟人修辞格，因为全诗描绘的都是人死而复生的故事，包括他们的行为(第一、三节)和对话(第二节)。将死人写活了同样是针对无生命事物的拟人化修辞。

作品鉴赏

这首诗是狄金森风格的一个典型体现。从主题来说，美与真，本来就是生活和艺术所追求的同一事物的两个方面，两者相辅相成，缺一不可，正如济慈所言：

"美即是真，真即是美。"①所以在诗中，美与真(为美而死的我和为真而死的他)在墓穴里隔墙相遇，两者一见如故，相谈甚欢，相见恨晚，因为他们本就是一家人。从诗歌叙事来看，诗人是以死后复生的超自然形式来讲述该故事的，颇有一种倩女幽魂般的美妙和神秘在其中，还有一种跨越千年的历史厚重感，使我们不禁想起了蒲松龄的《聊斋志异》和电影《神话》中的那种魔幻浪漫与神奇穿越。从格律形式来看，该诗以规整的抑扬格四音步与抑扬格三音步交替发展，但各行的尾韵却又极其不讲究，仅第一节有 abcb 的民谣风，其他各节都再无任何形式的押韵，堪称半格律、半自由化素体诗。从语言形式来看，本诗行文简洁、形象、生动，第二节竟然全由三句人物对话的直接引语构成，堪称一绝。此外本诗还夹杂着 11 个破折号，并省掉了相应的标点符号；然后还有 11 个首字母大写的名词，给人耳目一新的感觉。最后，从诗歌所反映的人生观来看，本诗通过墓穴场景的描述呈现了一种魔幻现实主义与浪漫主义精神，也反映出女诗人在孤独清冷的世界中那份对人生与艺术的执着追求。

---

① 孙梁. 英美名诗一百首[M]. 北京：中国对外翻译出版公司，2001：229.

📖 诗作二

I Am Nobody
我乃无名辈

I'm nobody，who are you?	我乃无名辈，不知君为谁？
Are you nobody too?	君也无名辈？
Then there's a pair of us.	我俩终一对。
Don't tell! They'd banish us，you know.	千万别吭声！免遭众人锤。
How dreary to be somebody，	出名多乏味，
How public，like a frog	青蛙般公开，
To tell your name the livelong June	漫长六月里
To an admiring bog.	大名报上来，沼泽也钦佩。

（诸莉　译）

📖 诗作三

A Thought Went up My Mind Today

A thought went up my mind today— 一念今又现，

That I have had before— 昔日长相知；

But did not finish—some way back— 至今未了愿，

I could not fix the year— 不记是何年。

Nor where it went—nor why it came 此念何处去，

The second time to me— 今又为何来，

Nor definitely, what it was— 我亦无头绪，

Have I the art to say— 何来技巧猜？

But somewhere—in my soul—I know— 灵魂深处知

I've met the thing before— 我俩曾相识；

It just reminded me—'twas all— 如今来提醒，

And came my way no more— 从此就两清？

（诸莉　译）

📖 诗作四

Wild Nights—Wild Nights!
暴风雨之夜

Wild Nights—Wild Nights!	暴风雨夜!
Where I with thee—	与你一起,
Wild nights should be—	暴风雨夜
Our luxury!	我俩奢靡!
Futile—the winds—	风大无虞——
To a heart in port—	心在港湾——
Done with the compass—	罗盘不需,
Done with the chart!	海图免谈!
Rowing in Eden—	荡桨伊甸——
Ah, the sea!	大海何惧!
Might I but moor—tonight—	或许今夜
In thee!	我停你区!

（诺莉　译）

📖 诗作五

I Started Early—Took My Dog
很早我出发——牵狗去看海

I started Early—Took my Dog	很早我出发
And visited the Sea—	牵狗去看海——
The Mermaids in the Basement	海底美人鱼
Came out to look at me—	探头看我来——
And Frigates—in the Upper Floor	战舰水面行
Extended Hempen Hands—	伸出大麻手——
Presuming Me to be a Mouse—	把我当老鼠——
Aground—upon the Sands—	搁浅沙滩上——
But no Man moved Me—till the Tide	无人惊扰我
Went past my simple Shoe—	海潮爬上鞋——
And past my Apron—and my Belt—	淹过我围裙——
And past my Bodice—too—	没过我胸衣——
And made as He would eat me up—	似要吞下我——
As wholly as a Dew	如吞一露珠
Upon a Dandelion's Sleeve—	落在花瓣叶——
And then—I started—too—	然后我转身——

And He—He followed—close behind—　　　　而他紧随后——

I felt His Silver Heel　　　　　　　　　　感受银鞋跟

Upon my Ankle—Then my Shoes　　　　　踏到我双踝

Would overflow with Pearl—　　　　　　鞋冒小水珠——

Until We met the Solid Town—　　　　　相遇小镇上

No One He seemed to know—　　　　　　无人他相识——

And bowing-with a Mighty look—　　　　对我鞠而视——

At me—The Sea withdrew—　　　　　　海潮终后撤——

（诸莉　译）

Unit 20 *Edwin Arlington Robinson*

埃德温·阿灵顿·罗宾逊

　　埃德温·阿灵顿·罗宾逊(1869—1935)，美国 19 世纪末、20 世纪初的大诗人，也被誉为是美国"承前启后"的诗人；既秉承格律传统，又开启了英诗的现代口语风格时代；早年因家门不幸而生活拮据，不得不从哈佛大学辍学，一边到处打工一边写诗，后得到总统西奥多·罗斯福的青睐及朋友们的接济得以维持生活并继续创作，生活逐渐得到改善，直到去世；罗宾逊生活在一个物欲横流、人情冷漠的时代，但他坚决反对物质主义，竭力倡导信仰和秩序；早年生活的坎坷经历使诗人形成了比较悲观的人生态度，又受叔本华、哈代等悲观哲学影响，使得其诗歌作品常常带有悲剧色彩，主题也多以失败为主。

📖 **诗作一**

Cliff Klingenhagen
克里夫·克林恩黑根

Cliff Klingenhagen had me in to dine	故人家宴邀，
With him one day; and after soup and meat,	上过汤和肉
And all the other things there were to eat,	以及各菜肴，
Cliff took two glasses and filled one with wine,	满上酒两杯，
And one with wormwood①. Then without a sign	苦艾与葡萄；
For me to choose at all, he took the drought②	举杯无迟疑，
Of bitterness himself, and lightly quaffed③	苦艾畅饮掉，
It off, and said the other one was mine.	余我酒葡萄；
And when I asked him what the deuse④ he meant	不解问其故，
By doing that, he only looked at me	相视答而笑：
And smiled, and said it was a way of his.	行事素如此。
And though I know the fellow, I have spent	我俩长相交，
Long time a-wondering⑤ when I shall be	何时也如他
As happy as Cliff Klingenhagen is.	快乐且逍遥？

（诸莉　译）

✍️ **语言注释**

① wormwood：*n.* [植] 苦艾；苦艾酒；苦恼，苦恼的原因。

② drought：*n.* 长期缺乏，严重短缺；<古>口渴；干旱，旱灾。

③ quaff：*v.* 大口地喝，痛饮。quaff it off，大口地喝掉。

④ what the deuse：究竟是什么；到底。deuse，一些体育比赛中的平分。

⑤ a-wondering：一直想知道，好奇。a-，处于……状态或过程中；在……之上；朝
　　着；用于加强语气。

? 思考题

1. Why does Cliff fill one cup with wine, another with wormwood?

2. Why doesn't Cliff give me any chance to choose at all?

3. Why does Cliff take the drought of the bitterness and lightly quaff it off?

4. Why does the speaker ask him about the reason of doing that to him directly?

5. What will you do if treated like this by your friend?

6. Will you do the same as Cliff Klingenhagen about the wormwood?

7. What does the speaker really think of his friend at the end of the poem?

8. Do you like making friends with people like Cliff Klingenhagen? Why?

✎ 节奏、韵律图示

Cliff Klingenhagen

行数 (Line)	五音步抑扬格 (Iambic Pentameter)	韵式 (Rhyme Scheme)
1.	Cliff Kling | enha | gen had | me in | to dine ▲ ▲　△ ▲　△ ▲　△ ▲　△ ▲	a–/aɪn/
2.	With him | one day; | and a | fter soup | and meat, △ ▲　△ ▲　△ ▲　△ ▲　△ ▲	b–/iːt/
3.	And all | the o | ther things | there were | to eat, △ ▲　△▲　△ ▲　△ ▲　△ ▲	b–/iːt/
4.	Cliff took | two glas | ses and | filled one | with wine, △ ▲　△ ▲　△▲　△ ▲　△ ▲	a–/aɪn/
5.	And one | with worm | wood. Then | without | a sign △ ▲　△ ▲　△ ▲　△▲　△▲	a–/aɪn/
6.	For me | to choose | at all, | he took | the drought △ ▲　△ ▲　△▲　△ ▲　△ ▲	c–/aʊt/

7.　Of bit │ terness │ himself, │ and light │ ly quaffed　　d-/ɑːf/
　　　△ ▲　　△ ▲　　　△ ▲　　　△ ▲　　　△ ▲

8.　It off, │ and said │ the o │ ther one │ was mine.　　a-/aɪn/
　　　△ ▲　　△ ▲　　△ ▲　　△ ▲　　△ ▲

9.　And when │ I asked │ him what │ the deuse │ he meant　　e-/ent/
　　　△ ▲　　△ ▲　　△ ▲　　△ ▲　　△ ▲

10.　By do │ ing that, │ he on │ ly looked │ at me　　f-/iː/
　　　△ ▲　　△ ▲　　△ ▲　　△ ▲　　△ ▲

11.　And smiled, │ and said │ it was │ a way │ of his.　　g-/ɪz/
　　　△ ▲　　△ ▲　　△ ▲　　△ ▲　　△ ▲

12.　And though │ I know │ the fel │ low, I │ have spent　　e-/ent/
　　　△ ▲　　△ ▲　　△ ▲　　△ ▲　　△ ▲

13.　Long time │ a-won │ dering │ when I │ shall be　　f-/iː/
　　　△ ▲　　△ ▲　　△ ▲　　△ ▲　　△ ▲

14.　As hap │ py as │ Cliff Klin │ genha │ gen is.　　g-/ɪz/
　　　△ ▲　　△ ▲　　▲ ▲　　△ ▲　　△ ▲

注：本诗为意大利比特拉克五音步抑扬格(petrarchan iambic pentameter：△▲)，仅有两处例外，都是人名，为扬扬格(spondee：▲▲)：1-1 和 14-3，即第一行第一音步和第十四行第三音步。另外，本诗尾韵为比特拉克十四行诗韵式 abba abba cde cde，只是第六、七行的押韵不太规则(序号顺延为 cd)，所以后面六行的序号顺延为 efg efg。

📑 修辞解析

本诗语言平易朴实，十分口语化，只是运用了两个诗歌常用的修辞手法：跨行连续和行中停顿。

1. 跨行连续(Enjambment)

所谓跨行连续，就是句意和语法结构从一个诗行或对句跨越到下一个而没有标点符号来表示停顿①。该诗一共运用了 8 个跨行连续手法(1-2 行，5-6 行，6-7 行，7-8 行，9-10 行，10-11 行，12-13 行，13-14 行)。从句法上来看，诗人使用了比较松散随意和口语化的日常语言来表达自己，所以诗人常常需要跨越到下一行才能把一句完整的话说完。诗人在这种松散随意的口语化日常语言中找到了

① Chris Baldick. 牛津文学术语词典[M]. 上海：上海外语教育出版社，2000：68.

节奏感和韵律感，在不经意间完成了意大利比特拉克十四行诗的五音步抑扬格。诗人没有刻意打造紧凑而精美的书面语诗行，而主要运用了跨行连续的手法做到了这一点，证明了诗人的语言功底非常扎实。

2. 行中停顿(Caesura)

本诗中共有 8 个行中停顿(第 2、5、6、7、8、10、11、12 行)。行中停顿的数量较多也与上面的跨行连续相关，因为跨行过来的句子不可能正好在行末结束，而大概率会在行中结束，这就导致了行中停顿的出现。令人称奇的是，这么多的行中停顿也没有打乱整首作品的五音步抑扬格节奏。可以想象的是，这其实是诗人精心构造的貌似松散随意的口语化，完全符合严格格律要求的意大利十四行诗。

🔲 作品鉴赏

本诗全面反映了罗宾逊的诗歌创作理念：格律严谨的传统形式，通俗易懂的口语行文，平凡的生活场景与深刻的人生哲学。"'文艺复兴'"后的美国诗歌大多是反传统的"①，主要体现在对格律的背弃，诗歌全面走向了自由化。但 20 世纪初有一批觉悟了的诗人，他们借助传统的英诗格律形式来表现美国社会新生活，罗宾逊就是其中之一，比他年幼几岁的罗伯特·弗罗斯特毫无疑问也是这个阵营里的中坚分子。

本诗讲述了老友克里夫和"我"餐后小酌时，没有同"我"协商就抢喝了一杯苦艾酒而将一杯葡萄酒留给"我"喝，令"我"大惑不解。得知这是克里夫一以贯之的行为之后，"我"感叹道，虽然"我们"之间彼此很了解，但"我"还是不确定什么时候自己也能像克里夫一样活得大气、洒脱和快意？这句话既是诗人的酒后感言，也是对天下芸芸众生的发问：在名利面前，有多少人能做到先人后己、吃亏在前？多少人能有"我不下地狱，谁下地狱"的英雄气概？

本诗行文完全是口语化的，没有使用书面化语言，更没有华丽的辞藻和修辞格，可以说是一气呵成、娓娓道来。语言平易朴实、贴近生活，是完全的口语体。除人名外，该诗极好地遵守了十四行诗的格律，比很多经典的十四行诗还要严谨规范，不得不说这是诗歌创作史上的一个奇迹。

---

① 王文. 走向二十世纪的传统诗人——埃德温·阿林顿·罗宾逊诗歌创作述略[J]. 陕西师范大学成人教育学院学报，1999(6)：30-33.

诗作二

Richard Cory
理查·克里

Whenever Richard Cory went down town,	每当理查·克里进城来,
We people on the pavement looked at him:	我们都喜欢站路边看他:
He was a gentleman from sole to crown,	他浑身都很有绅士派头,
Clean favored, and imperially slim.	也干净整洁,威严消瘦。
And he was always quietly arrayed,	他穿着打扮总是很低调,
And he was always human when he talked;	说起话来却很有人情味,
But still he fluttered pulses when he said,	当他说"早安"时我们都
"Good morning," and he glittered when he walked.	很心动,他走路也潇洒。
And he was rich—yes, richer than a king—	他很富有——比国王还富——
And admirably schooled in every grace:	他每个动作都受过训练:
In fine, we thought that he was everything	总之,他一切堪称典范,
To make us wish that we were in his place.	我们真想如他那般完美。
So on we worked, and waited for the light,	因此我们苦干期待转机,
And went without the meat, and cursed the bread;	因饭菜无肉把面包诅咒;
And Richard Cory, one calm summer night,	理查却在一个夏夜回家,
Went home and put a bullet through his head.	用子弹把自己脑袋打透。

（诺莉 译）

📖 诗作三

Miniver Cheevy
米尼弗·契维

Miniver Cheevy, child of scorn,	米尼弗·契维打小被鄙视,
Grew lean while he assailed the seasons;	营养不良使他骨瘦如柴,
He wept that he was ever born,	他为来到世上而难受流泪,
And he had reasons.	他当然是有太多的理由。
Miniver loved the days of old	米尼弗最怀念旧时的辉煌,
When swords were bright and steeds were prancing;	那刀光剑影，战马嘶鸣;
The vision of a warrior bold	一个骁勇善战的勇士形象
Would set him dancing.	他自豪不已，欣喜若狂。
Miniver sighed for what was not,	米尼弗感叹未实现的荣光,
And dreamed, and rested from his labors;	梦里也想，忙中乐活;
He dreamed of Thebes and Camelot,	梦游底比斯国、卡美洛殿,
And Priam's neighbors.	和普莱姆的相邻城郭。
Miniver mourned the ripe renown	米尼弗哀叹自己没能出名,
That made so many a name so fragrant;	像某名人一样享誉世界。
He mourned Romance, now on the town,	他向往浪漫、放荡的生活,
And art, a vagrant.	想做艺术家，四处漂泊。
Miniver loved the Medici,	米尼弗也羡慕麦迪奇家族,
Albeit he had never seen one;	尽管从未见过家族一员,
He would have sinned incessantly	他也可能犯罪，坏事做尽,
Could he have been one.	如果他真有幸参与其间。

Miniver curse the commonplace

And eyed a khaki suit with loathing;

He missed the medieval grace

Of iron clothing.

Miniver scorned the gold he sought,

But sore annoyed was he without it;

Miniver thought, and thought, and thought,

And thought about it.

Miniver Cheevy, born too late,

Scratched his head and kept on thinking;

Miniver coughed, and called it fate,

And kept on drinking.

米尼弗根本看不起普通人，

他绝对看不上卡其制服；

他向往的是中世纪的荣光，

侠义武士穿的铁甲戎装。

米尼弗鄙视钱财却又爱钱，

因为缺钱时他无可奈何。

米尼弗是想而又想，又想，

一直想着如何不劳而得。

生错时代的米尼弗·契维，

抓狂挠头也还是想不透；

米尼弗干咳两声只好认命，

然后就不断地借酒浇愁。

（诸莉　译）

📖 诗作四

The Sheaves
麦　堆

Where long the shadows of the wind had rolled	风翻影不弃，
Green wheat was yielding to the change assigned;	青苗随季熙。
And as by some vast magic undivined	天有大魔力，
The world was turning slowly into gold.	满眼黄金衣。
Like nothing that was ever bought or sold	商货与之异，
It waited there, the body and the mind;	灵与肉不急；
And with a mighty meaning of a kind	天地含大义，
That tells the more the more it is not told	多说并无益。
So in a land where all days are not fair,	花无百日香，
Fair days went on till on another day;	好时慢流淌。
A thousand golden sheaves were lying there,	千穗风不荡，
Shining and still, but not for long to stay—	亮闪难久长——
As if a thousand girls with golden hair.	宛如千妙女，
Might rise from where they slept and go away.	远去发飘扬。

（诸莉　译）

诗作五

The House on the Hill
山上的古屋

They are all gone away
The House is shut and still,
There is nothing more to say.

斯人早已去，
老屋门紧闭，
再无啥可叙。

Through broken walls and gray
The winds blow bleak and shrill：
They are all gone away.

透过灰残壁，
寒风凄厉啸，
房主早搬离。

Nor is there one to-day
To speak them good or ill,
There is nothing more to say.

今此全离去，
是非无人说，
再无啥可叙。

Why is it then we stray
Around the sunken sill?
They are all gone away.

为何仍徘徊？
塌陷门窗外，
人都已离开。

And our poor fancy-play
For them is wasted skill,
There is nothing more to say.

自作多情戏，
于人技多余，
再无啥可叙。

There is a ruin and decay
In the House on the Hill：
There is nothing more to say.

空有断垣壁，
山上古屋里，
再无啥可叙。

（诸光 译）

220

参 考 文 献

［1］Chris Baldick. 牛津文学术语词典［M］. 上海：上海外语教育出版社，2000.

［2］Gillespie Sheena，Fonseca Terezinba，Sanger Carol. Literature Across Cultures［M］. Boston：Allyn and Bacon，1998.

［3］Tilley M P. A Dictionary of the Proverbs in England in the Sixteenth and Seventeenth Centuries［M］. Ann Arbor，1950.

［4］狄金森. 暴风雨夜，暴风雨夜［M］. 江枫，译. 北京：人民文学出版社，2008.

［5］冯翠华. 英语修辞大全［M］. 周煦良，译. 北京：外语教学与研究出版社，2005.

［6］辜正坤. 英文名篇鉴赏金库(诗歌卷)［M］. 天津：天津人民出版社，2000.

［7］豪斯曼. 豪斯曼诗选［M］. 北京：外语教学与研究出版社，2014.

［8］胡壮麟，等. 西方文体学词典［Z］. 北京：清华大学出版社，2004.

［9］黄杲炘. 英国抒情诗 100 首［M］. 上海：上海译文出版社，1998.

［10］蒋洪新. 英诗新方向——庞德、艾略特诗学理论与文化批评研究［M］. 长沙：湖南教育出版社，2001.

［11］李正栓，等. 英美诗歌教程［M］. 北京：清华大学出版社，2004.

［12］刘守兰. 英美名诗解读［M］. 上海：上海外语教育出版社，2003.

［13］刘新民，杨晓波译. 每当少年因相思嗟叹——A. E. 豪斯曼抒情诗选［M］. 上海：上海三联书店. 2020.

［14］马可·奥勒留. 沉思录［M］. 李娟，杨志，译. 上海：上海三联书店，2008.

［15］吕煦. 实用英语修辞［M］. 北京：清华大学出版社，2004.

［16］罗伯特·路易斯·史蒂文森. 一个孩子的诗园［M］. 李翔，译. 北京：作家出版社，2015.

[17]罗良功. 英诗概论[M]. 武汉：武汉大学出版社，2002.

[18]聂珍钊. 英语诗歌形式导论[M]. 北京：中国社会科学出版社，2007.

[19]彭予，马丽娅. 弗罗斯特：工业时代的田园诗人[J]. 中国社会科学院研究生院学报，1994.

[20]孙梁. 英美名诗一百首[M]. 北京：中国对外翻译出版公司，2001.

[21]屠岸译. 十四行诗集[M]. 上海：上海译文出版社，1981：129.

[22]宋炳辉. 徐志摩译作选[M]. 北京：商务印书馆，2019.

[23]余光中. 天真的歌：余光中经典翻译诗集[M]. 南京：江苏凤凰文艺出版社，2019.

[24]张秀国. 英语修辞学[M]. 北京：北京交通大学出版社，2005.

[25]赵毅衡. 新批评———一种独特的形式主义文论[M]. 北京：中国社会科学出版社，1988.

[26]诸莉. 从形式到内容———鹰（片段）的文学性解读[M]//外语教育. 武汉：华中科技大学出版社，2010.

[27]廖永煌. 《海恋》赏析[J]. 外国文学研究，1995(1).

[28]王金玲. 从拉斐尔前派画家罗塞蒂的女模特看其女性观[J]. 美与时代（下），2011(1).

[29]王文. 走向二十世纪的传统诗人———埃德温·阿林顿·罗宾逊诗歌创作述略[J]. 陕西师范大学成人教育学院学报，1999(6).

[30]余光中. 被诱于那一泓魔幻的蓝[J]. 华中科技大学学报（人社版），2002(2).

[31]豆瓣小组. 斯多葛学派[EB/OL]. (2006-06-11)[2023-04-08]. https://www.douban.com/group/topic/179798213/? type=like&_i=0104384N9kdY9.

[32]陈黎. 一首够直白的英文情诗：致我羞怯的情人[EB/OL]. (2007-09-01)[2023-05-01].https://www. douban. com/group/topic/1925300/? _i = 5146464VyxiTkB.

[33]柯勒律治. 古舟子咏（中英）[EB/OL]. (2017-03-16)[2023-05-06].https://www.douban.com/note/611312068/? _i=0256778YszHM9o.

[34]廖康. 三读朗费罗[EB/OL]. 豆瓣小组. (2012-04-01)[2023-06-07].https://www.douban.com/group/topic/28593907/? _i=5081555VyxiTkB.

［35］百度百科. 陌生化［EB/OL］.［2023-07-06］. https：//baike. baidu. com/item/%
　　　E9%99%8C%E7%94%9F%E5%8C%96？formModule＝lemma_search-box.

［36］孙蕴春. 英诗汉译 79：耶稣升天节［EB/OL］.（2020-04-24）［2023-07-09］.
　　　https：//www.52shici.com/posts.php？id＝276862.

［37］百度百科. 象征主义［EB/OL］.［2023-07-09］. https：//baike. baidu. com/
　　　item/%E8%B1%A1%E5%BE%81%E4%B8%BB%E4%B9%89/1780147？fr＝
　　　aladdin.

［38］伊娃·格林. 朗读诗歌《上坡》（情迷英音第 61 期）［EB/OL］. 网易云音乐.
　　　（2019-11-28）［2023-08-15］. https：//music.163.com/#/program？id＝2064182540.

［39］William Blake. The Chimney-sweeper，1794［EB/OL］. 英语作文大全.（2018-
　　　12-13）［2023-08-04］. http：//www.dioenglish.com/writing/essay/99803.html.